"We're two breaths away from being lovers."

"And I know it because we've been lovers before," Sawyer said, continuing. "I might not remember when or why, but I remember that."

Rebecca's knees started to buckle. She grabbed on to his last words like a drowning man. "What do you remember?" She forced the words through the vise that her throat had become.

"I remember this," he said, his thumb brushing over her lips. He lowered his head alongside hers and drew in a slow breath. "I remember the way you smell. The way you feel."

Afraid to move, afraid to stay, Rebecca closed her eyes.

"Come on, Bec, tell me the truth before I go insane."

So his instincts might be flying off the charts of accuracy, but he didn't truly remember.

His mouth covered hers before she could finish his name. And when he finally lifted his head, Rebecca couldn't lie. "Yes," she whispered hoarsely. "We were lovers."

Dear Reader,

Back by popular demand, MONTANA MAVERICKS:
RETURN TO WHITEHORN reappears in Special Edition!
Just in time for the Yuletide season, unwrap our exciting 2-in-1
A Montana Mavericks Christmas collection by Susan Mallery
and Karen Hughes. And next month, look for more passion
beneath the big blue Whitehorn sky with *A Family Homecoming*
by Laurie Paige.

Reader favorite Arlene James makes a special delivery with
Baby Boy Blessed. In this heartwarming THAT'S MY BABY!
story, a cooing infant on the doorstep just might turn two virtual
strangers into lifelong partners...in love!

The holiday cheer continues with *Wyoming Wildcat* by
Myrna Temte. Don't miss book four of the HEARTS OF
WYOMING series, which features a fun-loving rodeo champ
who sets out to win the wary heart of one love-shy single mom.
And you better watch out, 'cause *Daddy Claus* is coming to
town! In this tender tale by Robin Lee Hatcher, a pretend couple
discovers how nice it might be to be a family forever.

Rounding off a month of sparkling romance, *Wedding
Bells and Mistletoe* by veteran author Trisha Alexander launches
the CALLAHANS & KIN miniseries with a deeply emotional
story about a forbidden passion—and a long-buried secret—
that can no longer be denied. And dreams come true for two
tempestuous lovers in *A Child for Christmas* by Allison Leigh—
the next installment in the MEN OF THE DOUBLE-C RANCH
series.

I hope you enjoy all these romances. All of us here at Silhouette
wish you a joyous holiday season!

Best,

Karen Taylor Richman,
Senior Editor

Please address questions and book requests to:
Silhouette Reader Service
U.S.: 3010 Walden Ave., P.O. Box 1325, Buffalo, NY 14269
Canadian: P.O. Box 609, Fort Erie, Ont. L2A 5X3

ALLISON LEIGH

A CHILD FOR CHRISTMAS

SPECIAL EDITION®

Published by Silhouette Books
America's Publisher of Contemporary Romance

For everyone who believes that love will find a way.

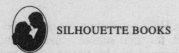

SILHOUETTE BOOKS

ISBN 0-373-24290-5

A CHILD FOR CHRISTMAS

Copyright © 1999 by Allison Lee Kinnaird

Visit us at www.romance.net

Printed in U.S.A.

Books by Allison Leigh

Silhouette Special Edition

Stay... #1170
The Rancher and the Redhead #1212
A Wedding for Maggie #1241
A Child for Christmas #1290

* Men of the Double-C Ranch

ALLISON LEIGH

started early by writing a Halloween play that her grade-school class performed for her school. Since then, though her tastes have changed, her love for reading has not. And her writing appetite simply grows more voracious by the day.

Born in Southern California, she has lived in eight different cities in four different states. She has been, at one time or another, a cosmetologist, a computer programmer and an administrative assistant.

Allison and her husband currently make their home in Arizona, where their time is thoroughly filled with two very active daughters, full-time jobs, pets, church, family and friends. In order to give herself the precious writing time she craves, she burns a lot of midnight oil.

A great believer in the power of love—her parents still hold hands—she cannot imagine anything more exciting to write about than the miracle of two hearts coming together.

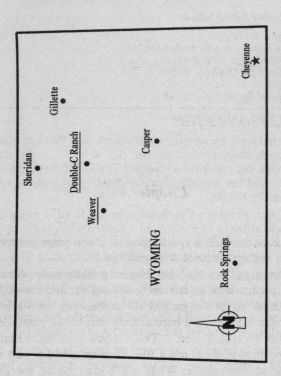

WYOMING

Cheyenne

Gillette

Sheridan

Double-C Ranch

Weaver

Casper

Rock Springs

All underlined places are fictitious.

Chapter One

"Listen, Delaney, I think I've got a patient turning into my parking lot. I'll call you back when I've got more time to talk." Dr. Rebecca Morehouse cradled the phone between her shoulder and ear and tossed the medical file of the patient she'd just seen on a pile of similar files stacked haphazardly across the small desk in her reception area. "Yes, I know you don't understand how a small town like Weaver could fill up my time so thoroughly. What can I say? Being the only physician in a hundred-mile radius keeps a girl busy."

After hanging up, she glanced out the big plate-glass window overlooking the parking lot in front of her office. The vehicle was just parking, and Rebecca slipped her tired feet back into the low-heeled black suede pumps she'd kicked off after seeing her last patient out the door.

She knew that her dismal mood had more to do with

the unfortunate news she'd just given her last patient than any real dissatisfaction with the way her days were filled. Even calling her friend, Delaney Vega, hadn't totally lifted her somberness.

Perhaps Delaney was right. That it was time for Rebecca to start actively seeking some fun. To accept one of the dates she was offered—and always refused—on a regular basis. To go out and simply have some fun.

She heard the muted sound of truck doors closing and absently smoothed her hand down the front of her white lab coat. How long had it been since she'd put aside her mountains of responsibilities and just enjoyed herself?

Too long. Not since she'd been in school. Not since—

"Don't go there," she murmured to herself. "You're just tired. And upset that there are some things even *you* can't cure." She pocketed her gold pen and looked up, her professional smile in place, when she saw who'd come into her office. "Hello, Jefferson. I didn't expect to see you today."

Jefferson Clay's wife, Emily, was only one of her obstetrical patients. Emily's two sisters-in-law, Maggie and Jaimie, were pregnant also. It seemed that the Clay men had been awfully virile this year. She frowned a little at that errant thought, and tucked her hands in the pockets of her lab coat. "Is Emily all right?"

Jefferson nodded, still holding the door. All Rebecca saw from her angle was another tall figure slowly walking across the snow-shoveled sidewalk. "Em's fine," he said, still watching out the door. "We've got a new patient for you, though."

Finally, the other man reached the entryway. She felt the blood drain from her head and she reached for the edge of the desk, once again knocking askew the pile of files.

Now that the second man was inside, Jefferson let the door swing closed and crossed the small reception area, a large manila envelope in his hand. "Records," he said briefly.

Rebecca automatically reached for the envelope; knew that her fingers closed over it and held it. But her mind, jarred out of its horrified dysfunction, started racing.

She'd known this could happen. She'd weighed the possibilities. The likelihood. Made a calculated decision based on a decidedly low risk. She just hadn't expected, hadn't thought—

"This is my brother," Jefferson was saying and the brother in question finally focused his gaze from perusing her comfortably furnished reception room to studying her face. "Sawyer."

Rebecca waited for the derision to cross Sawyer Clay's face. But it didn't come. He just stared at her, his dark blue gaze intent. Her heart stopped. She had never thought he'd forget, even though it had been years. But there was no trace of recognition in his eyes. A tight knot of anger formed in her stomach. Anger at herself for assuming he'd remember. Anger at him for not doing so.

Jefferson rubbed his jaw, glancing at his brother who grimaced when he caught the look. "Might as well tell her," he said, his low voice raspy. "That's what we're here for."

Rebecca's fingers tightened on the large envelope, which experience told her contained medical records and X rays. She couldn't help staring at Sawyer. He had several neat stitches on his jaw, and if the way he was holding himself was any indication, he'd suffered bruised ribs at a minimum.

"Sawyer had an accident," Jefferson told her. "Maybe you ought to just read the file there."

Sawyer's lips thinned, and he stepped closer, sucking the oxygen right out of her lungs as he did so. "What my...brother—" he hesitated over the word as if it didn't come naturally "—is trying not to say is that there's a new town freak." He smiled and Rebecca's fingers curled at the wealth of frustration she recognized in that faint movement of his lips. "Me."

She blinked, glancing down at the envelope in her hands. It wasn't often that Dr. Rebecca Morehouse was at a loss for words anymore. But then, it wasn't often that the good town doctor came face-to-face with the ghosts of her past. "Well, we treat everyone equally," she managed, then blinked again at the wisp of amusement that flitted through Sawyer's eyes.

Amusement. But no recognition.

That possibility had never once occurred to her. How foolish. She turned on her heel and led the way back to her office. "Come inside and have a seat," she said, pulling on her cloak of training with no small measure of comfort. Both men followed her, and Rebecca couldn't pretend not to be relieved—though she was fairly certain she hid that fact behind her mask of professionalism.

Sitting behind the wide mahogany desk she'd brought with her from New York City helped. It had been her husband Tom's desk and sitting there she could almost feel his presence. Standing behind her, his hand gentle and comforting on her shoulder. Giving her strength as he'd done so well when he'd been alive.

She blinked and made herself focus on the materials

she slid from the envelope. It wouldn't do for her to just sit there and stare at Sawyer, even if it was her first instinct.

Jefferson shrugged out of his heavy coat and sat in one of the chairs on the other side of her desk. But Sawyer stood, peering at her diplomas hanging on the wall. As if he could find, hanging there, the secrets of life.

Her stomach churned as she read the neatly typed records.

"He was unconscious for nearly a week after the car accident," Jefferson said. But Rebecca had already read that much in the report, and she looked up to see Sawyer watching her with a speculative expression. The man should be sitting down.

No. He should still be in bed. In the Maryland hospital where he'd been taken nearly three weeks ago after an accident that would surely have killed him had he not been thrown clear before the car exploded. He certainly shouldn't be standing here in her office, staring at her without one breath of recognition in his eyes.

"I can still speak." He directed the comment at his brother. "I didn't forget how to string a few words together into a sentence."

Rebecca felt more than heard Jefferson's sigh as he rose. "Then speak," he said evenly. "And stop standing there like a bump." He picked up his coat. "I'll wait outside."

She wanted to call out and tell Jefferson not to go. But such behavior was not only unprofessional, it was cowardly. So she folded her hands together atop the surface of her desk and returned Sawyer's look with a steady one of her own. "Captain, please sit. I'm getting a kink in my neck watching you."

His eyes narrowed. "'Captain'?"

She swallowed, nudging the medical report with her knuckle. "That's what it says here." Considering what she knew about him, she was surprised it hadn't said *Admiral.*

He started to rub the stitches on his jaw, then seemed to think better of it. "Don't call me that."

"That's what you are." Capt. Sawyer Clay, United States Navy.

He shrugged, grimaced, then sat. Rebecca noted his pale coloring and the faint sheen of perspiration on his forehead. Swallowing, she rose and walked behind his chair, reaching for his coat.

"What are you doing?"

She lifted her hands peaceably. "You'd be more comfortable without your coat," she said. "Both now and when you put it back on to go outside."

He surrendered the leather bomber jacket with a slight frown. She tossed it over the other chair, then resumed her seat behind the safety of her desk. "Why are you here, Captain?"

Sawyer eyed the cool woman sitting across from him, her hands folded neatly together atop the file of stuff he'd brought with him. His brother—just telling himself he had siblings seemed odd—had told him that the town doctor was young and female. But Jefferson hadn't said that she was startlingly beautiful. He hadn't said anything about lustrous brown hair waving to the shoulders of her white lab coat that, he'd *also* noticed, covered a pale yellow sweater that clung to some mighty interesting curves. Nor had he said anything about wide-set golden-brown eyes that watched a man from beneath level brows in a perfectly oval, creamy face.

"Captain?"

He shifted. He still ached in every joint of his body. "Isn't it obvious why I'm here?"

Her eyebrows rose a fraction. "You suffered a head injury as a result of an automobile accident."

"You didn't finish reading."

"No, I—"

"Have we met?" He didn't expect her to blanch the way she did. He'd thought Jefferson had said the doc was relatively new to town. But he might have gotten it wrong. God knew his brain wasn't firing on all cylinders right now. "Sorry," he said abruptly. "My brand of humor these days."

She frowned, making a narrow crease appear between her barely arching eyebrows. She looked back down at the report, obviously reading what she hadn't yet come to. Her beautiful face revealed her growing shock.

"Amnesia," he said flatly. "Hell of a note, isn't it?" His attention focused on her lips when they pressed together for a moment, drawing his interest in a way he was pretty sure she wouldn't appreciate. "Bet you don't have many cases like mine come through your doors."

Finally she looked up from the report. "No," she admitted, her voice husky. Then she briskly cleared her throat. "This must be very frustrating and upsetting for you. But most cases of amnesia resolve themselves after—"

"Save the techno jargon," Sawyer interrupted. He'd already heard more than he could stand from the doctors at the hospital. "I'm only here 'cause the powers that be said they'd haul me back east in restraints if I didn't get medical care out here. There's even a form in there that you'll have to fill out and send in." And another form that she'd have to fill out if—*when*—he was up to snuff and could report back for duty.

"Why *are* you here?" she asked. "Surely you were advised not to travel."

"Apparently Jefferson has some clout," Sawyer said carelessly. He didn't care what means his brother had used to secure his hospital release the way he had. One more minute in that hospital bed with the nurses from hell and he'd have jumped out the third-story window for relief.

"I see." But clearly, the lovely doctor did not, and her expression said so. She rose and shuffled the contents of the envelope into a pile, which she tucked into a folder she pulled from a desk drawer. "Let's take a look."

He followed her along the short hallway that broke off into two examining rooms that faced each other. The door at the end was closed, and he immediately wondered what was behind it. He already knew it wasn't her office.

Figuring out he had an intensely curious nature had been just one of many discoveries over the past several days since he'd regained consciousness. Whether that curiosity had more to do with the fact that he hadn't recognized a single person around him, much less his own reflection in a mirror, or with his ordinary nature, he didn't know.

"Captain?"

He realized she was waiting and walked past her into the room, getting a faint whiff of her perfume. It tantalized his senses.

Soft.

He drew in another breath without thought as he dropped his coat onto the side chair by the door.

The scent was heady.

Familiar.

It was all he could do not to grab her. "What perfume are you wearing?"

Her eyes widened a fraction. She stepped into the exam room, moving toward the counter across from where he stood. She left the door open, he noticed. "I really don't see—"

"I recognize it."

Her lips, soft and full enough to warrant a second look from any man worthy of the term, parted a breath, then firmed. She turned to the file folder she'd carried in with her and looked at it as she pulled a pen from her lapel pocket. Her thick hair slid down her cheek. "I see."

He closed his hand over her arm, startling them both. "No, I don't think you do. I've smelled that perfume before. What is it?"

She looked pointedly at his hand around her arm and he released her. Reluctantly.

"It's a custom blend," she said crisply. "But I'm sure there are similar elements in many fragrances, which is probably what your senses are picking up on."

Sawyer stared at her. She could say whatever she wanted in her crisp, professional, cool voice. Perhaps there was even some truth in her statement. How was he to know? He only knew that the scent of her fragrance plucked some chord deep within him.

It was the first familiar thing since he'd woken up in that damned hospital bed.

She held her gold pen in her slender hand, turning

it over and over between her fingers. Her nails were short and unpainted. Practical for her profession, he supposed. Then he had a sudden vision of those long, cool fingers running over him.

Those hands were on his shoulders now, nudging him back onto the exam table. "Captain? Are you feeling dizzy?"

"No," he lied, catching her wrists between his fingers and receiving another frigid look, which he ignored. He thought perhaps he was used to ignoring people's frigid looks. It wasn't a comforting thought; made him wonder just what kind of man he was.

He looked down at her slender wrists. Her skin was pale and soft compared to his darker, tanned hands. He waited for that vision to come again, then wanted to curse when it didn't. He looked up to find her eyes studying him warily. "*Have* we met?"

Rebecca's heart stopped. Oh, God, this was worse than anything she'd ever dreamed. Any nightmare she'd ever suffered.

She twisted her hands, and he released his hold on her wrists. She barely kept herself from rubbing them. Not because he'd hurt her, but to stop the warm sensation of his touch that lingered. "No," she stated flatly.

His dark blue eyes narrowed, as if he was trying to see into her mind. Into her lie.

She turned away and snatched up the pen she'd dropped. "I need some medical information," she said evenly, "in addition to what you've brought."

He made a rough sound and Rebecca dared a look at him, silently chastising herself for letting her emotions get in the way of her profession. "I'm sorry," she said, not sure why she truly was—other than that he was a human being and he was suffering. "This must be very frustrating for you."

"You might say that."

She pushed her thumb against the end of her pen. "Tell me what has happened since your accident."

He rose from the table, and Rebecca braced herself against the waves of restless frustration emanating from him. "I woke up in a hospital bed with no idea who I was, where I'd come from or where I was going. They told me I'd been in a car accident, that I'd been alone and that there were no other vehicles involved." His voice was deep. His words clipped.

"Physically." She knew what the report said. She wanted to hear it in his words, though.

"I banged my head hard enough to knock my memory right out of me. They traced my fingerprints to identify me, 'cause it was faster than trying to find something identifiable on the car. Apparently I've got quite a file with the government."

That was no surprise. The fact that she hadn't heard about his accident through Weaver's well-developed grapevine was. "The hospital notified your family then? It's a wonder they didn't all troop to Maryland."

"I told the hospital not to notify them."

"Why?"

If he thought her curiosity out of place, he didn't say. "Just more strangers."

"Strangers or not, they're your family. They're concerned for you."

He shifted. Picked up a box of tissue and set it back down. Rebecca waited. "That's what Jefferson said," Sawyer finally admitted. "Only his words were a little less tactful. Apparently he—my brother—didn't care what requests I'd made. And it's just as well. 'Cause I was going nuts in the hospital. Apparently I didn't show for a meeting a few days ago with someone Jefferson knows, and he made it his business to find out why. Which is why he ended up in Maryland, where he arranged my escape.''

She squelched the traitorous curl of sympathy and clicked her pen. ''I believe in treating the whole patient, Captain Clay, and—''

''Don't call me that.''

''Excuse me?''

''My name is Sawyer, so I've been told. If you have to call me something, use that.''

Rebecca looked down at her blank medical form. ''Very well.'' She started writing with a hand that barely trembled. Yet that faint trembling annoyed her immensely. She set the pen down with a snap and reminded herself again that she was a professional. She'd taken an oath. ''You sustained additional injuries?''

His eyes—a shade of blue that she'd never forgotten, no matter how hard and how long she'd tried—studied her. ''Bruised ribs. Some cuts.''

She motioned to the examining table, telling her stomach to stop jumping around like a third-year med student's, and stepped up to him, lifting his chin so she could see the sutured cut more clearly. Her fingertips tingled against the rasp of whiskers. He hadn't shaved. ''You should keep this covered for another day or two,'' she said.

''I didn't know where the bandages were.''

Rebecca swallowed at the wave that swept through her, despite her better sense. She didn't need to feel sympathy or empathy or any other ''athy'' but antipathy for this man. Yet that one statement drove right to the heart of her.

She stepped back, pulling her stethoscope out of her pocket. "I think we can take care of that before you leave," she said huskily. "Are you staying with Jefferson or Daniel?"

"No."

Meaning he was probably staying at the main house of the Double-C Ranch. The house where he'd grown up, on a cattle ranch some twenty miles away from Weaver. The house where, now, he didn't know where to look for bandages. She automatically warmed her stethoscope against her palm. "Remove your shirt and let me take a look at your ribs."

His smile was sudden and barely shy of wolfish. "I thought you'd never ask."

Never before had Rebecca wished so strongly that she had a full-time nurse on staff with her. But she was long used to such comments from male patients, she reminded herself. She knew how to handle them. Unfortunately, as Sawyer slowly pulled off his long-sleeved T-shirt, that ability seemed to desert her.

His shoulders were wide; his chest hard with roping muscle. And the sight didn't make her feel breathless. It really didn't. She was a physician. Well versed in the human form, male and female.

No, what affected her, she assured herself, was the angry contusions blotching the golden skin stretching over those hard muscles. Another set of stitches— eleven—crossed his shoulder. She carefully checked him over. His pulse was a little rapid, but that was to be expected.

She dressed his cuts and dropped several bandages into a small manila envelope, which she set on the table beside him. Then finally, thankfully, she was able to step back to her file while he pulled on his shirt.

"You have a prescription for your headaches?" She caught his look of surprise when he nodded. "I can see the discomfort on your face," she said. She certainly didn't want this man suspecting that she had some special intuition where he was concerned. The fact was, his entire body was braced against pain.

She rapidly completed the paperwork for the office visit and tore off his copy, handing it to him. "If you have an insurance card, we can submit that for you." Rebecca made the decision then and there to look for a part-time billing clerk.

He slowly took the yellow form from her. "I suppose I must have had one," he said, his voice suddenly weary. "And it was probably in my wallet, which stayed in the car that burned to cinders—"

"After you were thrown clear," Rebecca finished. She touched his arm gently, then barely kept herself from snatching back her hand when she realized what she'd done. It wouldn't do to draw this man's curiosity, she reminded herself sharply.

She waved toward the form. "Don't worry about that for now," she said, stepping out into the hall where she could breathe easier again. "We'll get everything figured out before long. The Maryland hospital will undoubtedly have all the information I need."

Sawyer's injuries would heal. He'd regain his memory.

He would disrupt the quiet, satisfying life she'd managed to create for her and Ryan. And then he'd go back to his life, leaving theirs in pieces.

Sawyer couldn't sleep. He lay in bed in one of the rooms he'd chosen in the basement guest suite of the house he'd been told he'd been raised in. Now he stared up at the dark ceiling.

That ceiling was like his mind, he thought.

Black. Empty.

No, not empty.

Murky.

That was it. His mind was one murky place.

What if he never remembered?

He shoved back the soft quilts and strode out to the sitting area, grateful that he had the whole suite to himself. Grateful that the room he'd been told he had as a kid no longer existed because of the remodeling his brother was doing upstairs. The last thing Sawyer needed were any witnesses to his decline into insanity. He much preferred the small measure of privacy the downstairs rooms gave him.

The sitting room's temperature was cool against his bare shoulders, but it felt good. It was a damn sight better than lying there in bed working up a sweat over his murky memory.

If he had to work up a sweat about anything, it ought to be for the beautiful Dr. Rebecca Morehouse. There was a woman a man could easily sweat for.

A touch as cool as a spring breeze.

Silky brown hair as inviting as...as what? He couldn't remember, he thought with unexpected wryness.

Eyes as hot as— Okay, he was stretching it there, too. He didn't imagine for one minute that those warm brown eyes of hers couldn't flame hotter than molten gold. But the fact of the matter was they'd been cooler than her touch. Distinctly cool. Okay, frigid.

Maybe that was her usual bedside manner. Maybe that was why she was practicing in the dinky town of

Weaver, rather than some busy city. He'd seen her diplomas and certificates hanging on the wall in her office. Some pretty big-name places that even his murky mind recognized. With credentials like that, she could probably hang out her shingle just about anywhere.

Why Weaver?

He knocked his shin on the corner of the television armoire and swore, fumbling for the little lamp that sat on the table next to the couch. He managed to knock it over before he found the damned little switch and he swore again.

Once the light was on he went around the breakfast counter and yanked open the refrigerator door hard enough to make the bottles of beer in the door rattle. He didn't reach for the beer, though he recognized the brand.

Was it *his* brand?

Did he even *like* beer?

He pulled out the quart of milk and flipped it open, automatically sniffing to see that it was fresh before drinking right from the carton. Then he stood there in the open door of the fridge and wondered at the ease of his actions. Was this what he often did in the sterile apartment in Maryland that Jefferson had taken him to after springing him from that hospital?

He'd walked, stiff and aching, through that apartment and even with the pain-medication-induced haze that clung to him, he had wondered who was pulling that great cosmic joke on him. Because he'd never seen the place before in his life.

He'd walked down the short hallway to the single bedroom with its large bed in the center of the room with the plain blue bedspread tucked about it with military precision. He'd wondered if there was a woman who shared the bed with him. Or women. He was certain there was no one "special." Not when the only visitor he'd had in the hospital that first week had been a man who claimed to be Sawyer's commanding officer. It had been that man who told Sawyer enough details of his life, of the accident, to keep him from going stark mad those first few days.

He'd gone into the adjoining bathroom of his impersonal home and stared at himself in the wide mirror that hung over the cold white sink and had looked at himself. The reflection had been no more familiar to him then than it had been all the times he'd stared at himself in the hospital mirror before Jefferson arrived and flatly told Sawyer that he couldn't hide from the family any longer. Jefferson used his considerable influence on the powers-that-be who finally deemed him physically fit to leave. Physically fit. Mentally blank.

No, that wasn't right, he thought as he stared into the milk carton. He wasn't a blank.

He knew who the president of the United States was.

He knew it was the twelfth of December.

He knew how to speak and read and drive a car— he'd talked Jefferson into letting him drive the rental around the hospital parking lot just to make sure.

But he hadn't known his own name until they'd told him in the hospital.

And here he stood at a strange refrigerator in a strange house with strange people in it, wondering if he often stood at his own refrigerator in the middle of the night wearing nothing but boxers, drinking straight from the containers.

If there *had* been a woman in his life, would she have scolded him? Would she have smiled and shaken her head and invited him back to bed?

There had been no hint of a feminine presence in that apartment anymore than there had been a feminine presence at the hospital during visiting hours. No lingering scent.

The only lingering scent in his mind was that which clung to Rebecca Morehouse's creamy skin.

He replaced the carton and shoved the refrigerator door closed. This wasn't getting him any closer to sleep.

Rather than go back to bed, he opened the armoire to reveal the television and sprawled on the couch, picking up the remote control from the coffee table. Thanks to a satellite dish, he had his choice of channels—hundreds of them.

Not a one held his interest and he finally settled on CNN, turning the sound way down. Listening to the murmur of the news channel was preferable to listening to the silence in his murky mind.

He heard a soft footfall overhead and wondered who else in the house wasn't sleeping at this late hour. Going up to find out held no appeal. It had only been two days since he'd arrived, but he was already fed up with the sympathetic, cautious expressions in their eyes.

There was Matthew. Another of his four brothers. And Matthew's wife, Jaimie, and their daughter, Sarah. There was also Squire Clay. His father. The man he had studied all during dinner the night he'd arrived, trying to see some resemblance. Some sense of familiarity.

All he'd gotten for his efforts had been a throbbing headache.

Rather than take up either of the offers he'd received from Jefferson and Daniel to stay with them, Sawyer had chosen to stay in this house. The "big house" they called it. Which, absurdly, made him want to laugh, since the only "big house" he could remember was some reference to prison in an old black-and-white movie. "The big house." Where he'd been raised.

But his first sight of the sprawling brick-and-wood house had brought about no blinding flashes of memory. Just the realization that he recognized the breed of cattle huddling in clusters beyond the fences. Jefferson had told him that Matthew and Daniel, who was the second youngest of his brothers, ran the Double-C Ranch jointly. That Jefferson and his wife, Emily, ran the spread directly east, breeding horses.

Matthew, Daniel, Em—names that Sawyer knew he should know.

Names he didn't.

So he'd declined both brothers' offers. The whole point of coming here had been to see if it helped him regain his memory. He'd supposedly grown up here. In the big house.

Had he felt like it was a prison?

He shook his head, feeling like a madman.

Maybe that was why he lived in Maryland, he thought. Because he didn't get along with his family. Because this place was a prison to him.

But that didn't feel quite right to him. From what he'd seen since he'd arrived, his brothers were all straight arrows. He respected that. Liked that. Even liked them when he wasn't analyzing to death all the blank spots in his mind. Their assortment of wives and daughters were okay, too. Sawyer didn't think he had anything against kids.

He just hated that look of expectation in their eyes— knowing he was disappointing everyone with his failure to recall his past. Them.

The yellow form that Rebecca had given him sat on the coffee table alongside the packet of bandages she'd given him. He picked up the form and looked at the imprinted name, address and telephone number.

A cordless phone sat on the side table by the lamp with the now-crooked shade. He picked up the phone and punched out the number from the form. He'd leave a message, he thought, even though he wasn't quite sure what he would say.

A fine idea shot to hell when the voice that answered was very much human.

"Rebecca Morehouse," she repeated when he failed to answer the first time.

"I want to see you tomorrow."

Rebecca sat straight up in bed at the commanding voice that penetrated the phone line. She hurriedly fumbled for the light switch beside her bed, pushing her hair out of her eyes. Talking to this man in the still of night was better done with the lights blazing. Her first thoughts were utterly selfish. Had he remembered? "Captain Clay?"

"I told you not to call me that."

She pressed her lips together. Thank goodness Ryan no longer awakened whenever the phone rang at all hours. "Are you all right?" she asked. "What are your symptoms?"

"Sleeplessness."

She blinked. Stared sightlessly at her ivory eyelet comforter. Saw in her mind the man on the other end. Would his thick hair be rumpled from his pillow? Did he still wear those khaki box— *Stop it.*

"Are you experiencing dizziness again?"

"No," his voice was steady and low and far too intimate. "I said I can't sleep."

"So you called me in the middle of the night to tell me?"

"No, I called to tell you I want to see you tomorrow."

If her heart rate didn't settle she was going to pass out. "I have some open time midmorning."

"Not for an appointment."

"I... Excuse me?"

"I'll meet you for lunch. What time?"

"Captain Clay, I don't think—"

"I asked you not to call me that."

She swallowed. Moistened her lips and pushed her hair out of her eyes again. "I'm not available for lunch."

"Supper."

"No."

"Why not?"

She drew up her knees restlessly. "You're my patient. It, uh, wouldn't be ethical."

"To sit across from me in a restaurant? I'm assuming, of course, that one of those places in town *serves* supper."

"Of course they do. This isn't the back of beyond."

"Could have fooled me."

There. That was the man she remembered. In between comments that she'd once thought had indicated fondness for this town he came from had been the ones that said he wasn't fond of it at all. It was one of the reasons she'd thought it would be safe. That knowledge that Sawyer Clay never planned to live his life in Wyoming.

He'd preferred the rest of the world.

"The next day, then."

She pressed her forehead to her knees. He might

have amnesia, but he was still the same man, she reminded herself. "No. If you need medical care, please say so. Otherwise, I'll say good-night now."

"What time tomorrow?"

"For what?"

"An appointment."

She switched hands on the receiver. Oh, to be a secretary. A data-entry operator. Anything but the only physician for a hundred miles. "Eleven."

"Done. Good night."

She held the phone out and looked at it when he hung up. "Damn you, Sawyer Clay," she whispered to the buzz of the dial tone. "I won't let you destroy my life again. Or my son's."

Chapter Two

After hanging up with Rebecca, Sawyer managed a few hours' restless sleep before he rose around dawn. Perhaps it was his habit to rise early, since he'd been doing it "ever since he could remember."

What was that now? Two weeks? He took a rapid shower, feeling no inclination to linger under the hot spray despite the relief it brought to his aching muscles. He hoped that ache would go away. Assumed it was all attributable to the accident. Maybe it was partially because of his age. Jefferson had told him he was the oldest of the Clay brothers. Forty-three.

A good decade older than Rebecca Morehouse, if her smooth skin was any indication.

The thought of seeing her again gave him something to look forward to. Even if it was only inhaling her fragrance, taking some insane measure of comfort in its familiarity. Or trying to figure out if her cool manner was reserved strictly for him, or for all of her patients.

He raked his wet hair back with his fingers, eschewed the razor, replaced his bandages with fresh ones, then dressed in jeans that could have been two years old or twenty, for all he knew. He yanked on a thick black cable-knit sweater and headed upstairs to the coffee he could already smell.

Matthew, the brother with the short-cropped blond hair and the ice-blue eyes, was drinking a cup at the table, his attention on a pile of mail he was methodically working his way through. He looked up when Sawyer entered the kitchen. "Morning."

"Looks like night to me." Sawyer reached for one of the plain no-frills mugs hanging from a mug tree on the counter and filled it to brimming with the piping-hot brew. He pulled out one of the chairs and sat down, squinting over the steam as he sipped gingerly from the mug. Matthew watched him for a moment, then turned back to the envelope in his hand. "Okay, what did I do different?"

Matthew shook his head and gave a brief glance to the contents of the letter, then tossed it aside to one of the piles. "How you feeling?"

"Well, just dandy, Matthew. How are you feeling today?"

Matthew sighed and dropped the mail. "Okay. Dumb question. Sorry."

Sawyer set his mug down and scrubbed his hands down his face, feeling the bandage on his jaw. The bristles from two-days' growth of beard. "No," he said abruptly. "I'm the one who is sorry." He stared at his mug, circling his hand around it. "Tell me something, Matt. Anything."

"I thought we were supposed to let things come to you in their own good time."

"I'm not asking for the secrets to world peace," he snapped. "Just *something!*" Sawyer could tell from his brother's hesitation that he'd been warned not to feed him too much information about his past. The doctors in Maryland had sternly warned Jefferson, who had obviously dutifully passed the warning on to the rest of his family, that Sawyer's mind needed to assimilate the memories as they came naturally. Forcing them or feeding them might only cause more harm than good.

"Well," Matthew considered slowly, "you always were a crabby S.O.B. in the mornings. That doesn't appear to have changed."

He knew he deserved that. Didn't even take offense at it. He lifted the mug and sipped. Blew on it. Sipped.

"You used to sit in that chair there," Matthew added after a moment.

Sawyer looked at the chair across from the one he'd taken.

"And you drank your coffee from the saucer, like Squire."

"What?"

Matthew rose and opened one of the cupboard doors, pulling out a flat china saucer. Then he grabbed Sawyer's mug and tipped coffee into the saucer. "You drank it this way."

"Like a damn cat."

"I didn't say you lapped at it, idiot. I said you drank it." He carefully lifted the saucer, showing what he meant.

Sawyer snorted. "What for?"

Matthew set the saucer beside Sawyer's elbow and returned to his chair and his own coffee. "Squire drinks it that way, too. Probably because it's the fastest way to inhale hot coffee when you're in a rush to get somewhere. You didn't do it that way everywhere or every time I ever saw you drink coffee, but it's what you did around here. You wanted something? That's what you're getting.''

His brother gathered up one of the piles of mail and dumped it into the trash beneath the sink. ''You want to come out with me this morning?''

''To do what? It must be colder than a witch's—''

''It is. Which is why I need to make sure the water hasn't frozen over for the stock. You don't want to, that's fine. I just thought since you were hunting for—''

''Did I do it in the past?''

Matthew grinned. ''Not if you could help it.''

''Hated it?''

''Pretty much.''

Sawyer rose, mug in hand. He left the saucer untouched where it sat on the table and followed his brother into the mudroom that connected to the kitchen. ''Sounds like a good enough reason to me. But I want to be back in time to get to Weaver by eleven. I'm seeing Rebecca then.''

Matthew paused while shrugging into his heavy coat. ''You up to this, then?''

''I'm starting to creak with the aches in my muscles,'' Sawyer admitted grumpily. ''But I'm not seeing Rebecca because of my aching muscles or feeble mind.''

''Then why?''

Sawyer reached for his own coat. ''Because I want to know why her perfume smells so damned familiar.''

Matthew chuckled. ''She's a nice woman, Sawyer.

She's treated all of us at one time or another since she came to Weaver a couple of years ago. But if you're thinking you're gonna get beyond her professionalism too far, you might want to rethink it. From what I hear, 'just friends' is her favorite phrase.''

Since Sawyer didn't remember who his ''friends'' were, that didn't bother him too much.

Matthew opened the storm door and stepped out into the frigid air. Sawyer gritted his teeth against the cold rush and pulled his collar up around his neck, yanking on the gloves Matthew shoved at him. He grabbed his coffee mug for one last slug, feeling it burn all the way down. It was little comfort against the icy wind that blew relentlessly into his face as he followed his brother into the darkness.

Rebecca was painfully aware of the clock ticking inexorably toward eleven. The morning should not have dragged. She saw four patients. Set one broken wrist and put off Bennett Ludlow, the only attorney in the area, who'd apparently set his sights on her and couldn't get it through his thick skull that she wasn't interested. She had more success keeping Bennett from dropping by her office, as he insisted he wanted to do, though, than keeping Ryan occupied when he grew impatient with the inclement weather and wanted to put aside his math books.

''Mo-om.''

It was interesting the way her son could make the term a two-syllable word. ''Ye-es?''

''Let me walk to Eric's.''

Since he'd asked that question three times already, he knew the answer. Rebecca finished writing her notes on the broken wrist and added the file to her growing pile on the desk. Soon, she promised herself, she'd take care of that bulging stack. "It's snowing."

"Not that hard."

"Too hard for you to walk by yourself, young man."

Ryan rolled his eyes and slumped back on the waiting-room chair, one long leg slung over the side. Rebecca noted that his jeans were getting short again and hid a smile. Her son was growing by leaps and bounds this year; making up with a vengeance for being the shortest kid in his class, even if he was a year younger.

"If it's snowing so hard, how come you got patients coming in?"

Good point. Rebecca set down her pen and fixed her gaze on her son. "Go back to our apartment and eat the lunch I left for you. After my next patient, I'll drive you over to Eric's. Okay?"

"What time?"

That was Ryan. Always wanting more details. More specifics. Perhaps that's why he excelled in mathematics. She'd learned what she'd had to learn to pass her studies. Ryan learned what he wanted to learn in math because he chose to.

But even Ryan drew the line at studying all morning during his winter vacation. He was in the fifth grade, having skipped the third, and he took math classes at the high school with kids nearly twice his age.

He was thriving here in Weaver. No longer getting into trouble with a group of friends, older and looking for millions of mischievous ways to gain attention.

"Mo-om!"

"Eleven-thirty. Good enough?"

"Yep." Ryan hopped off the chair, tucking his thick calculus book under one arm and an electronic game in his other hand, and bounded through the door that led to their private apartment.

The associates she'd had in New York would have been shocked at Rebecca's setup—Delaney included. And it might have been a little unorthodox, considering that one end of her property was a motel, complete with six rooms that she still rented out; the rooms she'd fashioned into the comfortable apartment that she and Ryan now called home; along with her medical office and small surgical clinic. But it worked for them.

She'd never really planned on being a hotel magnate. The slim business the motel did was just fine with her. She'd refurbished the rooms simply because she couldn't abide the sixties-style decor, and since the town offered no other overnight accommodations, she'd left the remaining rooms available.

It wasn't as if she needed the motel income. Tom had left her financially set. Ryan's college fund was already well established. Rebecca wasn't rich by any standards. But she and her son would never starve, either.

Her immediate paperwork completed, she rose from the desk and wandered over to the window overlooking the small parking lot. The snow was still falling, though not as heavily as it had been earlier. Perhaps he wouldn't drive into town in this weather.

She could only hope.

Ten minutes later, she knew it was a vain hope, because she recognized the truck that wheeled into her parking lot. Maybe one of his brothers had driven him in. Rebecca was pretty sure that old brown Blazer was Matthew's.

But only one man climbed from the vehicle, and he had no cowboy hat on his head. Rebecca was also reasonably sure that Matthew didn't go anywhere without his hat and that he hadn't dyed his blond hair dark, with silver streaks at the temples.

She returned to the desk, brushing her palms down the sides of her lab coat. When Sawyer pulled open the door, she was busy with the supply order form she'd hastily dragged onto the desk. Cold air whipped into the room with him and she slowly looked up, proud of the cool smile she knew she had pinned on her face. "You're early."

"Five minutes." He shrugged out of his jacket, hanging it on the brass coat-tree near the door and brushed the snowflakes from his hair as he approached the desk. "Were you raised in snow country?"

Rebecca nearly snapped the pencil she held in two. "I beg your pardon?"

"No one would choose to live in this stuff unless they'd grown up in it."

She set her pencil precisely in the center of her order form and rose. "I've lived in an assortment of locations," she said, deliberately revealing nothing of import. It was none of his business that she'd grown up all around the world, following her missionary parents where they went until it had been time for her to start junior high. Then she'd been in a series of boarding schools in the United States. "And I *did* choose to live here." She lifted his medical file from the hot file where she'd placed it that morning and headed back to an exam room. "I find the snow beautiful. Very fitting for the Christmas season."

"Oh, yes. Christmas." Sawyer smiled, though it didn't reach his dark blue eyes. "And I even remember the reason for celebrating it. Santa Claus, right?"

Rebecca eyed him.

"A joke, Bec. A joke. I remember my old Sunday-school lessons. Don't remember ever *going* to Sunday school, though."

Bec. Good heavens. Rebecca set the file on the counter in the exam room and turned to face him, her arms crossed as she leaned casually against the counter. As soon as she found the time to do the remodeling that would add the third exam room she needed, she'd be sure to make the rooms larger. This one seemed far too close for some reason. "What can I do for you today, Captain?"

He shook his head, his lips twisting. "Aside from ditching the rank?"

Rebecca couldn't very well tell him that it would be a cold day before his name passed her lips again. "You requested an appointment. You must have some reason. Have your stitches become inflamed? Are you dizzy? Headache plaguing you more than usual? What?" She'd poured over the reports that he'd brought with him from the hospital, spoken with his doctors in Maryland and had spent hours more poring over her medical journals. Purely from a professional stand-point, of course. When she'd learned that his only vis-itors in the hospital had been his commanding officer, then later Jefferson, who'd thoroughly ignored the wishes of the patient and the rules of the hospital to get in to see him, she hadn't felt her heart squeeze at the lonely life that suggested. She hadn't. If Sawyer hadn't had a parade of people concerned for him, it was because he wanted it that way.

"There is something plaguing me."

She waited, carefully containing her impatience to get out of this small room and farther than five feet away from him.

"Your scent."

She felt her cheeks grow cold as the blood drained from her head. If she'd been alone, she would have stuck her head between her knees until the dizziness passed.

If she'd been alone, she wouldn't be dizzy in the first place.

"That is hardly an appropriate comment for your physician, Captain Clay." She smiled as she deliberately used his title. Reminding herself that everything in his life had taken second place to his one and only love.

"Blame it on my murky mind. Appropriate comments and behavior are out of my control just now."

"Murky mind?"

"Yes." He leaned his own hip against the exam table, mirroring her crossed-arm pose. "Murky. As in gloomy. Cloudy. Dark."

"Dismal," Rebecca added. "Yes, I know what the word means. And it's natural that you'd be feeling some depression over your—"

"I'm not depressed, Bec." He dropped his arms, and approached her. Rebecca stiffened and he stopped a few steps away. "I'm pissed," he said in his clipped, raspy voice. "If you'll forgive the term. Thoroughly and royally aggravated. And quite frankly, punching my fist through a wall sounds like a mighty fine idea—"

"Daniel punches walls."

"Except the muscles in my shoulders and arms are so damned stiff and sore that... What did you say?"

Rebecca brushed a lock of hair out of her face and eyed the small-print wallpaper border that circled the room at chair-rail height. "Daniel punches walls."

"Daniel. My brother, Daniel."

"Yes. He's broken a few bones while he was at it. I don't recommend it as a source of dealing with aggravation, however. Daniel hung a punching bag in his basement, I believe." She tucked her hands in her pockets. "Perhaps he'd let you use it."

"Why was he punching walls?"

"Well, only one wall since I've known him. I believe you'd do well to ask *him* that."

"Is he unhappy?"

"Daniel? No, actually, I believe your brother is over the moon these days. He got married less than a month ago, you know. Maggie is lovely and her little girl, J.D. is a sweet child. Plus they are adopting Angeline, too, I believe."

"So I hear. I'm told I was involved in some case, or I suppose I'd have been here for the wedding. Are you seeing someone?"

Rebecca's eyebrows rose at the abrupt change of topic. "I don't really think that's important here."

"Squire sings your praises, you know. At least he did all last night at supper. He's single. Has he sought you out?"

Rebecca blinked. Squire Clay was admittedly a handsome, vital man. But he was old enough to be her father. And she'd been very careful of any contact she'd had with the Clays of the Double-C Ranch.

She'd chosen Weaver deliberately, deciding that the risks were worth the safety and well-being of her son, but that didn't mean she'd be foolish enough to seek out trouble.

She deliberately looked at the narrow gold watch circling her wrist. The diamonds circling the face glittered under the overhead light. "If there is nothing else

I can do for you, I do have other business this morning.''

"You don't like me much, do you?"

Truly shocked, Rebecca shook her head. She'd tried to be so careful. "You are my patient. I want to see you fully recovered from your accident." Her ears actually started to burn at that. "'Liking' has nothing to do with it."

His beautiful, hard face lit with amusement. "You know the problem we have here, don't you?"

"I couldn't possibly say," she responded evenly.

"Ever since I can remember, you've been the most interesting person I've met."

If he only knew. Rebecca managed to smile at his ironic words. "I should think everyone you *meet* would be of interest. The more you immerse yourself in your old life, the more familiar things may become for you."

"If it was my old life," Sawyer said, "I'd still be in Maryland, apparently. I guess I haven't been around Weaver much in years."

He'd certainly been absent for two solid years, Rebecca knew. It was unfortunate that had changed. But if she kept her distance, she'd also keep her secret. She'd tried, more than once, all those years ago to tell him. But he hadn't listened. Hadn't wanted to listen. The only thing he'd wanted had been his career.

So if there was one thing she was determined to do now, it was to keep that truth from Sawyer Clay, one way or the other. He didn't deserve to know the truth. Not after all these years.

She flipped open his file and completed another office-visit form, tearing out the yellow copy and handing it to him.

"If you'd have lunch with me, we wouldn't have to resort to this pretense of professional visits."

Rebecca paused in the hallway, looking back at him. Six feet, one inch of trouble. That was Capt. Sawyer Clay. Six feet, one inch of trouble she did not need. Six feet, one inch of trouble she couldn't afford to let get under her skin. In her head. In her heart. Never again.

"I'm not interested, Captain Clay. I hope that doesn't offend you. But I do not date."

"Pity."

"Depends on your perspective, I would say."

The dark blue eyes that roved over her were frank in their appreciation. And they did not move her one iota. No, they did not.

She moistened her lips and turned away, heading blindly for the reception area. The sooner she got this man out of her office the better.

"Hey, Mom, I know it's not eleven-thirty yet, but Eric's mom said if I get there before then, she'll take us to the pizza parlor for lunch."

Her heart stopped and she barely kept from crying out to Ryan not to come into the office. But he was already there, bounding through the connecting door, exuberance in his stride. "I thought you were going to eat the lunch I left for you."

Ryan's smile was wide, the dimple in his cheek flashing. "I did. But I can always eat pizza. Can't we go a few minutes early?"

Rebecca was painfully aware of Sawyer standing behind her. "I'm with a patient, Ryan. I'll let you know when I'm ready."

Ryan, who knew better than to interrupt his mother

with a patient unless he was personally bleeding to death, made a face. "Sorry."

Rebecca softened. Ryan always did that to her. He was her son. Her shining joy. "A few more minutes, okay, Ry?"

He nodded, scooping his hair off his forehead and tugging the Mets ball cap back on his head. He started to turn back to the apartment. Rebecca started to breathe again.

And Sawyer stepped from behind Rebecca. "Is this your son, Bec?"

She swallowed. Hard. "My name is Rebecca. Or Dr. Morehouse. Or even Doc. Take your pick." Sawyer stopped right next to her, his shoulder brushing against hers and she sidled to the side.

"And what's my name?"

"Cap—" His smile widened when she swallowed the rest. "Yes," she decided to answer his question. "This is my son. Ryan."

Her son took that moment to suddenly become the polite young man she'd always wished for. He removed his cap and stuck out his hand. "I'm pleased to meet you, sir."

"Okay, pod person." Rebecca jostled Ryan's shoulder before Sawyer could shake her son's hand. "Who are you and what have you done with my son?"

Ryan rolled his eyes and managed to shake Sawyer's hand anyway. "I know who you are. Sawyer Clay, huh? My friend Eric says you used to be a SEAL. That's pretty cool. Was it anything like that Demi Moore movie?"

"Ryan thinks Demi Moore hung the moon." Rebecca put her arm around Ryan's shoulders, casually nudging him back toward their apartment. "The only thing he knows about that movie is that he's not old enough to watch the video.'' Then she realized Sawyer didn't have a clue who she was talking about. ''She's an actress.''

''With phenom—'' Ryan dropped his lifted, expressive hands at his mother's raised eyebrows, and flushed. He stuck his cap back on his head. ''She's real pretty,'' he finished.

''Go get your coat and boots,'' Rebecca suggested and watched until Ryan disappeared back through the connecting door. She walked over and shut it.

''How old is your boy?''

''Nine.'' She didn't want to discuss her son with this man. She'd have preferred it, actually, if the two had never even met. But the damage was done. And anyone in town could have told him her son's age. ''As you heard, I need to go on Mom duty for a while. So if you'll excuse me...''

''He seems tall for his age.''

''You have recall over the average heights of the nine-year-old male?''

''You really are a cool one.''

She moved across to the coat-tree and removed his jacket, holding it out for him. ''I trust you'll let me know if you need me? Medically speaking,'' she added, noticing the gleam in his eyes.

''Medically speaking, I think my need is only growing, Dr. Morehouse.'' He took the coat from her, his fingers deliberately brushing against hers. ''You have a fine-looking son. You must be very proud of him.''

Oh, this was ridiculous. She didn't really feel her throat knotting, did she? ''Thank you.'' She cleared her throat of the knot that couldn't possibly be there. ''I am proud of Ryan.''

"And Ryan's father?"

Rebecca shoved open the door, heedless of the brisk wind that carried snow in over her taupe pumps. "He's gone."

Sawyer didn't take the hint immediately. Rather, he ignored it. She could see that in his expression. "Divorced?"

"My husband died two years ago," she said coldly. "And I prefer not to discuss my private life with my patients."

He finally stepped through the doorway, his hand covering hers where it held the door open. "All your patients, or just me?"

It didn't matter, suddenly, what it revealed. She yanked her hand from beneath his warm palm, dislodging his hold on the door, as well. "Just you."

She pulled the door closed and snapped the lock into place.

Knees shaking, she crossed the reception area to the connecting door leading to their private apartment. The only reason she made it was knowing that if she collapsed in one of the chairs in the waiting room the way she wanted to, Sawyer would see her, since he was watching through the windows.

She didn't need to look over her shoulder to see him standing there; she could feel his dark blue gaze burning through her lab coat and taupe sweater beneath.

She shut the connecting door with no small amount of satisfaction. There were no windows on this side for Sawyer to see into.

Thank goodness.

Ryan was already bundled into his snow boots and was tugging on his thermal mittens. Rebecca pulled on her own coat and changed her pumps for more practical, lined boots. They went out the door at the back of the building—the door that, in spring and summer, opened into their own private yard, complete with tire swing for Ryan, though she suspected by now he'd figure he was too ''cool'' for the swing. Her Jeep was in the garage. Ryan pulled open the door while she started it up, letting the engine warm for a few minutes.

By the time she finally pulled out and around the building, she figured Sawyer would be gone. And she was right.

''Hey, Mom. What's wrong with him?''

''Who?'' She turned onto Main, the central street of Weaver that ran outside her office, driving cautiously even though there was no traffic to speak of.

''Sawyer Clay.''

Her hands tightened over the steering wheel. She passed the high school and turned onto Third Street. ''Ryan, you know we don't discuss patients.''

''Yeah, but—''

''He was in a car accident,'' she said. Ryan rolled his eyes. He already knew that, courtesy of his grapevine source, Eric. Eric's father owned the feed store, and if there was a central place of gossip, the feed store appeared to be it. Either there, or Ruby's Café or Colbys. Colbys had a restaurant now as well the bar, but nobody could make the mistake of calling the place a restaurant first and foremost. It was a bar.

Rebecca hated the place, even though she personally liked Newt Rasmusson, who owned the dive. She ended up treating more injuries from the brawls that occurred inside Colbys' walls than she wanted. It really was the only type of violence she'd encountered here in Weaver. And perhaps violence wasn't really the correct term, either. Most of the fights involved a few whiskeys too many and someone poaching on someone else's girl rather than the violence for the sake of violence that she'd seen too much of in New York.

Still, she much preferred her obstetric side of things. And with the three Clay wives all currently expecting as well as a half-dozen other women in town, that area of her practice was alive and well.

"Do you think he's married?"

Rebecca's foot pressed a little too hard on the brake, and her Jeep slid a foot or so as she halted in front of Eric's house. "What?"

"Sawyer Clay. Do you think he's got a wife? I bet he knows lots of cool stuff. From the SEALs and all. They're like total warriors. Right?"

Ryan was fascinated with the testosterone-blessed men of Weaver and the surrounding ranches. He gobbled up stuff like fishing and hunting and ranching like a starved puppy. Naturally he'd think a former SEAL would be heaven-sent. "I have no idea if Captain Clay is married," she replied briskly. Actually, if the man had ever acquired a wife, she'd eat her hat. The man she'd known had been too single-minded to take on those particular responsibilities. "Nor do I care. I'll pick you up at four-thirty, okay?"

"Naw. Eric's mom said she'd bring me back after supper."

"But she's also taking you for pizza for lunch."

"Cool, huh?"

"Cool," Rebecca repeated halfheartedly. She missed her son when he was gone over supper, but she also was pleased and proud of the friendships he'd made. Spending time with these people was good for Ryan. She watched her son jog up the snow-shoveled walk to the front door, which opened before he reached it.

She returned Eric's mother's wave and slowly drove back to the office.

Sawyer Clay married? Not likely. The only thing he'd been wed to had been his precious career.

And she knew from personal experience that nothing and no one could ever get in the way of *that*.

Chapter Three

"**W**hy just me?"

Even though her office was closed, Rebecca had put aside her supper to answer the phone when it rang, thinking it might be Ryan. Instead, she'd heard Sawyer's voice on the other end.

She now slumped down in her seat, wishing she could just hang up on him. Wondering why she didn't do just that. "You're very forward." That part of his personality hadn't been forgotten along with the memories.

"Pushy, you mean."

"Take it however you like, Captain."

"Have dinner with me."

"I believe we've played that song already."

"Call me persistent."

She'd call him a hazard. "I'm hanging up now, Captain."

"Do you like a man in uniform, Rebecca?" His voice was low. Husky. And it wrapped around her despite her resistance, stilling the motion to hang up. "You keep dwelling on the *Captain*. Maybe I should have brought one of those uniforms with me to Wyoming. You like the shoulder boards? The collar? You just into eagles, or what?"

She'd seen him in all manner of dress from his skivvies to full dress, long before he'd attained a captain's rank. Even back then, in a contest between her and the uniform, the uniform won. Hands down. "I prefer civilians, Captain."

"What did your husband do?"

Her fingers tightened on the receiver. "He was a neurosurgeon."

"Sounds...elegant. I'll bet he owned his own tux and drove a Lincoln Town Car."

"He was brilliant." And he had owned two tuxedos and driven a Jaguar.

"What was his name?"

"Tom."

"Good, solid name."

"He was a good, solid man." And discussing him with Sawyer Clay seemed the height of lunacy. Tom had been everything to her that Sawyer had not. She didn't know how she'd have gone on if Tom hadn't been a visiting lecturer at her school; hadn't made it a point to seek her out because of his long-standing friendship with her parents. He'd helped fit her heart back together after it had been shattered to pieces by Sawyer. He'd been there for her when Sawyer had not. He'd helped her transfer schools from California to New York, where he lived, helped her find an apartment, helped her focus on the reasons she just couldn't curl up and die after Sawyer had finished with her. He'd understood that she couldn't bear to remain in California where Sawyer would one day return. He'd given her his support and eventually his heart.

She cursed the burning behind her eyes. "Goodbye, Captain."

"Wait—"

Rebecca hung up. Then did the unthinkable and took the phone off the hook. It buzzed with the dial tone, then started beeping annoyingly. She turned the phone on its side and disconnected the receiver from the base. Silence.

If she was needed, she could be paged.

Sawyer tapped the cordless phone against his palm. He'd get to the bottom of the lovely Dr. Rebecca Morehouse. The challenge of the task intrigued him. Energized him.

"What's got you smiling?"

Sawyer looked up to see Matthew's wife entering the kitchen. Jaimie. She looked as if she had a basketball tucked under her bright green sweater. "When is your baby due?"

"March." She smiled easily at him, her person fairly vibrating with energy. "Squire is down visiting Gloria, and Matthew has succumbed to my wifely demands for pizza. We're driving into Weaver in a half hour or so. Want to join us?"

"As long as there are no anchovies."

Her head tilted. "You don't like them?"

"Can't stand them." He realized it was true. He knew he didn't like anchovies. "I'll be damned," he murmured.

"No, I think you'll be remembering," she corrected.

"On our way home tonight we're going to pick out a Christmas tree, so be sure to dress warm."

"Christmas tree." Sawyer's bit of good humor dwindled. "I wonder what I was doing last Christmas. I wasn't here."

"No," Jaimie confirmed gently. "Actually, if Emily and I succeed in our plans, this house is going to see a big, old-fashioned Christmas celebration. With all the family and the children gathered together here, instead of us all doing our own thing. It will be a basically new experience for all of us."

"Why?"

Jaimie hesitated, and Sawyer knew she'd been cautioned, as well.

He shook his head impatiently. "Forget I asked."

"Sawyer, I wish there was something I could do to help you."

The horrible thing was Sawyer knew she meant it. These people, these strangers who called themselves family, would quite obviously turn somersaults if they thought it would help him. The notion of being dependent on someone else's help, however, tasted bitter. Family, strangers, whatever. He felt like a man who was used to taking charge. Solving the problems. Not letting someone else do it for him. "Tell me about Gloria," he suggested. "That ought to be safe enough, right?"

So Jaimie filled him in on Squire's occasionally storm-filled relationship with The Widow Day. How they'd met when Squire had a heart attack several years back. "He spends half his time in Casper with her," Jaimie finished. "Unless they've had an argument. In which case, he'll come storming back here, and stomp around muttering about stubborn women and such. Then he'll cool off and trot on down there again.''

"Doesn't she come here?''

"Occasionally. We all just wish he'd be done with it and marry her.''

"Why hasn't he?''

Jaimie lifted her shoulders, as if to say, Who can explain Squire? "I'd better get Sarah ready to go to town,'' she announced, excusing herself to tend to her young daughter. Sarah. Apparently named after Matthew's mother, Sarah.

His mother, too.

Restlessness eating at his nerves, he went through the dining room, past the wide staircase and into the living room. The room, despite the welcoming furniture, seemed to shout disuse to him. What interested him, though, was the large portrait hanging over the fireplace. Sarah Clay. His mother.

She'd been a pretty woman, he thought objectively, with her long blond hair and blue eyes. He could see the resemblance she'd passed on to Matthew and Jefferson and Daniel, too, though not quite as strongly. There was another brother, too. Tristan. He was the youngest and lived in California, so he'd managed to weasel out of Matthew that morning while they'd been freezing off their cookies in the cold dawn.

Then Matthew came in and chaos erupted as Jaimie scurried around after Sarah, bundling the little girl into her coat and boots. An hour later, they were seated in the noisy restaurant, which, considering the filled tables, seemed to be a popular place in the small town. Judging by the greetings Matthew and Jaimie received, Sawyer figured everybody knew everybody.

Except him.

There was a collection of video games and air hockey tables at one end of the restaurant, and Sawyer watched the kids as they huddled around the games. One ball-capped head earned a second look, and he realized it was Ryan. Rebecca's son.

He reached back for the icy mug of beer the waitress had set at his elbow a few moments earlier and glanced at Jaimie. She was an easier target than Matthew. "You know Ryan Morehouse?"

Jaimie nodded, busy unwrapping the packets of saltine crackers for Sarah, who was ready to eat the things, plastic and all. "Is he here?" She craned around, spotting the boy. "He sure is. That's Eric Fielding with him. Do you see Rebecca here?"

Sawyer shook his head, aware of the disappointment he felt. For a minute there, he'd thought he'd have another crack at the cool doctor. Then Ryan saw him, and waved so enthusiastically he knocked his own ball cap askew and Sawyer's mood took an abrupt upswing.

What was it about the Morehouse mother and son that lightened the darkness clinging to his mind? He swung his legs over the picnic-table-style bench and grabbed his beer. "I'll be back."

Ryan grinned when Sawyer approached. "Evening, sir."

"Sawyer will do," he suggested. "What're you playing there?"

Ryan bounced on his toes, watching over Eric's shoulder as his friend's fingers maneuvered the video controls. He began explaining the intricacies of the game. "Blow 'em away," was clearly the object.

"Ah man," Eric groaned as he watched the piles of fallen mutants surround his lone defendant. "Ryan, take it, man." He scooted carefully off the seat which was incorporated into the structure of the game. "Hurry up."

Ryan slipped into place, his hands nimble on the controls as Eric raced toward the rest rooms.

"I thought you were coming here for lunch," Sawyer said. "Don't tell me you've been here all this time."

"No way. My mom would have a hissy."

Sawyer couldn't quite envision Dr. Morehouse in such a state, but it definitely inspired interesting possibilities.

"This is our second time here, today," Ryan continued.

"Hi, Ryan."

Sawyer watched Ryan's hands jerk on the control. His man bit the dust, but the boy didn't notice. How could he when his eyes were bugging out at the young girl who'd stopped to greet him. Sawyer hid his smile in his beer and watched as Ryan's throat worked for a second before a garbled "Hi" came out.

She dimpled prettily, her brown eyes never veering from young Ryan. "Are you having fun on vacation?"

"Uh, yeah. Sure." Ryan's knee jiggled, a sure sign of adolescent nerves. "You?"

"Yeah." The girl seemed ready to go on, but she heard her name called and rolled her eyes. "I gotta go before my dad has a cow."

"Yeah, sure. I'll...uh...see you around."

"Yeah." She smiled at Ryan, reluctance obvious as she backed away toward the man waiting near the entrance.

Once she was gone, Ryan's whole young body sighed. "Oh, man. That was Melanie. She's like, you know, totally hot."

"She likes you, too."

"Oh, wow. Ya think?"

"Definitely possible." Sawyer lifted his beer, then nudged the lovesick boy's shoulder. "Mind if I have a try at that?"

Ryan blinked. "The game? Have you played it before?"

"Not that I recall," Sawyer said dryly. "Is there some age limit prohibiting old men from playing?"

"You're not old," Ryan scoffed as he slid from the seat. He flipped some magical lever and the seat scooted back, allowing for Sawyer's considerably bulkier form. "Now Ruby Leoni from Ruby's Café? *She* is old. Like a hundred or something."

Sawyer laughed. And maneuvered into the game. He dropped some quarters into the slot and placed his hands on the controls. "Okay, master chief," he said to Ryan, "let's rock and roll."

Suzanne Fielding called Rebecca around seven-thirty with profuse apologies. She'd left the boys at the pizza parlor around six and had planned to pick them up by now, but her six-year old daughter suddenly took sick. Rebecca offered to go by and take a look at Eric's sister, but Suzanne said she was sure it was just the "flu that was going around." Instead, she asked if Rebecca could pick up the boys from the restaurant.

So Rebecca pulled on her coat and hat and gloves and got her Jeep out again for the short drive to the restaurant. She scurried into the town hot spot, her eyes immediately picking Ryan out from the kids milling about.

Unwinding her scarf from her neck, she started for her son who hadn't yet noticed her. She smiled when

Ryan hooted and pounded enthusiastically on the roof of the video contraption he stood next to. "Oh, man," she heard him say reverently. "Even Eric hasn't gotten to this level. Wait'll he sees it."

She didn't hear the words, only the low timbre of the response her son received, and her steps faltered. Then annoyance flowed hotly through her veins. The nerve. The gall.

She walked up beside the game, going to the opposite side of Ryan and looked at the man crammed inside. As usual. Acting the hotshot just like he used to do. "I should have known better than to think you'd respect my refusal to see you," she said tightly.

Sawyer looked up at her, his dark blue eyes narrowing. "Excuse me?"

"You just blithely do whatever you want just like you always—" She snapped her mouth shut, horrified at her lack of control. Ryan was staring at her as if she'd grown two heads. And Sawyer...

"Like I always...what?" he asked silkily. He looked up at her with his eyes intent and she felt as if *she* were the one pinned into that contraption of a game. "Bec?"

She swallowed, pushing her hands into her pockets. "Like the captain you are," she finished, knowing it was weak.

She was a physician. She wanted this man restored to full health.

She was also a woman. She hoped he never remembered. Ever.

"Ryan, why don't you finish off the game?" Sawyer suggested, catching her elbow when she started to scoot back from the game.

"No," Rebecca said hurriedly, stiffening under his

touch but refusing to jerk out from it the way she yearned to do. "I need to take Ryan and Eric home."

"Mo-om! Not yet! We're in the middle of the game."

Rebecca barely heard her son's fervent plea as Sawyer climbed from the game to tower over her. "Ryan, don't argue—"

But her son had already assumed the controls and was muttering over the game. Eric appeared, waving at her, then exclaimed over something Ryan had apparently succeeded at.

"Let 'em play," Sawyer said softly.

No matter what it displayed, she yanked her elbow from his hand. "This does not concern you."

"Considering you fly off the handle and start screaming at me that I'm plotting some—"

"I do not scream."

"Could have fooled me, Bec."

He didn't need to touch her to make her blood run shrieking through her veins. All he had to do was call her that. Next thing she knew he'd call her "sweetness" and then "sweet Becky Lee." And he'd remember just where they'd been when he'd said those words. When his voice had been husky with tenderness, then rough with passion.

She trembled. Hated herself for it and forced her mind toward coherency. "Stay away from my son."

The command was as effective as a slap. But she should have known that Capt. Sawyer Clay, former Navy SEAL, hotshot intelligence expert and God knew what else wouldn't be deterred by a verbal slap.

"Why are you afraid of me, Bec?"

She wished she could retract everything she'd said to him. Pull it back in where he couldn't wonder and puzzle over it. When he'd just think she was the stand-offish town doctor. "That's ridiculous." She made herself look him in the face. "I'm only…concerned that you have no regard for my disinterest."

Sawyer nearly laughed with amusement. The doctor was trying so hard to recover her composure. He far preferred her brown eyes spitting gold flames between her thick lashes than remaining encased in ice. "Concerned. Sweet Becky, you wanted to tear my head off and we both know it." He caught her elbows when every speck of color drained from her face and her knees buckled. "Whoa."

She lifted a trembling hand to her forehead. "Ryan," she said. "I have to get him…home. And Eric."

She frowned and Sawyer knew instinctively she was on the edge of tears. He nudged her toward the lone, unoccupied table sitting in the middle of the video games. "In a bit." She sank onto the bench—a sure indication she was not herself. He hunkered down in front of her, ignoring the protest in his sore body and curled his hands around hers. They were cold. "What's gotten you in such a tizzy? You hate uniforms that much?" Her fingers curled, but he didn't let her go.

"You're not in uniform," she said after a moment. Her lashes swept down, and he knew she was looking at their hands. "Sawyer, please."

Maybe his crouched position was cutting off the blood from his brain. Maybe he was having a stroke. Maybe he was going stark raving mad.

He'd heard those words before.

Heard them spoken by this woman and the realization made his head tighten as if it were in a vise. Sweet Becky. The endearment echoed hollowly through his aching head. *Why?* "Who are you? Why do I know you?"

Now that he was the one reeling, she seemed to regain her composure. "You don't," she said, a shadow of her former crispness returning to her demeanor. "If you'll excuse me, I must take my son and his friend home."

She tugged at her hands, and this time, Sawyer let her go. He pulled himself onto the bench and watched her aim straight for her son. Ryan's argument was short-lived, but Sawyer recognized the frustration in the boy's eyes as he and his young friend trudged after Rebecca, who sketched a wave toward Matthew and Jaimie, but didn't slow her progress toward the exit.

Sawyer was frustrated, too. There was more to Dr. Rebecca Morehouse than met his eyes. One way or another, he'd find out what it was.

And how she figured in the memories locked inside his murky mind.

She was, hands down, the most beautiful woman he'd ever seen. The knowledge should have relieved him, that he had some sense of this, when looking at his own face aroused no familiarity.

All it did was eat at him. How could he know something so assuredly about a woman he'd never met?

Just as he knew one day he'd taste her lips and would hold her beautiful, curving body against his. Maybe it would bring some memory back into his murky mind. Maybe it wouldn't.

He strongly suspected that when he held her the way his gut urged him to, he wouldn't care if he remembered anything or not.

That just holding her, tasting her, loving her, would be enough.

Chapter Four

"You're a lot like him."

Sawyer looked up from the photo album opened on the kitchen table to see Jefferson's wife, Emily, standing in the doorway. He'd been thinking more about the previous evening at the pizza parlor than about the photos in front of him. "Like who?"

She smiled and tucked her rainwater-straight hair behind her ears. "Squire." She walked—waddled, really, considering the pregnant belly she had to counterbalance—toward the table and looked over his shoulder. "I recognized that old album," she explained. "From Squire's early days with Sarah."

Sawyer rose and pulled out a chair, wondering how she could keep her balance as she sat and exhaled a heartfelt sigh. Unlike Jaimie, who was leggy and tall, this sister-in-law was so short, he could have tucked her in his pocket. "How long you got to go with that kid?"

She folded her arms across her distended belly. "Nineteen days." She sighed. "And I came over to see Jaimie to distract myself from the interminable wait. But she's busy with Sarah just now." She scooted forward in her chair, reaching forward for the corner of the album. "That's your dad's wedding picture," she said. Her fingertip hovered over the youthful Squire. "They were only seventeen when they got married."

"Babies," Sawyer murmured.

Emily made a sound that could have been amusement or dissent. "Young or not, they managed to make the Double-C a successful operation." She raised her eyebrows, then turned the page of the album when Sawyer didn't protest. "They built this big old house and filled it with sons."

"Squire didn't remarry."

"No." She smiled wryly. "But we live in hope."

"I got that impression yesterday from Jaimie." He flipped back to the previous page with its larger, single photo and studied the black-and-white image. Squire looked wet-behind-the-ears young, yet there was nothing but confidence in his expression; and nothing but adoration in the long, gangly arm he had wrapped around his petite bride. "What day did they get married?"

"February 26."

If his wallet hadn't burned inside the car, he would have pulled it out to look at his driver's license. It irked him that he didn't know what day he'd been born.

Emily patted his arm and pushed back from the table, levering herself to her feet. "August first," she said.

His eyes narrowed.

"You may not remember me just now, Sawyer," she said softly. "But I know you. I can imagine what your mind is puzzling over, trying to fit all the pieces together until it comes back to you as memories rather than facts you've pulled from photo albums and such. Jefferson would behave the same way. You and he are the most like Squire."

"Jefferson looks like Sarah."

"He has her coloring," Emily agreed. "But his stubborn nature is pure Squire. Like you."

"I'm not stubborn."

"Perhaps," she allowed, though her soft smile said otherwise. "But memory or not, you are a man who knows what he wants. With confidence instilled in you right down to your bone marrow. We know it, even if you have temporarily forgotten.

"Tell Jaimie that I had to leave, would you please?" Emily said, glancing down at her watch. "She's upstairs with Sarah and frankly I can't stomach the idea of climbing them all just now. If I don't leave now, I won't make my doctor's appointment with Rebecca."

He figured what he knew about gestating females would have filled a thimble, even if he did have his memory. But Emily was obviously miserable, despite her serene expression and gentle smiles. He followed her through the kitchen. "Are you sure you should drive?"

"I drove over here from our place."

"But that's only ten miles or so."

"You and Jefferson." She shook her head, waving

away his concern. She reached for the coat she'd hung on a hook in the mudroom. "I'll be...*oh*—"

He took the coat from her nerveless fingers when she halted mid-stride and mid-sentence. "I'll call Jefferson."

"He and Daniel are gone for the day at some farm auction."

"Then I'll drive you."

"Sawyer, really, that's not necessary. You're barely out of the hospital."

He snorted, watching the way she was rubbing her slightly puffy hand over her massive belly. "And you look like you're ready to go *to* the hospital. I'll drive. I remember how," he said dryly. "Get yourself bundled up while I start your truck."

There were two other cars parked outside Rebecca's office and Sawyer pulled up next to them, then went around to help Emily. "You're not gonna have that kid *now,* are you?" The thought sent horror right to his toes.

Emily chuckled and shook her head. "Not on your life. Jefferson would never forgive himself if he went off to buy a tractor only to come back and find our son had already arrived."

He pulled open the office door, hoping Emily's certainty wasn't misplaced. "It's a boy?"

"That's what I think. Your brother, of course, disagrees with me." She unwound her scarf as they entered the empty reception room. "We won't know for sure until the baby arrives."

She didn't settle in one of the chairs as Sawyer expected, but apparently preferred to pace slowly back and forth across the gray, tweedy carpet. Twice, he suggested that she sit. And more than twice, he offered to get Rebecca. Emily just waved her hand, calmly telling him to relax, and continued to slowly pace.

Five minutes passed before an elderly woman appeared with Rebecca following. Sawyer watched Rebecca with her patient, calmly and warmly answering the woman's questions.

Rebecca even escorted the woman across the reception area, her steps faltering momentarily when she saw him sitting in one of the chairs. But she didn't take her attention from her patient, helping the woman into her coat and opening the door for her. She even waited until her patient was in her car and driving away before turning back inside.

Her eyes skated over him, focusing on Emily. "You made it," she said, smiling easily. "Come on back." She dashed one look over her shoulder as she waited for Emily to precede her back to the examining rooms.

Sawyer stretched out his legs, crossing them leisurely at the ankle. And smiled.

Rebecca's cheeks flushed, and she hurried after Emily.

Feeling better than he had all day, Sawyer closed his eyes, listening to the soft, piped-in music. He'd have figured she'd play country rather than this slow, bluesy jazz. His thoughts drifted along with the low, mournful wail of a sax.

Twenty minutes passed before Rebecca walked into sight. She went right to the desk, not acknowledging his presence with so much as a grimace as she sat. Her pen busily moved across whatever was on her desk.

He sat there wondering which of them would give in first. Then the familiar scent of her drifted along his senses. "Emily okay?"

The pen paused. "Yes." She didn't look up. Not until they heard wheels roll too fast and slow too abruptly outside the office and they both looked out the windows to see two tall men jumping out of a big black pickup truck.

Then the door flew wide and Jefferson stood in the doorway, Daniel right behind him. "Why is Emily here?" he barked. Rebecca didn't answer him fast enough and he was moving across the reception area, a faint limp in his rapid stride that took him right on past the desk. "Emily?" He called her name loudly.

Rebecca hopped up. "She's fine," she assured hurriedly. "Just more false labor."

"Where?"

"Room two." She'd barely gotten out the words before he brushed past her. They heard a door open, and a startled squeak. Then low murmurs and the door slammed shut again.

Daniel shrugged out of his sheepskin coat, his expression relieved as he grinned at Rebecca. "He saw their truck and steered my pickup right on over here," he said. "Not smart, considering *I* was in the driver's seat. How you doing, Doc?"

She smiled and answered Daniel, easily making conversation.

Easily making Sawyer's nerves knot. It obviously was no exaggeration that she reserved her icy bedside manner for him, alone.

Rebecca could have cried with relief when Jefferson and Emily finally appeared. Emily's cheeks were rosy, and her velvety brown eyes were sparkling. She looked thoroughly kissed, and the faint smear of lipstick still on Jefferson's face confirmed it.

Rebecca didn't dare look Sawyer's way. She handed

over the paperwork to Jefferson and reminded Emily of her next appointment, then busied herself with her appointment book while they all trooped out of her office, leaving her in solitary peace.

She heard one engine start, then watched thankfully when it drove away from her office. But her relief was short-lived when the office door opened once again and Sawyer stood there. She could see Daniel's pickup behind him in the parking lot, still parked crookedly over the curb. There was no sign, however, of Daniel.

He stepped through, pulling the door closed, cutting off the rush of cold air. "More patients today?"

"No." He turned to the door and flipped the lock and she chastised herself for not thinking to lie. "What are you doing?"

He shrugged out of his bomber jacket and tossed it onto one of the chairs. Most men in these parts wore sheepskin coats or parkas at this time of year. Sawyer Clay, of course, had to wear black leather that looked as soft and supple as a newborn baby's skin. Idiot macho man. He probably froze outside.

But she didn't care about that. She did not. "I asked what you're doing."

"Making myself comfortable," he finally said.

"Office hours are over."

He touched the bandage on his jaw. "I think these are ready to come out," he said easily.

She nearly told him to take them out himself. Nearly. She'd spent a sleepless night before, thanks to this man and the words that had come so easily to his lips in the restaurant. "Fine." She wheeled on her heel and went into room one. He came in and started to close the door. "Leave it open."

He closed it anyway. "Afraid to be alone with me?"

"Hardly." She yanked open the drawers, staring stupidly at the contents. What was she doing?

He reached past her and she nearly jumped out of her skin. His eyes were darkly blue and knowing as he dropped the bandage he'd pulled from his jaw into the trash receptacle. She snatched up what she needed from the drawer and slammed it shut with her hip.

He sat on the exam table and Rebecca wished she didn't have to get so close to him. But she couldn't very well remove the tiny sutures while keeping the safe distance of the room between them.

Oh, who are you kidding? The only safe distance from this man was afforded by hundreds of miles.

She pushed his chin until she could see what she was doing, and rapidly removed the stitches. "Done," she said. "What about the ones in your shoulder?"

"I took 'em out myself yesterday. They were itching." He pulled the collar of his button-down shirt to one side, showing her the healing wound. "No problems there."

"Good. Then you can go."

"Not yet."

Of course he wouldn't go. Sawyer Clay had never done anything he didn't want to do, in whatever time he chose, at his own convenience and no one else's. "Fine," she retorted. "Then I will." Her heart was pounding only because of annoyance, she assured herself. He didn't inspire anything other than annoyance in her anymore. She made for the door.

He stuck out one long arm, stopping her progress. She refused to struggle. That third room was *definitely* going to be considerably larger. "I don't enjoy being groped by patients."

"Since my hand is respectably around your upper arm, I hardly consider this groping."

His hand was around her upper arm. His knuckles, however, brushed against the side of her breast. But she'd rot before acknowledging the wave of heat that contact created.

"What is it about you, Sweet Becky, that pulls at me?" He was the one doing the pulling. Pulling her around to face him. Pulling her forward until she stood between his thighs against the cushioned surface of the table.

She swallowed, vowing to ignore him. If he didn't get a reaction from her, he'd tire of his prying. She'd given away far too much when he'd called her that at the pizza parlor. She wasn't going to fall for it again.

"And what is it about me, Dr. Morehouse, that pushes you away?"

She set her teeth, keeping her eyes trained toward the door. Toward freedom.

"Your heart is racing," he murmured. "Why is that?"

"Dislike." The word escaped.

It didn't seem to offend him. Just intensified the curiosity in his eyes. "Why? If we haven't met, as you say, then what have I done to inspire your dislike?" He shook his head and her eyes unwillingly focused on the strands of silver threading through the lustrous strands at his temples.

She'd always known his hair would be prone to waviness if he ever let it grow past an inch or so. She dragged her eyes back to the doorway.

"I don't think it's dislike," he continued. "I know it's not."

One of her eyebrows peaked. "You know nothing."

"Only because I can't remember."

"Because you don't know me," she said flatly. No more now than he had before. He hadn't really known her. He certainly hadn't loved her, despite his words. Because if he had, he wouldn't have ripped out her heart and trampled it underneath his polished shoes.

She'd been a med student focused on her studies, on the career she had mapped out in her head. They'd met in the emergency room over his bleeding leg, and she'd been lost after one look into his midnight-colored eyes. When he'd pursued, she'd been so easily caught that even now, years later, it still mortified her. One week she was a serious med student, the next she was making room in her bureau drawers for his skivvies. He'd never "officially" moved in with her, but he'd spent more nights under her apartment roof in San Diego than he had his own roof at the naval station. He'd been sexy and fun and difficult and cocky. But when he'd taken her virginity, he'd been gentle and loving and intense and commanding.

She'd thought he'd been honest, too. Believing his husky words of love. She was wrong.

He'd taken her love and her trust and her faith and dismissed them with a casual flick of his fingers. She would never forgive him for that. And she'd never give him a chance to hurt her son, either.

Never.

"I want to change that."

Rebecca's stomach plunged to her feet. But he wasn't talking about her unspoken thoughts. "Change what?"

"Knowing you."

"There is no point."

"I disagree."

"Then we'll have to agree to disagree." Why on earth couldn't the confounded man remove his hands?

"There are worse things in the world," he said. "None of which explains why your pulse is thundering so unevenly that I can see it beating like a wild bird trapped against your lovely throat."

"Wild birds don't like to be caged."

His lips curved faintly and Rebecca lowered her eyes, fiercely reminding herself why she couldn't succumb to his masculine appeal.

Then she realized he'd lowered his hands from her arms, and she was still willingly standing there. His thighs brushed her hips, hard and warm through his blue jeans and her lab coat and slacks.

Move away, move away, her mind cried. Go. Fly away.

Then his hand—long fingers and broad palm—slid through her hair, cupping her neck, while his thumb rested on her pulse. "Sweet Becky," he murmured.

A cry rose in her throat. *Don't call me that.*

"I won't hurt you."

You already have. But how could she tell him that?

Then his lips covered hers, and she forgot everything. Past, present and future.

There was only his lips against hers, gently brushing. Softly tantalizing. Soothing. Seducing.

She trembled wildly and grabbed for something, anything, to steady her reeling senses. But what she grabbed, what her hands plastered themselves to were his strong thighs. And his breath hissed and his head lifted. He ran his thumb across her lower lip, his shoulders lifting with the deep breath he drew. "You make me forget," he said, and his low words rumbled across her heart. "That darkness in my head goes away when I see you, Bec. Why is that?"

She shook her head, moistening her lips. "Don't."

He caught her face between his palms, his touch gentle and painfully familiar. Painfully new. "Take away the darkness, sweet Becky. Just for a while."

Tears burned behind her lids. When his mouth covered hers, she opened to him, unable to withstand the temptation. His tongue met hers, and she couldn't stop the soft moan that rose in her. Then his hands weren't cupping her face, but were running down the unbuttoned lab coat, slipping underneath to find her waist. To burn against her back when he delved beneath the hem of her red and green sweater.

As if by magic, he found the clasp of her bra and his fingers nudged it away, sliding over the thrust of her breasts. Finding and conquering the tips that tightened frantically against his sure fingers. His mouth left hers and she gasped for air, her fingers sliding up his chest, flexing uncontrollably over his shoulders, sinking into the satin heaviness of his silver-laced hair.

"It's okay, sweet Becky," he murmured, running a rain of fire along her jaw. Tasting the thundering pulse in her neck with his tongue.

Time swayed and blurred and folded.

"Ah, sweet, sweet Becky." Her lab coat slipped heedlessly to the floor and he drew her sweater upward.

She shivered and he shushed her, gathering her closer, ever closer. And it was that first time all over again when she'd been so frightened and eager and so in love with him that she'd do anything he asked of her. Her fingers pressed against his scalp, feeling the shape of his head, his ears. His hard, angled jaw and lean, bristled cheeks, hollowing ever so slightly as he gained the peak of her breast and drew the agonizingly tight nipple between his lips.

She arched mindlessly against him, and he helped her with his other arm slipping behind her waist, holding her on her toes for his hunger. Then his palm moved down over her bottom, shifting, rearranging until instead of standing between his thighs, he'd nudged one leg between hers, pulling her up hard and tight against him.

"I can't do this," she gasped, her forehead falling to his shoulder.

"Yes." His breath was rough, his kiss urgently crossing to her other breast, treating it to the same devastating attention. Then to her shoulder. Her neck again. Meeting her lips, delving, tasting, devouring. His palms surrounded her hips, his thumbs reaching toward the heat of her where his thigh pressed so intimately against her. "So good, Bec," he praised roughly when their lips parted for air. "Let it go, sweetness. Let me have it."

She would. Only because she loved him so. She'd give him what she wouldn't give any of her fellow classmates; her boyfriends. He was different from all of them. Older and experienced and so sure of himself. She felt the tightening in her belly spread and clung to him, grateful for the hands that moved her when she lost the ability to speak. To think. He notched his thigh higher between hers and swallowed her breathy cries with his lips…. Oh, she loved him—

"Mo-om! You back there?"

Rebecca's head whipped up and she stared at Sawyer with horror as the past slammed into the present. A present with years of disillusionment and tears and pain standing between them.

Her eyes burned, and she shoved out of his arms. But getting away from him wasn't enough. Not when he watched her, his eyes dark with a wanting that she remembered too well. Wanting that hadn't really been the love she'd foolishly believed it to be.

"Damn you, Sawyer Clay," she cursed hoarsely. And raised her hand before thought could stop her.

Sawyer caught her hand before it could connect with his face, however. The slap would have stung like hell, he knew, but the expression glittering in her golden-brown eyes hurt more. Such pain. Such hurt.

Such accusation.

She twisted against his hold, apparently forgetting the voice that had jerked them both to their senses before things got out of hand.

"She'll be out in a second, Ryan," he raised his voice loud enough for the boy to hear out in the reception area.

The color drained from her cheeks. She stared at him, no doubt unaware of the mute pleading in her expression.

Sawyer would have given everything he owned—if he could only recall what all that was—to have more time with her. More time to figure out why holding her felt like home. Why her eyes told him things he knew he should know, but didn't.

He didn't even know why he felt such sorrow in his gut. Only that he did.

He stood from the table and finished the job that she'd begun of yanking his shirt out of his jeans. Her eyes widened, then flickered away when she realized what he was hiding with the long shirttails. Then she seemed to realize her own clothes were far more disheveled than his, and whirled around, presenting her back to him as she fumbled her clothing back into place and snatched her lab coat off the floor.

He reached for the tangled sleeve, trying to help her, and she bared her teeth like a wounded kitten, backing away and finishing the task unaided. "The next time you need a doctor, drive to Gillette." Her voice shook almost as much as the hands that attacked the buttons on her lab coat.

He wasn't too worried about medical care, just now. "This isn't over," he warned.

"Yes, it is." She raked her fingers through her hair. Fumbled with her stethoscope, the pen that had fallen out of her pocket. "It was over before it even started."

"You admit it, then." He felt as if he were standing on the precipice of a bottomless abyss.

She yanked open the door. "I admit nothing." She ran her fingers through her hair once more and hurried out to the reception area.

Ryan was sitting on the desk, swinging his legs. The pleasure Sawyer felt when the boy's eyes lit at the sight of him knocked him sideways for a bit.

"Hey, Sawyer!" Ryan hopped off the desk. "Wicked slash on your jaw, man. Bet that hurt plenty."

"That's enough, Ryan." Rebecca gestured toward her son, obviously trying to hustle the boy out of the office.

Ryan, however, had a mind of his own. "You think maybe you can go with me to the pizza parlor to play video games again? I'd sure like to see you reach the sixth level again."

"Ryan! Captain Clay is not here to entertain you. Go set the table for supper."

Ryan's blue eyes widened at his mother's vehement

tone. He gathered up his young frame, only a few inches shorter than his mother's. "Jeez, Mom, what's—"

"We'll work out something, Ryan," Sawyer promised before the boy said anything to send his mother toppling over the edge. "Better do as your mother says."

Ryan made a face. But he didn't argue. "Yes, sir." He headed back through the open door that Sawyer now realized must lead to their living quarters.

Rebecca whirled on Sawyer the second Ryan was out of earshot. "I don't need your interference with my son."

"I will figure it out. Or I'll remember," he said as he picked up his coat from the chair where he'd left it. The relief fairly rolled in waves from Rebecca's slender frame when he unlocked the office door. "Rebecca—" God, he hated the way she stiffened when he spoke her name, vowing right then and there to get to the bottom of the animosity that went beyond discomfort over what they'd shared in the examining room. "For what it's worth, I am sorry. Not for what happened in that little room back there. But for whatever it was I did in the past that's got you upset."

Her lips tightened, and she didn't look away fast enough for him to miss the liquid glimmer in her eyes. Her jaw worked, then her words finally came. "I don't like being attacked by my patients," she said tightly.

The statement enraged him, just as he figured she'd intended. And knowing it, the anger dissipated, leaving his head aching and his gut clenched. Before he could say another word, however, Rebecca turned and went through the doorway that Ryan had used, slamming the door behind her.

Raking his hands through his hair, Sawyer briefly debated going after her. But she probably would call the sheriff, and then he'd have to explain things he couldn't even explain to himself. Retreat and regroup, he reminded himself.

So he let himself out the door, making sure it locked after him. Then he climbed stiffly behind the wheel of his brother's black pickup and drove out of town. He had to get some answers to the questions plaguing him.

Had to.

Chapter Five

Jefferson had told Sawyer that the horse ranch he and Emily owned was east of the Double-C a bit, and when Sawyer neared the main entrance of the Double-C, he drove the black truck right on past. Another ten miles or so and the road curved and dipped and he spotted the river-stone pillars that held a heavy gate, opened wide. He slowed and turned in, his sharp gaze taking in the gold plate affixed to the center of the gate as he drove past. Clay Farm, it read.

He parked in front of the house and stared for a few minutes at the single-story dwelling, but his mind was still back at the doc's office; still focused on the tears that had collected in Rebecca's eyes when he'd apologized for things he couldn't even remember.

A gust of wind rocked the truck as he got out, lowering his head against the biting wind when he headed up the wide stone steps leading to the front door. He knocked twice and waited, looking back over his shoulder at the snowy landscape. From what he could see, Jefferson's operation was first-class all the way.

The creak of the door snagged his attention again. Jefferson stood in the doorway. Now that he was here, Sawyer didn't know what to say. Which annoyed the hell out of him.

Jefferson smiled faintly as if he knew precisely what Sawyer was thinking and stepped back, opening the way into his home. Then he turned and led him through an arched doorway into a spacious kitchen.

"How's Emily?"

Jefferson hooked open the refrigerator door and pulled out two long-necks. "She wanted a nap once we got home. Which is a good thing since she hasn't been sleeping well at night lately. The baby keeps her awake." He held out a bottle. "What's keeping *you* awake?"

"What isn't?" Sawyer took the bottle and automatically popped the top off against the sharp edge of the granite counter. A part of his mind noticed the faint smile that reappeared on Jefferson's face as his brother twisted off the cap and tossed it alongside the one from Sawyer's on the counter. "I just want—" He shook his head, the knot in his gut growing. "Hell, I don't know what I want. My life back. Then I'd sleep."

Jefferson watched him for a moment, then turned on his heel and led him over to a long room with windows that offered a panoramic view of snow and sparse trees and mountains off in the distance.

Jefferson lowered himself, grimacing slightly, into one of the deep chairs alongside two long couches. "Might as well sit, Sawyer," he suggested.

But Sawyer prowled around the room, wondering if

he'd ever look out at that snowy landscape and feel some sense of familiarity. Even though he was here, ready to talk to Jefferson, it wasn't because he felt some inner kinship to the man. It was simply that he'd *known* Jefferson the longest, since he was the one who'd been at the hospital back east. Still, asking the question wasn't easy. He started to rub his chin, then stopped at the painful tenderness of the healing cut. "How do I know Rebecca Morehouse?" He deliberately loosened his tight jaw. "Aside from now, that is."

"Got me."

Sawyer looked over his shoulder at the man. His brother who had barged his way into the hospital even when Sawyer had told his doctors he didn't want his "family" to know he was there.

"Seriously. Rebecca came to Weaver a few years ago when the town finally got its act together enough to conduct a search rather than wait in vain for some doctor to decide he or she couldn't live anywhere else in the world. Other than a few details, I have no idea what her life was like before she came to Weaver."

"I know her." He almost expected his brother to laugh at the statement, but Jefferson didn't. Sawyer stepped around the couch and sat down, placing his beer bottle on the table. "I do."

"Okay."

"That's it? Okay?"

"What else do you want me to say?" Jefferson drew his feet off the table and sat forward, too. He grimaced at the movement. "Wet winter makes my hip ache," he muttered. "Listen, Sawyer, you weren't exactly one for keeping the rest of us informed of every little thing in your life. Hell, you were gone as much or more than

I was. There's no way we could know whether or not you knew Rebecca before.'' He tilted the beer to his lips, then set the bottle next to Sawyer's. "Ask her."

"I have."

A spark of curiosity grew in Jefferson's expression. "And?"

Sawyer grimaced. "She wouldn't say." He clawed his fingers through his hair. Just lifting his arm made his chest ache, but the ache was nothing compared to the frustration churning inside him. Frustration from not knowing. Not knowing his family. Not knowing what he'd done to cause the tears in Rebecca's eyes. Frustration because his body knew Rebecca's, whether or not his brain did.

And dammit, her body had answered. He might not remember his own birthday, but he knew when a woman wanted his touch. He knew that this particular woman had wanted it. And he knew that he'd touched her before. *He knew it.*

Jefferson leaned back again in his chair, propping his boots once more on the table. Sawyer eyed him. "You're no more help than the rest of 'em."

"Did you expect me to be?"

Tired of Jefferson's hedging, Sawyer sighed impatiently and changed tack. "Why were you gone so much?"

"Work."

"That tells me a helluva lot, Jefferson."

Jefferson chuckled. And oddly enough, Sawyer found himself smiling, too. "We ran into each other now and then, professionally speaking," Jefferson allowed.

"You were with the teams?"

"No."

"Then what?"

"Does the name Coleman Black ring any bells for you?"

Sawyer thought. His eyes narrowed. He felt as if he should know the name. There was a hint of familiarity in the ring of it. "No."

"He's the guy you were supposed to meet with and didn't. He couldn't reach you when he called and so he started checking. He didn't get much from your commanding officer. Cole knew Daniel had just gotten hitched and that Tris was out of the country so he called me. I flew to Maryland and, despite your welcoming smile, sprang you from the place."

"Why was I supposed to meet with Black?"

"Who knows? It probably had to do with the case you were working on last Thanksgiving. You and Cole are the only ones who can answer that. He heads up an agency called Hollins-Winwood. Maybe that name is familiar?"

He shook his head, feeling a fresh throb set up residence inside his temple. "No."

Jefferson smiled faintly. "Wish I could forget its existence, too," he said. "I used to be in special ops for them. Private. Dan was, too, for a while. Tris, however, hasn't learned better, yet."

"How'd you get involved in something like that?"

Jefferson waited a beat. Then decided to answer. "The intel community is surprisingly small," he said. "I got recruited out of school by Cole because of…certain skills he'd learned I possessed." His lips twitched, without humor. "You and Cole go way back even if neither of you advertise the fact."

Sawyer looked at his brother. Jefferson was the middle brother of the five Clays. But the cynical glint in

Jefferson's eyes only came from a lifetime and then some of seeing things people weren't meant to see. And he knew instinctively that Black had learned about Jefferson's "skills" because Sawyer had told him.

"So you didn't hang around the ranch, either. What brought you back?"

Jefferson reached for his beer and leaned lazily back in his chair again. But the laziness was deceptive, Sawyer noticed. And recognized it, because it was something he understood. Something he identified with.

"Got a little too beat-up," his brother said. Then he smiled wryly, his expression lightening. A decade of hard living disappeared from his face. "Emily."

A rustle near the door brought Sawyer's attention around, but he realized that Jefferson had been aware of the sound long before he was.

Emily walked into the room, her gait slow. She smiled at Sawyer but quietly glowed when she stopped next to her husband's chair, her hand easily falling to his shoulder. "Did I hear my name?"

Jefferson's hand covered hers and Sawyer barely heard Jefferson's response as he eyed the couple, so clearly two parts of one whole.

He couldn't help but wonder if he himself had ever felt that way. Had ever felt that complete. Wondered if there was a woman out there somewhere who completed him. A woman he couldn't remember.

The only face that swam into his mind was the beautiful one of Rebecca Morehouse.

He realized Emily was speaking to him and focused with an effort on her invitation to stay for supper. He pushed to his feet and shook his head. "Thanks, but I've already got plans." They didn't question him. Emily simply told him that he was welcome to join them anytime. He waved Jefferson back in place when his brother started to rise. "I'll find my way out," he said. "Thanks for the drink."

Leandra was playing in the hallway with a stack of colorful blocks which she'd spread around in an uncanny resemblance of a small town and she hopped up, scattering a tower as she did so. "You going byebye, Uncle Sawyer?"

Sawyer stopped, looking down at his niece. She resembled both her parents; her coloring from Jefferson, her delicate features from Emily. "Yes."

She smiled and held up her hands, clearly expecting him to do something.

A soft snort from behind told him that Jefferson had followed him to the door after all. "She wants a goodbye kiss," he said.

Right. Sawyer leaned over and dropped a kiss on her forehead, but she wrapped her arms around his neck and clung like a limpet. He had to scoop her up or let her fall, so he lifted her and she giggled against his cheek. Sawyer's arms tightened fractionally around her warm little body. God. Had he ever wanted children of his own?

Leandra smacked her lips loudly against his cheek, then wriggled around and Sawyer set her back on her feet, where she darted back into the center of her blocktown and immediately began rebuilding the tower she'd knocked over. Despite the fact that his brother moved rather gingerly, Jefferson folded his long length down onto the floor beside his daughter and began stacking red, blue and green blocks.

Feeling colder somehow, Sawyer pulled on his coat and left. He drove through the main gate of the Double-C and parked in front of the big house. The daylight was dwindling and golden light spilled from the windows. He supposed it presented a pretty welcoming picture, especially considering the light fall of snow that had begun halfway between the drive from Jefferson's place to here.

He wondered what kind of life he'd led that he couldn't even seem to appreciate the picturesque sight. Had he ever appreciated the ranch? Or had it always inspired the edgy knot of tension inside his gut that he now felt?

He made a rough sigh of impatience. Sitting here freezing wasn't accomplishing a damn thing. He suddenly knew what he wanted to do. He wanted to drive Daniel's truck right back into Weaver and find out if welcoming warm light shone from the windows of Rebecca's home.

Rebecca peered at the cookbook, checking the recipe for the delicate, lacy cookies. The photograph showed beautifully golden tubes, one end dipped in rich chocolate. What sat on her counter, however, more closely resembled charcoal briquettes.

She went into the pantry to get the trash can and carried it back to the counter, sweeping the flopped results from the counter into it. So much for this particular batch of holiday cookies.

It was probably better if she stuck to her usual peanut-butter cookies that she'd learned how to bake in high school economics. It was just that the photograph in the cookbook had looked so pretty. The instructions so impossibly simple.

"Hey, Mom, look who's... Oh, gross. Burned 'em again, huh?"

"Don't rub it in, kiddo." Rebecca dashed her hand

across the counter, sweeping the last of the ruined recipe into the trash and looking over her shoulder at the same time. Seeing the man standing behind her son shocked her so deeply that her fingers loosened and the narrow kitchen trash can slipped from her fingers, sending burned cookies and the empty cans of sloppy-joe mix she'd used for Ryan's supper skidding across the flour-dusted kitchen floor.

Ryan goggled. "Jeez, Mom."

Feeling heat climb her face to the roots of her hair, Rebecca yanked the trash can upright and started scooping up the cookies, dumping them back inside. Sawyer's boot stopped a rolling can, and he crouched down to pick it up and toss it into the can. Their fingers bumped when they reached for the last can at the same time and Rebecca quickly snatched it, tipping it into the trash can. She stood, brushing her fingers over the sides of her jeans. Sawyer rose, too and she decided that her kitchen was too darned small. First her exam rooms, and now her kitchen. If the man didn't stop coming around, she'd find the entire state too small.

She stepped back and bumped soundly against the counter behind her. Sawyer, darn him, didn't move. Just watched her with his eyes dark and steady.

Her son, on the other hand, giggled wildly. "Jeez, Mom. You take your klutz pills today?"

Cheeks hot, Rebecca looked past Sawyer to Ryan. "Don't you have some work to do? You promised."

Ryan's grin died. He rolled his eyes but went. Only a moment or two passed when they heard the distinct thud of a door being shut rather enthusiastically.

"What did he promise to do?"

Rebecca moistened her lips, turning away from Sawyer to grab the dishcloth from the sink and wipe down the sticky countertop. "Clean his room. It's an ongoing war between us." She thrust the cloth under the faucet and rinsed it. She wrung the cloth harder when she realized her hands were shaking.

"Typical of that age, I'd imagine."

She really wasn't standing in her kitchen like this with Sawyer. She wasn't. Annoyed with herself for letting him get to her, she pushed past him to snatch up the trash can, returning it to the pantry.

When she re-entered the kitchen, Sawyer was leaning against the counter, his arms folded across his wide chest. She stopped in the doorway between the pantry and the kitchen. "Why are you here?"

"I couldn't stay away."

It took some effort to ignore the jolt that went through her. She busied herself untying the chocolate-spattered apron from her waist. "That's quite a line, Captain. Does it work often?"

She looked up in time to catch the pained expression on his face, and wished she'd missed it. "Not in recent memory," Sawyer said blandly.

She wadded up the apron and tossed it on the counter. "I'm sorry."

He shrugged. "I didn't attack you, you know."

The empathy that had swelled inside her deflated like a popped balloon. "I don't want to discuss it."

He moved, uncrossing his arms, and Rebecca couldn't prevent the nervous start she gave. His mobile lips flattened and he held his arms out to the side, palms up. "Would you feel better if you frisked me? I'm not carrying."

"Oh, sure." The words came abruptly, without thought. "I really want to pat you down."

His expression eased, his lips twitching. "I'm crushed."

"I doubt it."

His hands dropped to the counter on either side of him. The position seemed to emphasize the breadth of his shoulders beneath his shirt. It was the same brown and black shirt he'd been wearing earlier that day. Had it only been that day?

She rubbed her fingertips across her forehead.

"You're tired."

She was. The last person she needed pointing it out, however, was him. "It's been a long day."

"So go sit down and relax."

While he was inside her home? There was a laughable thought. "I have to get some cookies baked. I promised to donate several batches for the community Christmas dance next week."

Eyebrows rising, he glanced to either side of him. "Oh. I see."

"Listen, Captain, I can bake."

"Okay."

"I *can*."

His lips twitched and despite everything she felt a chuckle rising within. "Okay, so sometimes I have a little trouble with it." The smile that stretched across his lips knocked her sideways a bit. She blinked and turned hurriedly to the refrigerator, pulling out the carton of eggs and setting it on the counter, alongside the tipped-over bag of flour.

Get him out of your house. The internal order lacked teeth. Particularly when she heard water running and looked over to see him washing the beaters for the electric mixer. She couldn't help herself. She stared. And stared even harder when he dried the beaters and popped them into the slots of the mixer. Then he started washing the collection of mixing bowls she'd left piled in the sink. "What are you doing?"

He kept right on washing at a dried smudge of cookie dough. "Being helpful. Don't you recognize it when you see it?"

Not when it's coming from you. She swallowed, and stuck the eggs right back into the refrigerator. Allowing him to remain in her home was pure madness.

Rebecca prided herself on being totally sane. She didn't have time in her life for madness. She certainly didn't have time in her life to deal with Sawyer Clay.

She didn't *want* to deal with Sawyer Clay.

"Too tired, after all, to bake more tonight?" He finished rinsing the last bowl and extended one arm, opening the third drawer from the top in the row of six, to find a clean dish towel. He spread the towel on the counter and turned the clean, wet bowls upside down on it, leaving them to air dry.

Rebecca dragged her attention from the drawer he'd opened with such unerring accuracy. She'd kept her dish towels in the same drawer in a half-dozen different homes, including the small San Diego apartment of long ago. After so many years of moving around as a child, she cherished order.

"Bec?"

She pushed her fingers against the pain between her eyebrows and walked out of the kitchen. "I'm tired," she mumbled as she passed him.

But in the living room, she stood in the middle of the room, neither settling on the comfortable sectional couch she'd purchased when she and Ryan had moved to Weaver, nor on the oversize recliner that Tom had praised but had never seemed to find the time to relax in.

Hands descended on her shoulders from behind and she pressed her fist to her mouth, stifling sound. Sawyer's long fingers kneaded her shoulders, his strong thumbs finding several little knots. "Relax, Bec," he murmured.

She was. Relaxing. She stepped forward, out from beneath his touch. "You shouldn't be here." She moved blindly, settling in Tom's chair.

"Where should I be?"

"Home."

He didn't respond. Just slowly moved around her living room, stopping to look at the collection of family photos hanging on the wall above one side of the sectional sofa. Then he moved to the bookcases and her jumbled mess of novels and magazines. He picked out one novel—a historical romance she'd finished reading a few weeks ago—and paged through it. She watched him, no more inclined to speak than he was. He replaced the book and pulled out another, a medical thriller. The shelves with her medical journals were as neat as a pin and he didn't spend one second looking through those.

He finally stopped when he came to the baby-grand piano she'd positioned in an alcove that ordinarily would have held a dining-room table, had she and Ryan had need of one. But the table in the kitchen suited them just fine.

"Do you play?"

"Badly." She rubbed her palms over the soft upholstery fabric covering the arms of the recliner. "It was Tom's."

"As in your husband. The Lincoln-driving neuro-surgeon."

Rebecca contained her irritation. She leaned her head back, watching Sawyer from beneath her lowered eyelashes. "He played beautifully."

"Good for him," Sawyer grunted. "A real saint."

"A good man," Rebecca corrected evenly. There wasn't one thing Sawyer could say against Tom Morehouse. He'd been good and kind, and had been taken from them far too early.

Sawyer had nudged out the padded bench and sat down, lifting the keyboard lid. He drew his fingers along the upper keys, creating a soft, tinkling ripple of sound.

Suddenly, Ryan blew into the room, his shoulder-length hair tousled. He darted across to the piano, slamming the lid closed with a sharp crack. Sawyer barely had time to draw his hands back.

Rebecca pushed out of the chair. "Ryan!"

"Nobody plays that but my dad," he said, his voice high and agitated. "Nobody." He turned around and glared at Rebecca, as if she'd committed some sin. But his dark blue eyes were glazed with tears, and Rebecca's heart ached. She reached out for him, but he darted away, dashing down the hallway and slamming into his bedroom.

Rebecca looked at Sawyer, seeing his concern, then followed Ryan.

She knocked on Ryan's door before opening it. He lay on his twin bed, looking every bit the little boy he still was. It had been slightly over two years since Tom's death, but Ryan was still a long way from accepting it, even though he seemed to have gotten over the angry mood swings that had immediately followed his father's death.

Crossing to the bed, she gently touched his shoulder, swallowing the pain of having him shrug away from her touch and sat beside him. "Did I ever tell you that Tom bought that piano for our second wedding anniversary?" She didn't expect a response from Ryan, and didn't get one. "He hired a private teacher to come to our home and give me lessons every Sunday afternoon. You'd crawl between the legs of the piano and all during my lesson, you'd sit there under the piano. Then, when the piano teacher decided teaching me was a hopeless endeavor, and Tom started playing it more, you'd sit under it then, too. Oh, you loved that piano."

"I hate it." The muffled statement was adamant. And thick with tears.

Rebecca touched her son's narrow shoulder, ran her palm soothingly down his back.

"He shouldn't have touched it." Ryan rolled over, accusation sharp in his young eyes. "You shouldn't have let him."

"I'm sorry, Ryan. I should have asked your mother before I opened the piano lid. It's not her fault."

Ryan's face colored and he swiped at the tears on his cheeks when Sawyer stepped into the room, stopping just inside the doorway.

Rebecca could see the dilemma pulling at Ryan. The sanctified memory of Tom versus his fascination with the former Navy SEAL who was very much alive and very much present. Ryan's lips tightened. "It's okay," he mumbled.

Sawyer took a step farther into the room at the same moment Rebecca's phone rang with a distinctive double ring. She brushed her hand through Ryan's tumbled hair and rose. "I need to get that," she said.

Sawyer stepped out of her way when she walked past him.

"That's the office ring," Ryan told him after a moment. "The weird ring is so she can tell if it's a regular call or a medical thing."

From the living room, Sawyer could make out the low, melodic tone of her voice as she answered the call. "Mind if I sit down?" He lifted his chin toward the straight-back chair sitting at a student desk, complete with an open laptop computer.

Ryan shrugged.

Taking that as an assent, Sawyer went over and sat down. He glanced at the computer. "You play a lot of games on this?"

"Some." Ryan sat up, crossing his legs Indian-style. "I e-mail some of my old friends from New York, too. But mostly I do homework on it."

"What grade are you in?"

"Fifth." Ryan shrugged again, picking at the torn knee of his blue jeans. "I skipped the third grade."

"No kidding? You must be pretty smart."

Again that shrug. "In math, maybe. I take some classes at the high school, and a thing on-line from a university in Texas."

"I'm impressed."

Judging from Ryan's grimace, Sawyer figured he hadn't said quite the right thing. He propped an elbow on the desk and looked at the boy across from him. "You miss your dad a lot."

Ryan swung his legs off the opposite side of the bed, presenting Sawyer with his back and stiff shoulders.

He fiddled with a Notre Dame ball cap that was on the bed, then jammed it on his head. "No big deal."

"I imagine it's like a part of you is missing. Your body is all there, but there's still a hole somewhere that used to be full-up and now isn't," Sawyer mused softly. "That's kind of how I feel."

"Your dad ain't...isn't..."

"No, Squire is still with us." He raked his fingers through his hair, thinking absently that he wasn't used to it being long enough to wave. "But I don't remember him."

Ryan looked over his shoulder at him. At least the tears were drying. "Huh?"

"Your mom didn't tell you?"

"She doesn't tell me nothing about her patients. 'Cept that you were in a car accident."

"Yeah. And now I have a little problem with my memory." There was an understatement.

The boy's body swiveled around to face him as well. "And you can't remember your dad? Jeez."

He couldn't recall so much more than Squire, but Sawyer didn't see the point in elaborating.

"Oh, jeez," Ryan said again. He sat forward on the bed, his young body leaning toward the desk. "I bet you don't remember Weaver or the rest of your family, huh?" He scrunched up his face, as if he were staring at a particularly repulsive—yet fascinating—bug. "Bummer. At least I *remember* my dad."

Sawyer squelched his unexpected chuckle. "What was he like?" He was afraid Ryan would retreat again into that ball of angry misery again. But Ryan surprised him when the boy shrugged and flopped back on his bed, crossing one gangly leg over the other.

"He was real smart."

"Guess you get your smarts from both your parents."

Ryan didn't respond. He just jiggled his foot for a long, silent moment. And when he did speak, Sawyer realized the boy had discussed his father as much as he wanted to. "You think my mom is pretty, dontcha," Ryan stated.

"Yeah."

"She won't go out with you. She doesn't go out with anybody."

"So I've heard," Sawyer murmured, wondering where the boy was going.

"My math teacher at the high school asked her out. She said no. Some rancher dude asked her out, too. And that lawyer guy, Bennett Ludlow, is always bugging her."

"You trying to tell me my chances with your mom are pretty slim?"

Ryan's foot stopped jiggling. "I think she misses my dad a lot," he said. "She's always talking about him and junk."

Sawyer saw Rebecca appear in the doorway, her face pale but composed. She'd obviously overheard her son's observation.

Ryan noticed her then. "You gotta make a house call?"

"Not this time." She walked over to the bed and bent over, kissing Ryan's forehead. His cheeks turned red before he darted a pained look Sawyer's way.

Stifling another chuckle, Sawyer stood. "It's getting late. I'll catch you later, Ryan." He crossed to the doorway.

Rebecca spoke softly to her son and followed him

into the hallway where she closed Ryan's bedroom door.

Sawyer headed into the living room, picking up his jacket that he'd left on the coat-tree near the door when Ryan had let him in earlier. He shouldn't have come here. Rebecca and her son didn't need his problems on top of their own.

He felt like a selfish bastard for pushing into their home. All he'd thought about was his own need to fill the spaces in his murky mind. He hadn't thought at all of what effect his actions would have on Rebecca. Or Ryan.

He reached for the doorknob. "I'm sorry, Doc. I didn't mean to upset your boy." He wanted to say more, but couldn't fathom what. "Good night."

Rebecca's arms tightened around her waist as Sawyer opened the door and headed out into the cold, dark night. She looked down the hall at her son's closed bedroom door.

The man striding toward his truck who couldn't remember her was the only person who'd gotten her son to say one word about Tom since his death more than two years ago. The bittersweet irony made her eyes burn.

She dashed to the door and threw it open, grabbing a coat on the way. She pulled it around her shoulders and hurried after Sawyer toward the truck that he'd parked beyond the garage. He'd already reached it, was climbing up into the cab.

Feeling her heart squeeze, she jogged up to the truck. "Sawyer." She put her hand on his forearm where he'd reached out to pull the truck door closed. "Wait."

Even through the barrier of his leather coat she felt his muscles tighten. Clouds obscured the moonlight, but there was enough light from the truck interior to see the wary set of his head.

"I... You don't have to leave," she said.

"It's best."

Best for her peace of mind, no doubt. But best for her son? She'd moved more than halfway across the country to provide her son with the best possible home she could. To try to help him through his grief. She moistened her lips. "Sawyer, tonight was the most Ryan has spoken of Tom in two years."

He lifted his arm away from the door, dislodging her hand. "Like I said. I never meant to upset Ryan."

Rebecca huddled inside the coat. "I know that." She did know it. Despite everything, she didn't believe that Sawyer—memory impaired or not—would deliberately upset a child. "But don't you see? You got through to him when I couldn't. I've done everything I can think of to help Ryan, but he still refuses to talk about Tom." She swallowed the hurt over that fact. It was a minor thing compared to the milestone Sawyer had achieved. "Yet he talked with you about him. He was upset about the piano, of course, but then he actually talked to you."

He looked at her, shaking his head. "You're gonna freeze like that. You've only got on socks."

"They're warm enough."

He just shook his head again and reached for the keys hanging in the ignition. The engine spat once, then purred to life. "Go inside, Doc."

She folded her hands together, not quite believing what she was doing. "Will you come back?"

He tilted his head, looking steadily at her. She couldn't read his expression, though, to save her soul. "Why?"

"I...Ryan—"

Sawyer shifted the big truck into gear. Detesting the panic that spiraled through her, Rebecca reached for his arm again. "Please, Sawyer. I, uh, I need to know. Will you come back? Will you talk again with...with Ryan?"

His hand covered hers suddenly, warm against hers despite the cold weather. "I don't know how to talk kids through the stages of grief."

"It doesn't matter. Sawyer, don't you see? Ryan—he's—oh, I don't know—*bonding* with you or something."

"And you hate it."

Yes, she did. Maybe she did. Oh, hell, maybe she didn't. "Ryan is the important one, here. Just be yourself with him." My God, what was she saying? She closed her eyes for a moment, nearly swaying.

"I don't remember myself," Sawyer pointed out, his voice rough. "For all I know, I could be the bastard your eyes accuse me of being. And spending any time with your son could cause more harm than good."

She realized he was still holding her hands. "I'm willing to take that chance," she whispered.

"At least you've stopped pretending there's nothing between us."

She bit back her automatic denial.

His thumb moved across the back of her knuckles. "I'll come back," he said after a moment.

The relief that rolled through her fought with a black wave of blind panic. And as she watched him drive away she wasn't at all sure which side was winning.

Chapter Six

She'd asked him to come back.

Unfortunately, her reasons were specifically related to her son. Sawyer had no illusions about that. Rebecca Morehouse didn't want him around because she wanted *him*. She wanted him around in the hopes that Ryan would talk to him about her late husband. She'd been so emphatic about her request that she'd even dropped the *Captain,* for once.

Prowling around the downstairs guest suite at the big house later that night, Sawyer had relived every moment from the time Ryan had let him into the Morehouse home, until he'd driven away, leaving Rebecca standing there in her stocking feet. He was probably dwelling on it because his efforts at probing into the dark abyss of missing memories only made his head ache.

Sawyer muttered an oath and dropped thoughtlessly

to the floor, executing his third set of push-ups. His rib cage felt on fire from the exertion, but he'd hoped that physical exhaustion would bring on the sleep that eluded him.

So far, the idea was failing miserably.

However, as a self-inflicted punishment for being jealous of a dead man, it had some merit.

Sweat dripped down his temples, and every muscle in his body strained. Teeth bared, he plowed through the last ten, then rolled onto his back and lay there on the floor, his heart thundering. God, there had been a time he could have done twice this many before—

He held his breath, probing tentatively like a tongue against a toothache for the memory hovering just out of reach.

Almost...

Almost...

He muttered an oath. It was gone.

Lying there on the thick carpet, Sawyer waited until his breathing was back to normal before sitting up. The sharp ache cutting through his chest had him swearing all over again.

He groaned and rolled over, pushing himself up to his knees, then to his feet, automatically tightening the string of his baggy gray sweatpants. Okay, so maybe he'd overdone it a bit. Maybe his bruised body wasn't ready yet for some things.

A vision of Rebecca Morehouse slid slyly into his thoughts. Pretty brown hair that gleamed brighter than moonlight over the ocean. Skin as soft and velvety as fresh dairy cream.

"Stupid," he muttered to himself. His body was all too ready for *some* things. Heading into the small kitchen, he yanked open the refrigerator door. Bottles rattled, but when he opened the lone milk carton, it was empty.

He dropped it in the trash and wearily trudged up the stairs to the main kitchen. It was dark, except for the dim light over the stove. Finding the milk in the fridge, he lifted it halfway to his mouth, then stopped when he heard a sound behind him. He turned to see Squire standing there. "Thought you were off visiting. Gloria, right?"

Squire, his father—God, what was wrong with him that he couldn't *feel* what everyone told him was so—ambled across the room and sat down at one end of the table. "I was," he grumbled.

Sawyer waited.

"Confounded woman," Squire added after a moment. He softly thumped his fist on the table, his manner distracted. "She wants to get married," he added abruptly.

"You don't."

Squire focused his attention more closely on Sawyer. "Hell, boy, that ain't it. Well, mebbe."

"So?"

Squire made a face. "So? So, we've been seeing each other for more than four years now. Ain't nothing wrong with the arrangement. But like a woman, she wants to fix what ain't broke."

Leaning back in his chair, Sawyer stretched out his legs, absently rubbing one hand over his rib cage. "You don't love her?"

"That ain't the point, boy." Squire's silvered head shook. "Gloria knows how I feel."

"Yeah. She knows you don't want to marry her."

Squire made an impatient sound. "I've been married. To your mama."

Sawyer thought about the portrait of Sarah Clay that hung in the living room. He'd ferreted enough information out of Jaimie to learn that Sarah had died when he'd been little older than Ryan Morehouse. "She's been gone a long time."

"Mmm."

"Jaimie told me that Gloria's got two daughters," Sawyer offered. "In college somewhere."

"They'll be here for Christmas Day. Well, not *here*." Squire thumped the table again. "At Gloria's place down in Casper, seeing as she's being so contrary."

"How come you haven't just moved down there?"

"This is my home."

"Why doesn't she come up here, then?"

Squire shifted. His boots scraped softly against the wood planked floor. "She visits."

Sawyer's lips twisted. "Nice arrangements if you can swing 'em."

"What the hell is that supposed to mean?"

Sawyer shrugged. "Just an observation."

"Of what?"

"You've got a good thing going. Why change it? Visit your lady friend when you feel like a little romance. But she's far enough away that she doesn't mess with the order of things."

Squire's jaw ticked. "Helluva thing to say, boy, when you admit you don't remember anything about the situation."

"I've got eyes."

"Yeah. And they're as judgmental as they always were," Squire said evenly.

Sawyer wasn't sure why he was pursuing this. But the urge was too strong to deny. "How would you describe the 'situation,' then? Is she your mistress or not?''

"Dammitall, Sawyer, what kind of a thing is that to ask? Gloria's got her life in Casper. She's a nurse.''

"Does she expect you to move to Casper?''

"She knows better'n that. Gloria's a fine nurse. Doc Morehouse has said she'd love to have Gloria at the practice with her in Weaver.''

"So she's willing to come here. But you probably haven't asked her to because you're obviously content with the 'situation' as it is.''

"Judgmental," Squire muttered. "Gloria's free to come here, or not. It's her choice. She's got a bee in her bonnet right now, 'cause her daughters are coming for Christmas. And for some confounded reason, she's decided she wants my wedding ring on her finger.'' Squire pushed impatiently to his feet. "Confounded woman,'' he said again.

Sawyer didn't have an answer for that. He was too busy wondering how he'd earned a "judgmental label'' from Squire. Then he realized that Squire's attention had focused on him once more.

"You in pain?''

He realized he'd still been rubbing his side and dropped his hand. "No.''

"If you were, you wouldn't tell me,'' Squire said, sounding neither amused nor angry about it. "Any more than you would have told us about the car accident if Jefferson hadn't found out about it.''

There seemed to be no point in answering.

Squire pushed his chair into the table and walked past Sawyer. He stopped long enough to drop his big hand on Sawyer's shoulder, and squeeze for a brief moment. "You never liked it much here, son, particularly after your mama died. And we didn't always see eye to eye. But I'm glad you're okay, and I'm glad you're home.'' He headed back through the dining room. ''Even if you are a judgmental chip off the block.''

Sawyer sat in the kitchen, feeling the cold night slowly seep into his bones. He rinsed out the mug and went back downstairs. The cordless phone sat on the coffee table in front of the couch and he eyed it. The desire to call Rebecca, to have her voice fill his head whether she was berating him or asking him to talk to her son about his late father, was strong. So strong that he deliberately turned his back on the phone and went into one of the bedrooms and shut the door.

Dawn was breaking as Rebecca drove past the high school. It had been a long night. A call from Judy Blankenship about her daughter, Taylor, had startled Rebecca out of a restless sleep, and she'd just spent the past two hours with the teen, who had been inexplicably hysterical and making herself violently ill in the process. Judy and Roy had been at their wits' end, which was why they'd called Rebecca.

Now, everyone was calm again—as calm as they could be, anyway, after learning seventeen-year-old Taylor was quite likely pregnant and more scared than her parents had been. The Blankenships would bring Taylor by her office later that afternoon. Even though it was Saturday, Rebecca felt it would be better for everyone concerned to have the pregnancy verified right away, rather than wait until Monday. The sooner they could concentrate on Taylor's health and the health of her pregnancy, the sooner Roy Blankenship would have something to concentrate on other than his livid anger at the boy who'd gotten his precious girl in the family way.

The gold light spilling from Ruby's Café beckoned appealingly as Rebecca turned into the parking lot that was already half filled with vehicles. She'd get some of Ruby's famous cinnamon rolls to take home to Ryan.

Ryan. Her parents had been working at a small mission hospital in Ethiopia when she'd become pregnant with him.

Once they'd gotten the news, they'd sent a cable exclaiming their love and support, even over the distance separating them. If they'd ever wrung their hands together and fretted over her, she'd never known about it. It was more likely that they'd simply expected her to handle her life as she'd always done.

Nor had they returned to the United States when she'd married or when she'd buried her husband. Rebecca didn't blame them. They were so totally devoted to bringing health care to impoverished areas that she'd have felt wholly selfish if she weren't proud of their work.

She parked the Jeep and sat behind the steering wheel for a moment. Despite her pride, however, she couldn't help thinking that seventeen-year-old Taylor didn't know how truly lucky she was. Some hands-on parental support might have made several periods in Rebecca's life easier to bear.

A thump on the hood of her vehicle distracted her and she looked up to see Sheriff Bobby Ray Hayes standing on the other side of her door. She pocketed her keys and climbed out into the bitingly cold morning. ''Good morning, Sheriff,'' she smiled.

The man took her arm and escorted her across the uneven parking lot. "Doc. You're out mighty early."

"House call." She preceded him into the cozy warmth of the bustling café. "I was on my way home and decided that I couldn't resist some of Ruby's rolls for breakfast."

The sheriff doffed his hat and absently returned the greetings that rounded the café when they'd entered. He swept his hand over his nearly bald head and headed for the counter where a few stools were available. "They are irresistible," he agreed.

Rebecca joined him at the counter, waving off the offer of coffee from Hope Leoni, who was helping her grandmother over the school holidays the way she always did, and placed her order for some rolls to go. She cast a glance toward the sheriff. She still had a hard time thinking of him as Bobby Ray, even though he'd invited her to call him that when she'd first arrived in Weaver. She couldn't help it. The man was old enough to be her father, and "Sheriff" fit him so much better than "Bobby Ray." It was what most people called him, anyway, considering that he'd held the office as long as anybody could remember.

"Sheriff, are you taking your blood-pressure medication like I told you to?"

The man shrugged, nodded and shrugged again. Rebecca wasn't quite sure what that meant. But considering the man's flushed face, she suspected he'd been more than a little lax.

Then Hope set a heaping plate of biscuits, sausage and creamy gravy in front of the man before scooting away shyly. "Sheriff," Rebecca chided softly.

"I can't help it, Doc. I been eating this every Saturday morning for as long as I can remember."

And changing some habits were nigh impossible. Rebecca just shook her head. Minutes later, she paid for her foil-wrapped package, and headed home. She saw the big black pickup truck the moment she drove around the end of her building. Sawyer sat on the back step, his breath creating rings around his unprotected head.

Despite the fact that she'd swallowed her pride and every protective feminine instinct she possessed when she'd asked him to return—begged, really—the reality of having him on her back step made her light-headed. She parked in the garage with inordinate care, then headed toward the back door, her black bag in one hand and the package of fragrant rolls in the other.

Sawyer rose to his feet when she neared. "Out on an emergency?"

She handed over her medical bag when he reached for it. "Nothing life threatening," she murmured, unlocking the door and going inside to the kitchen.

"Of course, some might say a morning without a batch of Ruby's cinnamon rolls is a dire emergency."

Rebecca's breath stalled. She glanced over her shoulder at Sawyer, who looked as startled as she felt.

He smiled without humor and pushed a silver-tipped hank of hair off his forehead. "I don't get it," he muttered. "The things that come back to me." He set her bag on the round oak kitchen table. "The things that don't."

Rebecca placed the rolls on the counter and unwound the ivory-colored knit scarf from her neck. She unfastened her coat, stiffening slightly when Sawyer went behind her and slid it from her shoulders. He laid it over the back of one of the table chairs, then did the same with his own.

As if she'd invited him to stay for rolls and coffee. Panic rose in her throat and she focused instead on what he'd said. But the sympathy that rose in her went beyond professional interest, unsettling her even more than his unexpected visit. "Don't force it, Captain," she said, her voice, at least, calm. "There is no reason to suspect that your memory won't fully return in time."

"It was Sawyer last night."

She continued filling the automatic coffeemaker with filter, coffee and water. He stepped up to the counter beside her, bringing with him the sharp cold scent of the snow-filled dawn combined with the clean scent of whatever soap he'd used that morning in the shower.

Coffee scattered across the counter when her hand shook. Thoughts of Sawyer and showers were completely unacceptable. She flipped on the appliance and dusted the mess she'd made into the sink. "I need to check on Ryan," she said hurriedly. "Have a roll if you want." Oh, now, you've gone and done it, she chastised herself as she hustled down the hall to her son's room. Invite the man to stay and share rolls. Smart.

Ryan was still sound asleep. She left him undisturbed and went into her own bedroom. Rebecca nearly groaned at her reflection in the mirror over her dresser. She'd pulled her hair up in a ponytail after she'd received Judy Blankenship's phone call, and now it listed to one side. She didn't have on a speck of makeup and her sweatshirt and sweatpants had once been a bright cherry-tomato red, but were now more like diluted tomato soup, and—

What was she doing?

She didn't care how she appeared to Capt. Sawyer

Clay. Her only interest in him was how he could help her son.

Turning away from her reflection, she left the haven of her bedroom. Her feet dragged as she neared the kitchen. The coffee was still dripping into the glass pot and Sawyer sat at her table, yesterday's newspaper spread across the table. He'd unwrapped the rolls and as she watched, he finished off the one he held in a satisfying bite.

She turned blindly to her cupboard and drew out two mugs. She didn't want to acknowledge how easily he'd made himself at home in her kitchen. So instead, she filled the coffee mugs and plunked one down beside his elbow. "What are you doing here this early?" Dammit, that sounded like she'd *expected* him, only later.

"You asked me to come back," he pointed out. His dark blue eyes glanced at the selection of rolls.

Rebecca huffed impatiently and pulled off another sticky section and plopped it on the napkin by his coffee. "You know that's not what I mean."

"I do?"

"Don't play obtuse with me, Captain. I know you too well." Too late, she realized her error.

He'd leaned back in his chair, leisurely stretching his long legs across half of her kitchen floor. To get past him, she'd have to step over those legs. It was either that, or sit down at the table. She chose neither; just stood there like a ninny in her own kitchen.

"Everybody knows me too well, except *me*," he commented. "Squire says I'm judgmental."

Surprise buffeted her. "'Judgmental'?" Stubborn, opinionated, driven, yes. "Why did he say that?"

He picked a slice of pecan off the top of the roll. "Who the hell knows," he growled.

Which reminded Rebecca unexpectedly of the Sawyer she'd once known. The one who, despite his demanding career and the oddball hours of coming and going that went with it, was as grouchy in the early mornings as a lion with a thorn in his paw. At least until he'd had a couple of cups of coffee.

Or *her,* she remembered painfully. He'd told her once that making love to her when he awakened was better than any amount of coffee. At the time, she'd been absurdly charmed.

Now, it just made her cheeks hot. She turned away from the seat opposite him and faced the sink with the bowl and beaters he'd washed the night before.

She flipped on the water and rinsed everything, then filled the sink with hot, soapy water. She tried pretending that Sawyer wasn't sitting behind her, less than six feet away. She tried pretending that she always washed perfectly clean dishes at this hour of the morning. She tried pretending that she didn't remember, exactly, how she'd behaved in her examining room with him.

But when she heard a familiar door creak, followed by footsteps and her son's sleepy greeting, she couldn't pretend anymore. Sawyer *was* there. He was. And no amount of wishing on her part would change that.

She rinsed the bowl and beaters and opened the sink drain, turning to see Ryan's expression when he found Sawyer sitting at their table.

Her son lit up like the Christmas tree they had yet to pick out for the living room.

She caught the speculative glances her son kept casting between Sawyer and her and wanted to groan all over again. Controlling the impulse—putting it off, anyway—she poured Ryan a glass of milk and plopped two rolls on a small plate for him. She dropped a banana beside the plate and said to the room in general that she was going to take a shower.

Sawyer watched Rebecca practically race from the kitchen. Pity. He definitely liked that soft, somewhat rumpled person. Even if he'd just spent five minutes wondering what she'd been wearing under that soft sweatsuit that clung to her curves in a thoroughly distracting way.

"Did you spend the night last night?"

Sawyer nearly spit his coffee across the day-old newspaper. "What?" Ryan casually picked up his banana and started peeling it. He didn't repeat the question and Sawyer couldn't pretend he hadn't heard. "Ryan, you were still awake when I left last night."

The bill of Ryan's ever-present cap shaded the boy's eyes. "Then why are you here so early?"

Sawyer looked at the boy. Ryan glanced up then, his eyes steady and far too grown-up for someone so young. "I have a hard time sleeping," he admitted after a minute. Truthfully.

Ryan nodded, as if it was something he fully understood. Perhaps he did. He'd had more grief in his life than some adults five times his age.

"I didn't sleep good at our apartment in New York," Ryan said. He set aside his banana peel, and bit off a chunk. "I got into, uh, some stuff at school, too," he said around his mouthful. He swallowed. "So Mom moved us here."

Sawyer wondered for a moment what kind of 'stuff' Ryan had gotten into. "You like it in Weaver, though, don't you? I know you've got some friends. Eric, right? And Melanie."

Ryan flushed at the mention of the girl they'd seen at the pizza parlor. "I like it here okay. Do you?"

"Do I what?"

"Like it here. In Weaver, I mean." Ryan grinned slyly. "I know you like it *here*. You know."

Sawyer thought about it. He had nothing against Weaver. The small town had its own measure of charm. But then, considering the limited experience he had at his command...

"Maybe you're not sleeping good 'cause you don't like the house you live in," Ryan suggested, finishing off his banana in a wolfish gulp. "Our apartment was real big and nice and all, but—"

"You missed your dad."

Ryan nodded after a moment. "That's what Dr. Delaney said. She's a psychiatrist who's friends with my mom," he muttered. His shoulders wiggled impatiently and he reached for his rolls, diligently picking off each and every pecan. "Wanna help us pick out our Christmas tree today?" His eyes sparkled when he suddenly changed the subject. "Mom promised we'd get it today, 'cause if we don't, all the best ones'll be picked out. The Christmas dance is next weekend, and Eric says that his dad—he owns the Christmas-tree lot next to the feed store—is gonna donate whatever is left to the dance."

Rebecca walked into the kitchen on the tail end of Ryan's invitation. She watched Sawyer reach over to Ryan's plate and snitch the pecans that her son had picked off his roll. She hid her smile when Ryan gasped. "Hey, those are mine," Ryan defended.

"You picked 'em all off," Sawyer countered.

"So I can eat 'em separately," Ryan explained. "I only eat the roll 'cause—"

"—I like the pecans more," Sawyer finished on a chuckle. "Me, too."

Rebecca yanked up the zipper of her hooded fleece overshirt with excessive force. "Ryan, finish up. We've got a lot of stuff to get done today. And I've got a patient coming in this afternoon."

"But it's Saturday."

"Right. And if you don't hustle your buns, we won't get our Christmas tree today."

Her son made a face, but he scooped up the rest of his pecans and walked out of the kitchen, happily crunching the nuts in his mouth.

She considered it the height of irony that she wished Ryan was still in the kitchen once he was gone and she could hear the hiss of the shower from the hall bathroom. Fiddling with the zipper tab on her blue-and-pink-plaid overshirt, Rebecca looked at Sawyer, then away. But his image, sitting there at her table, was clearly reflected in the gleaming black door of her wall oven.

He'd turned up the cuffs of his dark blue denim shirt and as he flipped a page of the newspaper, she couldn't help looking away from the reflection to the real thing. His wrists were long and surprisingly narrow to support such broad, square-tipped fingers. Golden-brown hair dusted his forearms and—

Good grief, what was she doing? Thinking? She smoothed her hair back into its fresh ponytail and moistened her lips. "That's yesterday's news, Captain."

"Paper's always been a day late in these parts," he said absently. He folded over the last page and looked up at her, his expression watchful. "Look, Rebecca, I know you heard your son invite me along on your great

Christmas-tree hunt, but I'm a big boy. You don't want me to go along, say so.''

"I—"

"I never was one much for the fuss surrounding Christmas," he added. Then made an impatient sound, scrubbing his hands down his face.

If he'd recognized the sad pang that swept through her, he'd have been horrified. But his low, gravelly voice, so matter-of-fact, made her want to weep. He'd told her once about his mother's death on Christmas Eve when he'd been only a few years older than Ryan. "You're welcome to come with us," she said huskily.

Afraid something in her tone alerted him, she held her breath when his eyes narrowed faintly in speculation. But he just nodded after a moment. "Thanks."

She felt her smile wobble around the edges, then die completely when Sawyer suddenly stood. He pressed one hand to his side at the abrupt motion and Rebecca bit the inside of her lip, wanting to reach out to steady him, but knowing he wouldn't appreciate it. Sawyer grabbed up his coat, wrapping those long fingers around the scarred black leather.

"What time?"

Her cheeks heated when she had to drag her attention from his hands. "What time for what?"

"Christmas-tree hunting."

"Oh, in a few hours."

"I'll come back then."

Now that he was going, her breathing came a little easier. "Are you driving back to the Double-C?"

He paused, his hand on the doorknob. "I s'pose that would make sense," he murmured. He opened the door and stepped out into the bright morning. "See you in a while, Bec."

He closed the door and Rebecca sank back against the counter. "Rebecca Lee Morehouse, you are out of your tiny little mind."

She refused to chase after Captain Sawyer Clay. There was no earthly reason to think that he wasn't perfectly contented driving back to his family's ranch. No reason at all.

The squeak of the door opening made her jump guiltily. Sawyer stood there. "I want to rent one of your motel rooms," he announced abruptly.

Rebecca's jaw loosened. "You must be kidding."

His lips tightened. "No, actually, I'm not."

"But—but, that'll defeat the whole point of your coming back to Wyoming!"

"I came back to regain my memory. The only thing staying at the ranch does is make me more crazy."

"You're not crazy," Rebecca protested. "You're suffering—"

"Dammit, Rebecca, I know exactly what I'm suffering from. I don't need your professional opinion on it. What I need is some place I can sleep at night, and the ranch ain't it. Now, are you going to rent me a room, or not?"

Folding her hands together at her waist, Rebecca reminded herself that she was long over Sawyer Clay. His return was a shock, certainly—one that she'd foolishly, complacently, expected never to happen. And she was supposed to be highly intelligent.

"Rebecca?"

Oh, Tom, tell me what to do. She pulled her hands apart, tucking her fingertips into the front pockets of her blue jeans. "Yes." She forced the word out. "I'll rent you a room."

Chapter Seven

Later that morning, Rebecca gave serious thought to calling Delaney Vega, and not just for a gossipy chat. But she knew what Delaney would say. The same thing she'd been saying ever since Rebecca had shocked her entire network of associates when she'd made the move to Wyoming—that Rebecca was afraid to step away from the past, and equally afraid of stepping into it.

So she hovered in the reception area of her office, pretending that she wasn't peeking out the front windows as Sawyer and his brother, Daniel, unlocked the room at the far end of the building and carried in a duffel bag and a couple boxes of groceries. The far room was the only one with a kitchenette. Rebecca could only be grateful for the facade of distance between that end room, and this end, where she and Ryan dwelled.

She moistened her dry lips, and breathed deeply, trying desperately to banish the knot with the fluttery edges from her stomach. She should have known better than to come here to Weaver. She should have known better than to come to Wyoming at all. She should have—

"Mo-om!"

Rebecca whirled around, her hand pressed to her heart. Ryan stood behind her. She decided to ignore the knowing grin flirting at the corners of his mouth, and focused instead on the bundle of towels and sheets in his arm.

He looked at her hopefully and she shook her head. "No way, Ry." She herded him back through the office area to their private quarters.

He was so full of grumbles and earnest young competence at starting the laundry that she felt an overwhelming urge to hug and kiss him. But he'd let her know in no uncertain terms recently that he preferred to keep the huggy-touchy stuff to a minimum. So she contented herself with ruffling his hair where it fell over the collar of his oversize T-shirt. "You need a haircut."

Ryan closed the lid on the washing machine and pulled his hair back in his hand. "Uh-uh. If I get it cut at that barbershop in town, you know old man Murphy'll cut it too short. Then my streak'll show again."

"Sweetheart, an inch off that mop wouldn't hurt a thing." She knew Ryan was overly sensitive about the narrow streak of stark-white hair that grew at the very nape of his neck. His hair was long enough that unless he specifically lifted it up, the white was completely hidden. But still, there was a limit. "At least agree that we'll get it cut before the dance."

Ryan made a face. But he didn't disagree. And when

the knock came on their kitchen door, he yanked it open. The wide smile that lit his face made the nervous knot return full-force to Rebecca's belly. Ryan looked at Sawyer with as much delight as he'd looked at the department-store Santa when he'd been three years old.

"Ry, go on and get your coat and stuff," she suggested, nudging him out of the open doorway.

Grinning, he bounded out of the kitchen. Rebecca looked at Sawyer, then just as quickly looked away. She reached around him and pushed closed the door before more frigid air could stream into the warm kitchen. "We'll, uh, be ready to go in a few minutes." Her gaze kept sliding back to his hands, those incredibly masculine hands. So she deliberately busied herself with unloading the dishwasher. "I trust the room is satisfactory."

She paused in the act of pulling a slender drinking glass out of the dishwasher rack when Sawyer settled one lean hip against the counter right on the other side of the opened dishwasher door. "It's fine," he said.

She pressed her lips together, quickly turning to put the glass and its twin into the cupboard. She reached back for the clean plates.

"I remember when the rooms here had burnt-orange carpet, avocado-green bedspreads and wagon-wheel lamps."

The plate she held slipped out of her hand, right back into its spot in the dishwasher rack where it clattered against the others. She thought for a moment that she would choke against her heart, which seemed to have risen right into her throat. "You...remember what the room looked like?"

He shifted with a soft creak of cold leather, and

cupped his hands over the edge of the counter on either side of him. "Yeah."

Rebecca closed her eyes. Oh, please, please, please.

"Pretty damn weird," he said. "As soon as I walked into that room, it was like I was looking at two photographs, side by side. The room, looking the way it does now. Navy blue and burgundy. And the other photo of the room the way it used to look. I distinctly remember waking up to that orange and green with one hellacious hangover."

She felt dizzy. She closed the dishwasher door and lowered herself carefully onto one of the kitchen-table chairs. She pushed out the words. "Did you remember anything else?"

She looked up when he made a rough noise. And looked past her self-preoccupation, her own fear, to see the frustrated disgust on his face.

He was shaking his head slowly. "Other than chugging one too many beers when I wasn't even of age? Not one thing." He looked down toward the floor, and Rebecca was appalled at the wave of emotion that buffeted her. He'd never been one to drink and drive. His eyelashes, unfairly long and thick, cast faint shadows on his hard face, portraying a vulnerability that her intellect knew didn't exist.

But her heart—oh, her foolish heart—had its own ideas. Before she knew what she was doing, she'd risen and touched his arm, covered with that battered leather bomber jacket. "It'll come back to you, Sawyer. Be patient. Give it time."

"Patience," he murmured. "It doesn't seem to be a particularly strong trait of mine."

Rebecca knew for a fact that Sawyer had once exhibited patience like no one she'd ever known. What else could a man possess that would allow him to remain motionless in freezing waters, or endlessly still in rat-infested hovels in order to avoid detection on the countless ops he'd lived through as a SEAL. She also knew that, at heart, Sawyer was a man of action. He was a man who did what needed to be done. And getting it *done* had been his particular forte.

The knot in her stomach this time was formed of conscience versus self-protection. The sooner Sawyer remembered everything, the sooner he'd also remember her.

"Okay, I'm ready. We're gonna get the hugest tree there, right?"

Saved by the son. Rebecca snatched her hand away from Sawyer's arm, and stopped herself just short of rubbing her hand down her thigh to ease the tingles in her palm.

"As long as the *hugest* tree is no taller than seven feet," she agreed. She pasted a smile on her face and looked up at Sawyer, focusing somewhere around his left ear, because that, at least, didn't set off any impulsive, unwanted sympathies. "We'll have to drive," she said, carefully cheerful as she retrieved her coat and led the way out to the garage. "Because I have no desire to drag the hugest Christmas tree all the way back here from the tree lot."

"I told you it would fit."

Rebecca looked from the beautiful, fragrant tree that cleared her ceiling by a bare six inches, to Sawyer and Ryan, standing on the other side of the tree. They looked back at her with twin "I told you so" expressions. "Yes, Captain, you did tell me. Of course, you had to cut off the bottom set of branches, but that's a mere detail.''

Sawyer's lips twitched. Ryan's shoulders shook with the giggles he was trying to suppress.

Rebecca just tossed up her hands and shook her head. ''Clean up your mess,'' was all she said as she turned back toward the kitchen. She'd started a pan of hot chocolate earlier when they'd come in after two entire hours spent in the cold. They'd quibbled over the qualities of each and every tree in the lot before Sawyer had hustled her and Ryan into her vehicle and driven out to an area on Double-C property where they'd cut their own tree.

He hadn't *remembered* the place, he'd told her when her curiosity had been apparent. It was simply the place where Matthew and Jaimie had found their tree for the big house.

Despite her misgivings over the outing, Rebecca had to admit that she'd enjoyed herself just as much as her son had. She didn't know whether to be relieved, or give in to the fear such enjoyment wrought.

She was just pulling down three mugs when Ryan ran into the kitchen to ask if he could go outside and play with Eric and some other boys who'd come by. She nodded and took down two mugs instead. ''But be back here by four o'clock.''

Ryan rushed out in a bundle of energy and little-boy enthusiasm, leaving the kitchen very, very quiet. Heat collected at the base of her neck and she didn't need to turn around to know that Sawyer had entered the room. She poured the steaming cocoa into the mugs and dropped a handful of miniature marshmallows on top. She turned toward him, determined to ignore the awareness blossoming inside her.

A cluster of slender pine needles was caught in the thick silver-tipped hair at his temple, a reminder of the struggle to get the tree through a doorway that hadn't been designed to accommodate the width of an enormous fir. "You've got a tree branch in your hair," she told him lightly and dashed her hand lightly across his hair, knocking the pine needles free before pushing one of the mugs into his hand.

He looked down at the steaming drink, at the marshmallows that were melting into sweet little blobs. "Marshmallows."

She moistened her lips and stepped past him, out of the kitchen. Idiot, she called herself. She'd unthinkingly fixed the hot chocolate from scratch using the very recipe that Sawyer had introduced to her all those years ago. The recipe his mother had used. Why couldn't she have just boiled water and emptied some of those prepared cocoa mixes into it?

"The tree is lovely," she said, walking over to where it stood in the corner of her living room. "But it really wasn't necessary to cut one of the trees from your family's ranch—"

"My mother fixed cocoa this way."

Rebecca nearly choked on her words. She swallowed and schooled her features, then glanced over her shoulder at him. "Oh?"

Then he looked up at Rebecca, and his expression turned deliberately wry. "At least, I think she did."

Oh, she couldn't take this. This swinging pendulum of emotion. Fear...sympathy. Hate...wanting— *No. Don't go there, Rebecca.* She turned back to look at the tree with unseeing eyes. "Well, I hope it tastes all right." She held her own mug wrapped between her hands, but all desire to drink it had fled. "You've seen the results of some of my kitchen adventures."

She knew he was approaching her—more from the panic swelling in her chest than from anything else. And pasted a smile on her face. "I'm sorry to put you to all that work and then abandon you, but I do have a patient coming in any minute, now." It was only a slight exaggeration, but her conscience tormented her anyway. "There's stuff in the fridge for sandwiches if you're hungry. Or frozen pizzas, I think, in the freezer. You know boys, always wanting something like that to eat and the least I can do is feed you after all this work on the tree, but I've got to go into the office—"

Sawyer kept himself from staring, barely, at the rapid words spewing from Rebecca's lips. What had sent her into this tailspin of panic? Because there was no other word to describe the look in her wide eyes; the delicate flare of her nostrils. "Actually, I will grab a sandwich, if you don't mind," he said blandly. "Before I head on over to my room. Ham is more appealing than peanut butter." He pressed his hand to his ribs, not having to entirely conjure up the wince at the aching there. But it was nothing compared to the unfulfilled ache in his lower regions from spending the morning with her.

Her color drained even more. Not exactly the calming reaction he'd hoped for. She'd set down her mug and had placed her slender palms on his shoulders before he could react.

"I *knew* you were taxing yourself with that tree," she muttered. She tugged at the hem of his shirt and yanked it up, right out of his pants.

He nearly yelped when her fingers flitted delicately over his rib cage. Instead, he grabbed her probing hand and held it away from himself. "Bec—"

"Don't be silly. I've got to check your—"

"No."

She wiggled her fingers against his hold. "Sawyer, don't be childish."

"Trust me, sweetness, I don't feel the least bit silly or childish. And if you're gonna put your hands on me right now, it's not gonna be because you're my doctor."

Her fingers stopped wiggling. Color stained her cheeks, and her slender throat worked over a nervous swallow. Then she sucked in her lower lip for the barest of moments, and his attention focused fiercely on the moist curve.

He swallowed an oath. And simply went with the flow.

He lowered his head and gently caught that moist lip between his teeth. Tasted it with the tip of tongue. Explored the rest of her mouth, absorbed the lingering taste of hot chocolate.

She spoke his name against his mouth, and he shook his head softly, finally covering her lips fully. She swayed, leaned against him. Her fingers twisted in his shirt and he slipped his hands around her slender hips, gliding beneath the hem of her pretty pink-and-blue top. The thin turtleneck she wore beneath the top clung to her body and his palms swept up her back, feeling every slender muscle tighten at his touch.

She made a soft sound that went to his head like moonshine and he pulled her tighter against him, not caring anymore about frightening her off with his aroused state, just needing her against him. Needing her soft mouth against his, her taste in his mouth, her scent in his head. Her breasts were full and tight and pushed greedily against his hand when he touched her there. And her long, slender fingers were sliding through his hair, reminding him of that time—

A searing pain shot through his head, and he yanked back, swearing viciously.

Rebecca gasped and managed not to stumble. Horrified with herself, she turned Sawyer before he could crash into the tree he'd worked so hard to put up and nudged him instead to a chair. His eyes were so pained they were nearly black, and she wanted to cry when he pressed his palms to his temples so tightly that his knuckles whitened.

What was wrong with her? She was a physician, for God's sake.

She dashed into her office and grabbed her black bag. Then in her living room, she shut off everything inside her but the knowledge and ability to examine a man who didn't want her to do any such thing.

"Dammit, Rebecca, it's a headache," he finally roared, pushing her away and standing up from the chair. To his credit, he only swayed slightly, and didn't vomit even though his expression told her he was struggling mightily.

Since she had found no physical indication to say otherwise, she just sat back on her heels and looked up at him. "Go lie down, Sawyer," she suggested quietly.

He was squinting, as if the light bothered him and she rose, knowing she'd regret what she was doing, but not able to stop herself. She took his hand in hers and gently pulled him toward the hallway. "Come on."

Inside her bedroom, she left off the light and closed the drapes, feeling relief herself when Sawyer seemed to sigh with it in the darkness. She pushed him onto the bed, and leaned over, struggling for a moment to get off his boots.

"This is not what I pictured when I made it to your bed."

Rebecca snorted softly. "I'll bet." She didn't want to picture him on her bed at all, yet escorting him back to his room at the end of her motel had been the farthest thing from her mind. He needed rest, and he needed it now. Even if it was her bed. She left his boots on the floor by the bed and straightened. She touched his forehead gently. "Get some sleep."

His lips twisted, and she could see the glint of his eyes between his thick, narrowed lashes. "Haven't slept well since I woke up in the hospital."

Tears burned behind her eyes, and she hoped that it was dark enough that he wouldn't see. Her fingers strayed to his heavy, silky hair. "I can give you something—"

"No."

She wasn't surprised. She drew her hand away and walked to the bedroom door. "I'll check on you later," she said softly.

"That's probably what you tell your boy when he's got a stomachache from eating too much candy," he groused wearily.

"If you're good and rest like you're supposed to, I'll let you watch a movie later," she said, repeating the bribe she'd often used on Ryan.

A faint smile formed on his lips, before he threw one arm over his eyes and Rebecca let herself into the hall, closing the door of her bedroom behind her.

Leaving Sawyer Clay to sleep—or not—in her bed. He was just another patient, she reminded herself sternly. A patient who desperately needed a good stretch of sleep.

Only she felt a terrible yearning to be lying there

with him, and that scared her right out of her mind because she was supposed to know better.

Pulling her overshirt neatly down about her hips, she went out to her office and slipped on her white coat. Taylor Blankenship and her parents would be arriving any time now. And she was the town doctor, so she'd better just get her mind off the man in her bed, and on the patients in her care.

Taylor Blankenship was most definitely pregnant. Delivering the news to the teenager and her parents shouldn't have exhausted her as much as it did. But Rebecca came out of her lengthy appointment with them feeling nearly as disturbed as the stunned family did. It just hit too close to home, she decided, as she lingered at her desk long after the Blankenships left.

Particularly with Sawyer, presumably still resting in her bedroom.

Propping her elbows on her desk, she lowered her chin to her hands, and stared at the medical release form that had been in the packet of Sawyer's films—the form that would clear him, once again, for active duty.

Did Taylor know how fortunate she was to have parents who loved her and supported her no matter how badly their existence had been shaken? Did she have a clue of the struggles that she had ahead of her, despite that precious parental support?

Rebecca dropped one hand, smoothing her palm across the cool, silky surface of the desk. She'd been older than Taylor when she'd been pregnant, certainly. Though her parents had been away, she'd had Tom. Dear Tom, who'd gently pushed and prodded after she'd missed a few of his classes until she'd told him of her pregnancy. Who'd taken her under his wing so subtly that she'd barely known he'd been doing it until after she'd been well and truly there. He'd stood by her even after her half-dozen refusals to live with him. To marry him. And he'd been there three years later when she graduated med school, holding her toddler son in his arms, pride beaming in his eyes.

She'd married him two weeks later, and had never regretted it. Not even when he'd been dying of a virulent cancer that came on too hard and too fast for them to do one thing to stop it.

She knew what Tom, bless his peaceful loving heart, would say if he'd still been alive. He'd known her so well. In his calm and gentle way, Tom would simply have told her to do what she knew was right.

Her jaw throbbed and she realized she was grinding her teeth together. The problem was, Rebecca wasn't sure *what* was right anymore. Did she do what was right for Ryan?

Wasn't that what she was trying to do when she asked Sawyer to come back and encourage Ryan to remember Tom?

Or did she do what was right for her? Remembering the hurt Sawyer had caused her in the past; the pain and disillusionment that had been her heart's companion for longer than she cared to admit? Wasn't it only smart, wise, to stay on guard, to keep her distance, lest she repeat her mistakes all over again?

She pressed her thumb and forefinger to the bridge of her nose.

Of course, if Tom were still alive, she and Ryan wouldn't be living in this rural town in the middle of Wyoming. They'd be back in New York; Ryan flying through school subjects and her and Tom working seventy- and eighty-hour weeks, trying to fit a life somewhere into the few hours that were left.

Rebecca pushed to her feet, sliding the unsigned release form into her desk drawer. What she needed to concentrate on was doing the right thing for Ryan. Nothing more. Nothing less.

She glanced at her wristwatch as she closed up the office once more and headed back to their private quarters. It was well after four. Sawyer would have had plenty of time to rest, and he'd be able to go to his room at the end of the row. Once he was gone, she'd enlist Ryan's help in baking another batch of cookies. And Rebecca could try to pretend that the day had been no different than any other.

Walking through to her living room to find Sawyer sitting in Tom's recliner, a book open on his lap, startled her so much that it took her a few moments to realize that he wasn't reading, but sleeping. She blew out a soft breath and walked past his stretched-out legs.

Ryan's room was empty. As was his bathroom. He wasn't in the kitchen or the laundry room, or playing out in the backyard.

And it was getting dark outside.

She was in the kitchen pulling on her parka when Sawyer joined her, his eyes once again clear and sharp. She flipped the end of her ponytail out from the collar of her coat. "I have to go find Ryan." She wasn't too worried. He'd probably just lost track of time with his friends. They liked to hang out in the small park by the high school where there were some nifty hills to slide on. "This isn't the first time he's missed his check-in time." She pulled up her coat zipper. "Unfortunately, I'm going to have to ground him this time, 'cause I told him I would if he did it again."

"I told Ryan he could go over to his friend's house."

Rebecca went still, one glove held in the air. "Excuse me?"

"When Ryan checked in at four and asked, I told him it was okay to go over to Eric's house."

"Just like that."

His eyebrows drew together a fraction. "Got a problem with it?"

She tossed her gloves on the table beside her. "Yes, I've got a problem with it! You have no right to give my son permission to do anything!"

If she hadn't been so incensed, so utterly panicked, she might have paid more heed to the knife-edged angle of his tight jaw. "Just because you're renting a room here now, and you're my patient and—and— well, you just had no right!"

"I'm a damn sight more than just your patient," he said silkily.

Her stomach tightened. "What?"

"We're two breaths away from being lovers."

Her jaw loosened. "I don't *think* so."

"And I know it, because we've been lovers before."

At that, her stomach dropped away completely. She pressed her hip hard against the counter beside her, because if she didn't, she was going to fall right on her face.

"What? Nothing to say now, Rebecca? No denials, no flat-out lies?"

"Captain—"

"Goddammit, Rebecca, stop calling me that!" His big hands closed around her arms, crinkling the waterproof fabric of her parka. "My name is Sawyer. Use it. Like you used it before. When we were lovers."

She opened her mouth, but words wouldn't come.

Sawyer shook her slightly. "Quit hiding the truth from me, Doc. You and I have a history. And the want is just as bad between us as it ever was. I might not remember when or why, but I remember that."

Rebecca's knees started to buckle and she locked them furiously in place. She grabbed onto his last words like a drowning man. "What do you remember?" She forced the words through the vise that her throat had become.

"I remember this," he said, his thumb brushing over her lips. He lowered his head alongside hers and drew in an slow breath. "I remember the way you smell."

Afraid to move, afraid to stay, Rebecca closed her eyes, trying desperately to block out his low words. Failing miserably. She gasped audibly when his hand swept over her hip, up her belly and cupped her breasts. When had he undone the zipper on her overshirt?

"I remember the way you feel," he muttered. "Tell me I'm right. We were lovers, weren't we? Dammit, Bec, tell me the truth before I go insane."

So he didn't really remember. He might suspect. His instincts might be flying off the charts of accuracy, but he didn't truly remember. "Saw—"

His mouth covered hers before she could finish his name. He had tantalized her into kissing him earlier that day. Now he commanded it. And to Rebecca's dismay, she reveled in it. She pressed herself as tightly against him as he pulled. She fisted her hands in his hair, and took, just as much as he.

And when he finally lifted his head, both of them hauling in shaking breaths, Rebecca couldn't lie.

"Yes," she whispered hoarsely. "We were lovers."

Chapter Eight

She didn't wait for Sawyer to respond. She turned away, sweeping up her gloves and her car keys. "Lock the door on your way out," she said in the moment before she stomped out the back door, slamming it shut behind her.

Her boots crunched across the snow, and she didn't get over her fear that Sawyer would follow her until she was in her Jeep and driving down Main toward the Fieldings' home. And then, she was shaking so badly, she had to pull over and stop on the side of the road.

Engine still running, Rebecca folded her arms over the top of her steering wheel and pressed her forehead to her hands. What on earth had she been thinking when she'd moved to Wyoming? When she'd voluntarily planted herself and her son in territory that held more danger than a minefield?

The urge to collect Ryan and just keep on driving

nearly overwhelmed her. They could go north to Canada. East, back to New York. Anywhere, as long as it was away from Weaver, Wyoming—and Sawyer Clay, who had broken her heart once, and would do it again if she didn't do something to stop it.

At the Fieldings' home, she found Ryan and Eric thoroughly involved in some project in Eric's room. Eric's mother added her pleas to the boys' that Ryan be allowed to spend the night. So Rebecca cornered her son for a hug that was much too quick to satisfy her maternal needs.

"Jeez, Mom." Ryan rolled his eyes and grimaced, when Rebecca lingered. "I stay here all the time, what's the big deal?" He suddenly grinned, his eyes sharp and miles beyond her in scheming. "I bet Sawyer would eat supper with you," he suggested.

"I don't think so."

"But Mom, when I talked to him at four—"

"Something you had no business doing," Rebecca interrupted quietly. "If you want permission to do something, you don't run your plans by just anybody—you talk to *me*."

"Sawyer isn't just *anybody*," Ryan defended. "He's—"

"My patient and a motel guest," she said abruptly. "That's all."

Her son's eyebrows drew together in a painfully familiar fashion. "I don't know why you don't like him," he said hotly. "You were probably mean to him and now he'll go away just like Dad and—"

"That's enough." Grateful that she and Ryan were alone in Eric's room, she sat on the edge of one of the twin beds and pulled her son, front and center. "This has nothing to do with liking or disliking." Her words were brittle. "This has to do with you following our family's rules. You know you should have asked *me* for permission to come to Eric's house. And you know that comparing Sawyer to…to Tom is absolutely unfair. Tom didn't ask for cancer, darling. He didn't want to leave us any more than we wanted to lose him." Her heart ached over the impossible mess she'd made of things.

Sawyer was the one person her son would talk to about Tom, and he was the one person Rebecca knew was capable of walking away from people without a backward glance.

Ryan's jaw had cocked to one side as soon as he'd mentioned Tom. She could tell by that defensive, withdrawn look of his that more discussion would be futile. Just like it had been last night after Sawyer left. And frankly, she wasn't sure she was up to the task, either.

Sure that she was taking the easy way out, but helpless to make herself do otherwise, Rebecca dashed her fingers through the hair tumbling across Ryan's forehead. Her fingers lingered on his smooth cheek. He was growing so fast, her baby. Her boy. "You can stay the night," she said.

He darted forward and kissed her hurriedly. "Thanks, Mom." Then he ran out of the room, looking for his friend.

Rebecca followed, said good-night to the Fieldings, and drove home. She'd just turned into the parking lot when her headlights illuminated the end unit. The window was completely dark, with not even a slice of light showing from where the edge of the drapes would be.

He couldn't still be in her apartment, could he? Surely that was beyond even Sawyer. Still she hesitated, the engine rumbling smoothly in the dark evening. And when she turned around and drove back down Main, Rebecca figured she'd never experienced a more cowardly moment.

Sawyer stood in the dark motel room at the window and watched Rebecca's taillights as she drove away. He lowered his palm from the chilly windowpane and turned away. Now what?

He'd goaded Rebecca into admitting they'd been involved at some point in the past, but in doing so, he'd strengthened the wall she'd built between them—a wall that even a man with a murky mind could recognize.

He swore under his breath and sat down in the chair by the window. If he hadn't been so blindsided by that bloody headache, he had no doubts that the afternoon would have ended quite differently. But instead of sharing her bed, he'd been alone in it. And he'd slept soundly for a solid two hours, more soundly than at any other time since he'd gotten out of the hospital.

Yet when he'd wakened, one fresh-smelling pillow under his face and another fisted in his hand, the memory of another bed, another time, another place, had been swimming in his thoughts. He'd *felt* her in his mind. Known her taste, her scent. Known how her slender body had fitted against him, welcomed him.

But could he remember anything beyond that? No. And when she'd been ready to tear into him for overstepping the invisible boundaries she'd set, he'd torn back.

Not smart. And not his usual method, he felt certain.

One step forward, five steps back. He pushed out of the chair, jamming his fingers through his hair. He shrugged into his jacket, and slipped the room key into his pocket.

His mind didn't seem able to find its way out of the dark, so he did the only thing he could think of at that moment. Which was to, at least, leave the dark room behind.

The night air snapped and curled around him as soon as he left the protection of the motel room. The sky was impossibly clear, the moon slicing brightly across the town, as he walked down Main. He turned up his collar and buried his fists in his pockets, and walked.

Strands of festive lights and garlands hung across the windows of half the buildings. The arctic breeze churned at his hair, and he hunched his shoulders and quickened his pace, if only to get warmer.

It wasn't like he had any place to go.

He shut off his mind at that, and just concentrated on putting one boot in front of the other. Walking. Using up time. Tiring himself out so that he had some hope of coming within a hemisphere of the satisfying sleep he'd found among Rebecca's pillows.

He stopped walking, admitting the futility of trying to shut off his mind. Or of trying to put Rebecca *out* of it.

He realized he'd walked all the way to the end of Main and back up again, and now stood right in front of Colbys. And Rebecca's Jeep was parked there in the lot between a fifteen-year-old Chevy and a late-model sedan.

Full circle.

He crossed the lot and pulled open the door with cold hands. The warmth inside hit him like a blast furnace and he stood there for a second, absorbing it as well as the sound of country music wailing from a jukebox, and the smack and roll of balls zipping across a pool table into the corner pocket. A man and woman were slowly circling the patch of wood that masqueraded as a dance floor.

Sawyer's gaze moved from the dancing couple to the long, gleaming bar. Rebecca sat at one end, her feet tucked on the rungs of the high barstool. She held a tall, slender glass between her long fingers, and the muted light from the bar made her dark brown hair look nearly black.

As Sawyer watched, the bartender tossed a white towel over his shoulder and meandered down the bar toward Rebecca. He couldn't hear their words, but he could hear the low tones of her voice.

Whatever she'd said must have been amusing, because Newt Rasmusson—God, he remembered the short, wrinkled man and this bar—because Newt was cackling his crazy laugh before walking over to where the cash register was.

Rather than take the stool next to Rebecca, Sawyer headed toward the other end, and propped his boot on the sturdy brass rail that ran the length of the bar a foot up from the ground. "What do you have on tap these days, Newt?"

Newt's round face split into even more wrinkles as he grinned. "Same thing's always." He reached for a beer mug with his peculiar grace. "Heard you was back in town." He thumped the filled mug on the counter hard enough that if it had been anyone but Newt, Sawyer figured the beer would have sloshed right over the side. "Guess you had a real nasty accident, eh?"

"Bad enough," Sawyer answered. He had no desire to discuss the accident he couldn't remember. He unfastened his coat and leaned his elbows on the bar. A sideways glance told him that Rebecca was studiously ignoring him. If she turned any farther away from him, she'd be kissing the wall beside her. "Looks like business is as good in here as it always was."

Newt nodded, his attention already turned to the glasses he was polishing and placing on a shelf behind him. "Always was a need for a watering hole 'round these parts. Always will be." He slid a laminated, one-sided menu on the bar in front of Sawyer. "Got food now, too. Go on and order. On the house."

Sawyer tapped his hand idly on the menu, his attention straying once more toward Rebecca, and caught her peeking his way. Her shoulders went ramrod straight, and she knocked her knee against the wall beside her when she tried to act as if she hadn't been looking his way.

It would have been amusing, except there wasn't anything amusing about the way he felt. Nothing humorous whatsoever about the pain in her eyes whenever she looked at him.

He realized that Newt was still standing there, and ordered the first thing his eyes fell on. Newt nodded, and disappeared for a few minutes. Sawyer took his mug and turned away from his end of the bar, swallowing an oath when Rebecca stiffened even more. At this rate, she'd fall off the damned barstool. He continued on toward the empty booth that had been his original destination, no matter what Rebecca's posture indicated she'd feared.

He scooted the square table out from one side of the booth to give him more room, and shrugged out of his jacket, tossing it on the empty bench across from his. Then he sat, stretched his legs, and let his gaze wander once more around the bar, half-afraid of what he'd remember. Half-afraid of what he wouldn't.

Mostly, he watched Rebecca's back. Watched her sit at the bar, not moving, not drinking, until after Newt had set a platter of French fries and an enormous hamburger in front of Sawyer. She sat there while Sawyer plowed through the food, surprising himself with his hunger, and she sat there while he finished off his first beer, and was well into the second.

And then, she whirled around on her barstool, her color high, and marched over to his booth and slapped her palms down on his table. "Stop staring at me!" she hissed. "And stop following me!"

He set his mug back on the table. "Hell, Becky, running into each other is pretty much a given, considering how small Weaver is. What did you expect me to do? Hole up in that motel room of yours and not come out again until the moon turns blue? And watching you seems to be something I just naturally want to do."

She straightened, her eyes as brittle as a frozen caramel. "I changed my mind," she told him. "I don't want you to go near my son. I don't care *what* he talks to you about. You stay away from him!"

Anger zipped along his veins, but he remained casually slouched in the booth. "As far as I know, I'm not known for kidnapping young boys."

Sitting at that darned bar, determined to act as if she didn't care whether Sawyer was sitting behind her or not, had whittled Rebecca's patience—what there was left of it—to ground zero. "Well, I do know what you're capable of."

His hand wrapped around her wrist with such speed she hadn't even been aware of him moving. But suddenly, he was standing, then she was sitting in the booth and he'd sat down, too. His wide shoulders thoroughly blocking her way to freedom.

"And I'm sick of you holding it against me. So why don't you just tell me what it is I did to you? Then you can nurse your hate just as much as you want to."

"I don't hate you." The words came out despite herself.

"Maybe not. Except you don't like me. And you don't trust me. But you want me. So maybe that's what you hate."

His thighs pressed against hers and Rebecca wanted to scoot away, but there was no more room in the booth. She didn't want to look at him, but she did. Noticing the dark stubble on his hard jaw that nearly obscured that healing cut. The smudgy shadows beneath his dark blue eyes. The line across his forehead that seemed to have etched itself more deeply over the past few days. Even the silver tipping his hair seemed to be more apparent, though logic told her that was simply because his hair grew as rapidly now as it had in the past.

You broke my heart.

His eyes narrowed, and she realized she'd spoken the thought aloud. Fire swept up her throat to her ears and over her scalp until she was dying of it in the thick silence that followed.

He cocked his head to the side, as if he were trying to see into his own mind, his own memories. Then his dark blue gaze met hers and she felt her chest tighten. "I'm sorry, Rebecca," he said softly.

A tear squeezed out of her eye, and his shoulders moved in a sigh. He lifted his hand, and she barely kept from flinching away from him when his thumb caught that tear. But another followed rapidly on its heels when she found herself yearning to press her cheek against his palm.

"Sawyer, don't—"

A commotion sounded behind them, then Sheriff Hayes lumbered over to their booth. "Finally found you, Doc." His color was high, and despite the cold night, sweat had formed on his forehead. "Tried calling your number, even went by your place, but you were gone." He mopped his brow with his handkerchief. "Roy Blankenship's done beat up Dylan Reese."

"My pager," Rebecca realized aloud. She looked at Sawyer with horror. She'd forgotten her pager after she'd left Sawyer in her home. After she'd admitted they'd been lovers.

She moved, and Sawyer moved, too, out of the booth where he retrieved her coat and pushed her arms into it as they headed for the door. "How bad is it," she asked the sheriff as they hurried out into the night.

"Bad enough for me to haul Roy into jail, as much to keep Dylan's ma from taking a shotgun to him as anything," the sheriff muttered. "Dylan's at his house. You know, two doors down from the Blankenships'. I'll drive."

"I have to get my bag," Rebecca told him. "I'll meet you there." Ignoring Sawyer, she jogged to her truck and climbed in, gunning the engine. Before she could shift into drive, though, Sawyer had climbed in beside her.

"If I remember correctly, Roy Blankenship always did have a temper," was all he said.

It would take too much time to evict him from the seat he'd claimed. She drove back home, got her bag and the pager that was buzzing merrily with the sheriff's messages. They were at the Reeses' house within minutes.

Fortunately, Dylan's black eye and split lips would heal with no lasting damage. She wasn't so sure she could say the same about Taylor, who was standing out in the snowy yard, crying her heart out and begging Mrs. Reese to let her come in and see Dylan.

Aware of Phyllis Reese's angry eyes watching them from the front window as well as the curious attention of a couple other neighbors, Rebecca drew Taylor away from the house and walked up the sidewalk to the Blankenships' home, assuring Taylor that Dylan was going to be fine. "Where's your mom?"

"She drove over with Mr. Ludlow to get dad outta jail." Taylor sank onto the nearest chair inside her house and hugged her arms around herself and started crying again.

Rebecca set down her bag, fully aware that Sawyer had entered the house, too. That he'd closed the door and disappeared through to the kitchen. She scooted aside a stack of magazines on the cocktail table and sat down across from the teenager, staying with her until she'd calmed down and Judy had returned. Then there was Judy's fury to get through, because the sheriff wouldn't release Roy, even though Roy had been an upstanding citizen in Weaver for a lifetime.

Sawyer, amazingly enough, proved to be of help with Judy when Rebecca's efforts weren't successful. By the time he was through, sitting beside the woman, talking and listening much the same way Rebecca had done with Taylor, Judy was calm once more, and able to deal with Taylor's tears when they predictably started up once again.

It was well after midnight when Rebecca finally

parked in her garage. She'd had to stop at the sheriff's office and check over Roy, and she was exhausted.

Not because the injuries suffered by the two males had been severe. But because there had just been too many emotions flying. The Blankenships'. The Reeses'. Hers. Sawyer's.

She realized Sawyer had opened her door and was waiting for her to climb out of the vehicle. She didn't know why he'd stuck like glue with her from Colbys right on through the visit to the jail. It unsettled her, because it wasn't the behavior of the Sawyer she'd known. The Sawyer she *thought* she knew now. He'd let her do her work, but she'd been highly aware of his silent, yet tangible, support. And even though she recognized the irony of it, she did know, however, that the urge to lean exhaustedly against him when she slipped out from behind the wheel was strong.

Too strong to ignore. Too strong to submit to.

So she held her black bag protectively to her stomach and sidled past him, across the yard to the back door, which she'd left unlocked.

When she turned to look, Sawyer was walking away toward the end of the building and his room around the corner.

There was no earthly reason to sense the loneliness that surrounded him like a heavy cloak. But she did. She saw it. Recognized it.

Heaven help her, she felt it, too.

Chapter Nine

A full week had passed since Sawyer moved into the end unit of her motel. A full week during which the Reeses and Blankenships had observed a tentative cease-fire. A full week during which Rebecca had managed to bake the rest of the promised cookies for the dance and failed to get her son to the barber.

A full week since she'd spoken more than two words to Sawyer. Even if she did spend far too long standing in the darkness of her reception area, watching the end of the building. Watching him trudge across the parking lot, his hands tucked in the pockets of his leather jacket as he walked across the street, and down to Colbys. Watching, waiting for him to return later, either on foot, or being dropped off by the sheriff or someone else. Then watching, waiting some more until the rim of light around the drapes of his room was doused.

And now, here it was, Saturday again, and she was

supposed to be at the high-school gymnasium, decorating it for that evening's community dance along with the rest of the planning committee. And what was she doing? Carrying her boxes of cookies and beribboned garland out to her vehicle so she could get her rear over to the high school?

No. She was peeking out the window of her office, looking at that end unit again.

Resolute, she turned away, patting her pager where it was tucked against her waist. And after telling Ryan where she was going, she gathered up her boxes in the kitchen and carried them out to her truck.

Ten minutes later, she was sitting in the middle of the yawning gymnasium, surrounded by miles of Christmas-light strands. "Anatomy was easier than this," she muttered, as she tried to figure out how to remove the knots from the convoluted strands.

Sitting beside her, doing exactly the same thing, Maggie Clay laughed. "You're just cranky because you wanted to be the one to climb that extension ladder over there and hang the garland instead of untangle these lights."

Rebecca snorted. When she'd seen that ladder, she'd stated unequivocally that she had no intention of climbing such a thing. She gave up on the hopelessly tangled section and worked her way along the strand. "What in heaven's name possessed me to volunteer for the planning committee for this thing, anyway?"

Maggie chuckled. "I think it had something to do with avoiding Bennett Ludlow," she reminded softly. "You used the excuse of being on the planning committee to turn down his invitation to the dance."

Rebecca grimaced. Bennett was becoming a bit of a

problem, true. "Fat lot of good that did," she murmured back to her friend. "Seeing how he volunteered for the committee, too. Everyone knows he'd close down the elementary school given the least opportunity, yet he's on the committee for an event that is raising funds to keep it open."

"That's what you get for not just telling the man a flat-out no."

"I did," Rebecca muttered. "More than once." She tossed up her hands again at the impossible mess of lights. "This is hopeless. I could have just bought new strands for all the effort this is taking us."

Maggie scooted around and exchanged strands with Rebecca. "But then Vivian Porter wouldn't have been able to crow to the entire county how she donated all these wonderful lights to the dance. Here, these are ready to hang," she said easily.

Rebecca pushed to her feet, carrying the strands over to Bennett who was standing at the base of the extension ladder that Maggie's husband, Daniel, had scaled to the high beams of the gymnasium. She left the lights with Bennett, hurriedly excused herself before he could say a word, and returned to Maggie and the rest of the lights.

She sat down once again and attacked the knots anew. "So, how are you feeling?"

Maggie tsked. "You're not on duty now, Rebecca." But she smiled. "And I'm feeling just fine. My morning sickness is all gone, finally."

Rebecca was glad. She really liked Maggie, whom she'd gotten to know better since they'd both been involved in the planning committee for the dance.

"Is Sawyer coming tonight?"

"I have no idea. I've hardly talked to the man in a

week. Really," she added when she caught the sideways look Maggie gave her.

"That's interesting. Since Daniel says that whenever he talks to him, all Sawyer does is talk about you or Ryan."

"He wants his past returned to him," Rebecca said carefully. She finally freed a knot, and held it up, triumphantly. "Success. So what did Daniel think about the dress you chose for tonight?"

Fortunately, Maggie followed Rebecca's less-than-subtle change of subject, and the two women spent the rest of the time it took to untangle the lights discussing the much-safer topic of clothing.

Rebecca remained behind in the gym to finish tying the last few red bows in place after everyone else had already left. It took just a few minutes, then she put on her coat and dumped her scissors and tape back in the box she'd brought with her before letting herself out the automatically locking double doors.

"Let me help you with that box, my dear."

She nearly dropped the box in question at the voice behind her and whirled around to see Bennett smiling his big-toothed smile at her. "It's not heavy." She started past him toward the sidewalk that led around the building to the parking lot. "What are you still doing here?"

Bennett sidestepped, blocking her path. "It's the holidays, Rebecca."

Couldn't the man take a hint? "I'm aware of that, Bennett. If you'll excuse me, I'd like to get home to Ryan."

"I just wanted to be sure you'll save a dance this evening for me."

She wanted to tell him to take a flying leap. But

persistent or not, Bennett was a member of the community. So she swallowed her irritation. "Of course. If there's time," she couldn't help tacking on. She started walking again, hoping he'd move out of the way. He did. But only far enough to let her brush by as he walked along with her.

Her forced smile withered around the edges and she quickened her pace around the building, grateful beyond belief when the parking lot came into view. And the sight of Sawyer leaning indolently against the hood was such a relief that she overlooked the shock of surprise that came with it.

She strode across the pavement, the scissors and unused Christmas-tree ornaments rattling inside the box. "Sawyer," she greeted brightly. "Have you been waiting long?"

Fortunately, he didn't vocalize the curiosity sharpening his gaze and just stepped forward, taking the box from her. Rebecca automatically introduced the two men as she unlocked the back gate and waited for Sawyer to stow the box inside.

"Rebecca, my dear, Sawyer and I know each other, of course," Bennett said.

She turned just in time to see Sawyer's lip curl, mocking. "Guess not everybody in town is memorable," he said mildly.

Beneath the shoulders of his tidy wool coat, Bennett's shoulders stiffened. It didn't take a rocket scientist to see more trouble brewing, but it wasn't her place to tell Bennett of Sawyer's memory loss. Rebecca latched onto the sleeve of Sawyer's scuffed and scarred bomber jacket and pulled him toward the passenger side. "Got to get back to Ryan," she said to Bennett across the seat of the vehicle. "See you tonight."

Bennett sniffed and held the collar of his coat together with his manicured hand. She knew they were manicured, because Taylor—who worked part-time at Sally's Beauty Salon as well as for Rebecca at the motel—had told her he was a regular customer.

She unlocked the door and climbed in, pushing her keys into Sawyer's hands. "You can drive," she muttered. She simply didn't want to go back around to the other side of the truck, where Bennett stood.

Sawyer rattled the keys for a moment between his fingers that most assuredly had never seen a professional manicurist. Rebecca glanced at him, and sagged weakly against the seat when he walked around the vehicle and climbed behind the wheel. Bennett was heading for his own car.

Once behind the wheel, Sawyer started the engine and drove out of the parking lot. "You okay?"

At least he hadn't broached what had happened the week before at Newt's bar. "Of course." She adjusted the ends of her long, knitted scarf. "What were you doing at the school?"

"Rescuing you from Bennett Ludlow."

"I didn't need rescuing."

"Could have fooled me."

"Sawyer—"

"Ryan told me where you were." He slowed to a crawl until a trio of children could finish dragging their sled across the street. "I realize good manners should probably prevent me from asking you at this last minute, but I've got a feeling manners were never real big on my list."

"Asking me what?"

"If you'll go to the dance with me."

She stared at him. "You can't be serious."

"As a heart attack." His lips twisted. "Or a case of amnesia."

"I don't date." The usual response came automatically.

"Then just come back to my motel room and sleep with me."

She gaped.

He laughed abruptly. "Ah, Becky Lee, if you could see your face."

Rolling her eyes, more certain than ever that he was goading her, she turned and looked out the window. "You're spending a lot of time with Sheriff Hayes."

"You've been keeping tabs on me."

She'd only wanted to change the subject. Trust her to jump right into the fire. "I'm your physician, Captain Clay. I'm concerned about you overtaxing yourself. You're still recovering. You can't expect to have as much stamina as you ordinarily would."

"Bec, my stamina is just fine. And we're long past the 'Captain' stage, don't you think?" He pulled up behind her garage.

"I think you're more dangerous than Bennett," she said, and hopped out of the Jeep, pulling open the garage door so he could pull inside. Leaving him to it, she hurried through the kitchen door, found Ryan talking on the phone, just as he'd been when she'd left, then busied herself with that day's mail.

"You didn't give me an answer," Sawyer said from the direction of the kitchen.

There was no pretending she didn't know what he was talking about. "It's not a good idea."

"Yeah, but good ideas are often boring as hell. So live dangerously."

It must have been because she'd spent most of the

past week too aware of the distance between them. Because agreeing with him seemed ridiculously attractive. She swallowed as he advanced toward her. "I'm the town doctor. I can't live dangerously. I have a reputation to maintain."

A faint grin tilted his mobile lips. "This town talks even when there's nothing to talk about. There's not much else to do. Give 'em a thrill."

"There's lots to do around here." She defended the town she'd adopted as her own. "You always did have an attitude when it came to your hometown."

"And you ended up here. Quite a coincidence."

Rebecca turned to the tree and fiddled with an ornament that Ryan had made out of tongue depressors when he'd been in the first grade. A coincidence. "So did you remember Bennett?"

"Stop changing the subject."

She pushed her fingertips into the front pockets of her slacks and sighed. "Sawyer—" Her pager beeped.

Sawyer muttered an oath and paced impatiently around the living room while Rebecca went into her office to return the call. She came back within minutes with her bag in hand.

"I'll tell Ryan," he said. "That is, if you can trust me that far."

She hesitated, mother instincts warring with her physician's call. "I shouldn't be long."

He shrugged. "It's lunchtime. I'll grab something for your boy."

She blinked, sure that she should refuse. "Okay. Ah, thanks."

When she returned, Sawyer and Ryan were gone. Having lunch at Ruby's Café, according to the note Sawyer had taped to the refrigerator door.

Sitting around waiting for them only made her more anxious. But she didn't want to drive over to the café, either. To do so would only confirm Sawyer's mocking taunt that she didn't trust him.

And do you?

The question churned in her mind as she riffled through her closet, trying to figure out what to wear that evening. They still hadn't returned when she finally selected a royal blue sheath that had been shoved in the rear of the closet, so she decided to take a shower, which turned into a long bubble bath, instead.

When she came out and pulled on a clean sweatsuit, Ryan's bedroom door was closed and she could hear music coming from inside. But not his usual music. She listened. Tony Bennett, if she wasn't mistaken.

She shook her head and checked the dress she'd left hanging in the steamy bathroom. When she passed her son's room this time, the smooth voice coming through the door was distinctly out of place. "Ry, open up for a second." She knocked on his door, speaking above the music as she pushed open the door. "Since when do you listen to Frank Sinatra?"

The sight inside the room caught her broadside. Her son, cheeks flushed and ball cap twisted around backward, was carefully positioning his feet on the series of X's that had been taped to the carpeted floor. Sawyer, looking equally hot and frazzled, was standing to one side, near the bed they'd shoved out of the way of their impromptu dance floor.

Ryan turned even redder when he realized she was standing in the doorway, watching them. She looked at Sawyer. "I didn't realize you were here, too." She didn't know, in this instance, if ignorance was bliss or not. "I take it I interrupted some dance instruction?"

Ryan grimaced and flopped dramatically on his bed. "Melanie is gonna end up dancing with Jason Reese and I'm gonna stand there all night looking like a dork, 'cause there's no way I'm gonna learn this stuff."

"I told you that you ought to ask your mom to show you how to dance," Sawyer said.

"Dance with my own mom?" Ryan's voice rose.

Rebecca crossed her arms, leaning against the doorjamb. Amusement outweighed her indignation. "What's so appalling about that?"

Her son just groaned. Frank finished his song, and The Temptations filled the room with smooth sound.

"Maybe if you watched how it's done," Sawyer suggested, and Rebecca swallowed a nervous start when she realized he was looking expectantly at her.

"I don't dance," she said hurriedly.

He stopped in front of her, a glint of challenge in his dark blue eyes. "Yet you're on the planning committee for a dance?"

"It's a community event."

"Come on, Mom," Ryan said. "Sawyer says if I wanna impress a girl, I gotta be able to dance the yucky way. 'Cause women are all soft and funny about that sorta thing."

She couldn't quite deny the truth of that statement, even if she wasn't thrilled with the disgruntled male tone in which it was delivered. "Since when are you interested in what a girl thinks?"

Ryan's flush continued flourishing. "Jeez, Mom."

"I was just asking."

Sawyer chuckled under his breath and took her in his arms, pulling her over to the taped X's, moving easily with the music. "Maybe I shouldn't have asked you to the dance, after all," he said for her ears when she stumbled twice. "I don't have any steel-toed boots in my suitcase."

"Very funny." Her pulse pounded in her ears. "This isn't teaching Ryan anything," she said loudly and pulled out of his arms. "Ryan, come here."

Her son's expression was priceless. But apparently this Melanie he wanted to impress was more important than his feelings about dancing with his mother. So Rebecca found herself in the bittersweet position of teaching her son the box step in order for him to impress a girl who'd apparently stolen his young heart.

When Ryan jittered around his bedroom after a couple of successful sweeps of the temporary dance floor, Rebecca knelt down to pull up the masking tape from the carpet. Sawyer leaned over and helped.

She looked at his hands—long blunt fingers and strong, tapered wrists. Ryan was dancing behind them with an imaginary partner to music that played only in his head.

She brushed her wet hair behind her ears. "Yes, Sawyer. I'll go to the dance tonight with you."

Chapter Ten

"He sure does have a way about him, don't he?"

Standing near the punch bowl, Rebecca glanced at Sawyer's father. But her eyes didn't stray long from Sawyer, who'd succeeded in charming Hope Leoni out onto the dance floor. "Yes," she murmured. "He does."

"Where's Gloria?"

Squire's lips twisted. "She decided not to come tonight."

She took a closer look at him. He was a striking man, with his thick silvered hair brushed away from his hard, angled face. Though she'd tried to keep some measure of professional distance from the Clay family, the fact of the matter was that they, and the whole town of Weaver to boot, had welcomed her with disarming generosity. Squire had been on the committee that had hired her and basically funded the acquisition of the equipment in her offices. And Rebecca had been trying to get Gloria to agree to work in her office ever since.

It was pointless to pretend that she wasn't intensely interested in the Clay family as a whole. "Is she not feeling well?"

"Aside from being a confounded female, I'd guess she's fit as a fiddle."

Rebecca looked past the shrug he gave to see the strain in his expression. She set their drinks on the table and tucked her arm through his before she could think twice about it. "I seem to be in need of a dance partner. Would you be willing?"

He grunted. But he patted her hand and accompanied her onto the floor, and she felt a small bit of pleasure that she'd pleased him. "There's a nice turnout tonight, don't you think?"

He led her easily around the floor, reminding her strongly of Sawyer. "Pretty fair," he agreed.

"I do like the holidays."

"Haven't celebrated 'em too much myself," he admitted. "My boys' wives are working on changing that, though." His eyes took on a distant cast. "My wife died on Christmas Eve," he said abruptly.

Rebecca's heart squeezed. "I'm sorry."

"Was a long time ago."

"And time dulls the pain, but it doesn't make up for the loss."

"You lost your husband shortly before you came to us," he remembered. "I always thought you were too young and pretty to be a widow."

She smiled slightly. "And you were too young and handsome to be a widower."

His eyebrows worked. "Handsome," he snorted, the

tension easing from his shoulders. "Mind answering a question for me?"

"If I can."

"Would you get married again, if you had the opportunity?"

Rebecca realized she was watching Sawyer again and stumbled as Squire's words sank in. "I...well—"

"Of course, Gloria's lived a mite more'n you. Had a longer life with her husband than you did, before he passed on. And I—"

"You're thinking of proposing to Gloria?"

He didn't answer right away. One song changed to the next. "She says if I don't want to get hitched, she doesn't want to keep seeing me," he finally said. "Helluva thing to say, if you ask me."

"What do you want, Squire?" Rebecca asked softly, looking up into his face.

His gaze drifted toward the left and she knew instinctively that he was watching Sawyer. Then his attention drifted further and she guessed he was watching his other sons, Jefferson, Daniel and Matthew, who were at the moment occupying a round table with their wives and daughters. "Have you met my youngest boy?" he questioned, instead of answering.

"I've heard about him," she said. "From your family as well as an article here and there in the media." Tristan Clay, from all reports, was as rich as sin and as handsome as all his brothers combined and too fully grown to be called a boy.

"I wish my boys to be happy," he said. "Three out of five ain't bad, but it ain't enough."

"You're assuming that because they're unmarried, Sawyer and Tristan are unhappy."

"Sawyer always went his own way," Squire reflected, a faint smile on his lips. ''I said north, he said south. He knows more about ranching than some folks could forget in a lifetime, but he lit outta here before he'd even graduated high school.''

Rebecca started. She hadn't known that.

Squire didn't seem to notice, though, as he continued. ''Boy had half-a-dozen universities panting to get him into their mathematics programs, and all he could think about was seeing the world. Joining the navy. Don't know where that desire came from. And not just the service, either. No, sir. He had to be a SEAL. Comes from farmers and ranchers, and that boy wanted to live in a wetsuit treading water off the coast of some godforsaken country. And then he decides he wants even more excitement, getting into some even more hushed-up intelligence thing.''

''You're very proud of him.''

''Proud, sure. Understand him? No. And now he's got a crimped circuit in his brain that keeps him from remembering us, but he still walks his own path. Look at the way he moved into town the way he did.''

''Sawyer's condition isn't that uncommon, Squire. He sustained quite a trauma in that accident. There's no reason to think he won't make a full recovery.''

''And he'll leave his home behind again to go back to the life he wanted.''

The knot lodged in her throat doubled size. ''But if his naval career is what makes him happy, then you've gotten your wish.''

Squire's gaze narrowed. ''All right,'' he allowed. ''I wish they could be happy right here. On the Double-C, or in Weaver, at least.''

''That's understandable,'' she murmured. She knew that Sawyer would leave again. When he was fit again, she'd sign that release form. He'd return to the love that had always come first with him. His naval career. A thought that caused a pain in her midsection that she didn't want to come close to acknowledging. "So you want your sons to be happy. But what about Squire being happy?"

"Who says I ain't?"

She held his ice-blue gaze with her own, not flinching away in the least at his disgruntled tone. "I think you wish you were dancing with Gloria Day," she said mildly.

"Too smart for your own good, that's what you are."

"All those years in med school had to do something for me," she replied. "Life is too short, Squire," she said softly. "You of all people should know that."

He grunted. "Maybe I do, at that." His attention focused over her head for a moment. "Mebbe you need to remember that fact, too," he returned.

"Mind if I cut in?"

She realized Sawyer was standing behind them and felt as awkward as a gawky teenager when Squire thanked her cordially for the dance and surrendered her to his oldest son. She noticed that he didn't return to the table with the rest of his family, but headed, instead, for the exit. And Gloria, she suspected.

"Considering I brought you to this shindig, I was beginning to wonder if I was going to get you onto this floor or not."

Her heartbeat skittered around when Sawyer folded her hand in his. Considering the "practice" session earlier in Ryan's room, she ought to be over the worst of the shock of being in his arms. Only she wasn't. "I have a lot of duties here," she said, appalled at the breathlessness in her voice.

"Yeah, I noticed old Bennett keeping you company whenever he could. Thought you said you didn't date."

"I don't. And Bennett is just a—" She didn't know how to categorize Bennett. "Friend" would be overstating it on her part, though Bennett had made it abundantly clear he wanted more.

"Bennett is probably the same stuffed shirt he always was," Sawyer said. "More impressed with himself than any ten people in this town combined."

"I thought you didn't remember him."

"I remember he couldn't take no for an answer from more than one girl in high school. Watch out for him, Becky Lee."

She focused on the sinfully soft cashmere sweater he wore. Along with his finely tailored black trousers and the silver-tipped waves tumbling over his forehead, he was the epitome of rough elegance. "I'm a big girl," she said, as much to remind herself as him. "I'm perfectly capable of handling the likes of Bennett Ludlow."

"Sure. That's why you practically raced toward me earlier today when he was bugging you."

"It looked like Hope enjoyed her dance with you," she said deliberately. "Did she mention that she is a new teacher at the elementary school?"

"Changing the subject?"

"Seems wise."

His lips curved. "And you pride yourself on being wise and sensible and the ever-upstanding town doctor."

"Something wrong with that?"

He shook his head slowly, sliding his hand more

firmly around her waist. "I find it amazingly appealing," he said softly. "You look beautiful tonight, did
I tell you that?"

Her mouth ran dry. "I believe you mentioned it
when we left home."

"You look good in blue. But what I like most, I
think, is the length of the dress."

"The lack of it, you mean," she corrected dryly.
She'd debated that the dress was too short.

"You've got fabulous legs, Doc. Show 'em off, I
say." His fingers caressed the small of her back as they
moved slowly, barely dancing among the crowd. "It
does make a man wonder, though, what you've got on
underneath." His soft words stirred the hair at her temples.

Her cheeks heated. "You shouldn't say things like
that."

"Only speaking the truth."

She swallowed the moan that climbed into her throat
when he drew his warm fingers up her spine and back
down again. The cashmere was soft against her cheek,
but the chest beneath was wide and hard. "Sawyer."
She sighed. "This is madness."

"Madness is pretending we don't feel this."

She closed her eyes. Bing Crosby's voice swirled
around them, mingling with chatter and laughter and
the clink and tinkle of glasses and bottles. He led and
she blindly followed. "There is probably some woman
waiting for you in Maryland," she said somewhat desperately.

"There's not."

"Because you'd remember?"

"Because the only concerned face around me when
I was in the hospital was Jefferson's. No women came

to visit. I doubt I'd ever even had a woman inside that apartment that's supposed to be mine.''

Tears knotted in her throat. ''You make it sound so lonely.''

''I don't know. Maybe it was.''

''Your career meant the world to you, Sawyer.''

''If it did, why have I not recalled one thing about it? And why don't I care? You know what memory I want to regain the most, Rebecca?''

She realized they were no longer on the dance floor, but standing in the shadows outside the gymnasium, next to a row of lockers. The double doors he'd guided her through swung shut with a soft whoosh. ''What?''

He cupped her face in his broad, callused hands, his thumb brushing her skin. ''You. I want to remember you. And even if I never do, I'm glad for the accident, because I can know you now. I won't hurt you again, Rebecca. I can see in your eyes that it's exactly what you expect me to do. But I swear to you, I won't hurt you again.'' His thumb smoothed over her lip. ''Believe me.''

Weak, Rebecca curled her fingers into his arms. ''Oh, Sawyer. There's so much you don't—''

''Are you still in love with him? With your husband?''

''I loved him,'' she whispered. ''But he's gone. The last thing Tom would have wanted was for me to mourn him forever.''

''Was he your first love?''

She shook her head, dropping her forehead to his chest.

''Spend the night with me.''

''It wouldn't be right.'' Or smart or sane.

"We're not kids, Becky Lee. We're not Dylan Reese and Taylor Blankenship."

At that, the tears she'd kept at bay spilled over. If he only knew. "Ryan..." She couldn't finish.

"My room, then."

"You always were persistent."

"What else was I?"

"Willing to do anything to achieve your objective." She moistened her lips and tried to think rationally. "I think you're pushing your natural healing processes because you're impatient to put together the pieces of your memory. And I'm just a small part of the puzzle."

"And I think you think too much."

"Sawyer—"

"Shh." He pressed his lips to hers, halting the words.

Her rational mind shattered and all she could do was feel. Taste. Sigh against him and open to him when he sought more. Her fingers blindly explored cashmere-covered shoulders, felt his neck, so warm and strong. Felt his pulse thunder in tempo with hers, grazed his sharply angled jaw, the curve of his ear, slipped into the heavy silken hair.

His hands, on her hips now, pulled her tightly to him, and she murmured wordlessly when her body curved softly against his hard angles.

A sharp peal of laughter cut through the thick fog encircling them with all the finesse of a dull knife.

Rebecca gasped, pulling away, but Sawyer wouldn't let her go far, allowing her only to press her hands against his chest. "Sawyer, please. Someone will see. Let me go."

"After one question first. Who was your first love?"

"Sawyer—"

"Who?"

She looked at him, at the silver-tipped hair, disheveled because of *her* fingers. At the dark blue eyes, with faint shadows beneath them because of too many restless nights sleeping at the end of *her* building. "I suspect you already know the answer to that," she said huskily.

"I was. Where? When?"

That would be treading in far too dangerous waters. For a former SEAL who was used to danger, it was fine. But for the town doctor who'd worked hard to make a new life for herself and her son it was much too deep. "You said one question."

Sawyer grimaced, wanting to push, knowing he shouldn't. He reluctantly slid his hands from her hips. "I don't know what it is, Doc, but once again my patience seems to be nonexistent where you're concerned." He hauled in a long breath and shoveled his fingers through his hair. "Before you decide you're sorry you came with me tonight, if you haven't already, maybe we should go back inside."

He realized he was holding his breath when she smoothed nervous hands down her figure-skimming dress and nodded. He breathed again and turned back to the transformed gymnasium. "Doing what's right can be a real pain," he said softly.

He caught her elbow when she seemed to stumble. "Why would you say that?"

Why, indeed? An all-too-familiar throb reappeared in his temples, and he shrugged, pulling open the inner doors. "I have no idea. Just another one of those things that pops into my murky mind." He managed a faint grin and touched his finger to the little line that had formed between her level brows. "Put the doctor to rest, Becky Lee.'' Her smile was too shaky to suit him. ''Don't let a few kisses get you down.''

''It's not the kisses,'' she said in such a soft voice he had to strain to hear her. ''It's the 'Becky Lee.'''

And he knew then, why the name always came into his mind. A name that ought to belong to an innocent girl, rather than a grown, coolly professional doctor transplanted to Wyoming from a New York hospital. ''You got so mad at me the first time I called you that,'' he remembered slowly. ''I didn't know you were just a student or I wouldn't have given you such a hard time. But you turned positively green when you had to stitch up my leg—whoa, Doc.'' He caught her when she turned equally as green now as she had that long-ago day. He didn't know what was wrong with his brain that he could remember some things with such clarity, and other things—like just *how* long ago it had been—were out of his reach.

The look she was giving him was torn between horror and agony, causing a sharp stab of pain in his chest that had nothing to do with bruised ribs. And all he wanted to do was rid that well of pain from her golden-brown eyes, but he had no clue how to accomplish it. ''Ah, sweetness, it was a long time ago.'' Which didn't seem to help matters at all, and feeling totally inept, he wrapped his arms around her, rocking her slightly. ''Call me names or something, Doc,'' he murmured against her temple.

''Why?'' Her voice was choked, her palms on his chest caught between them. He felt her fingers curling. ''Why would I call you names?''

His laugh was humorless and short. ''I don't know. To make me feel better, I guess. You know this would be a helluva lot easier if you'd just spill your guts on what I did. Though I can probably guess.''

He tucked her head beneath his chin. Realized that smoothing his hand through her silky hair soothed him as much or more than it was meant to soothe her. "I was your first love and I broke your heart. No doubt through some monumentally selfish stupidity on my part. That much has become abundantly clear. But just as clear is the fact that you moved on. You were still a med student when we met, and now you're a respected physician. You and your husband—whom you obviously loved—had a son you'd do anything for, even to the extent of asking me to spend time with him just so he'll be able to remember his father more easily. Is that about it?''

Rebecca stirred and he let her go, feeling cold inside without her warmth against him. "Essentially," she said.

He watched her, probing the gray veil in his mind for more details, more explanations. Nothing. He leaned back against the cold wall of lockers and pushed his fingers in the front pockets of his trousers. "So where do we go from here, Becky Lee?''

Beneath silky royal-blue fabric, her shoulders straightened. "For now, back inside the dance," she said evenly. "Later, when you've recovered, I'll sign your release and you'll go back to your life.''

"What if I decide I want a different life than the one I've forgotten?''

She turned on a slender high heel and reached for the gymnasium door. "You can trust me on this one, Captain. You won't decide anything of the sort.''

Chapter Eleven

The rest of the evening passed in a haze, as far as Rebecca was concerned. She hovered behind the refreshment table, deliberately making herself busy. But her attention was on Sawyer, across the room, sitting at the big round table with his brothers and their wives, as if nothing untoward had happened that evening at all.

Every time he looked her way, she grabbed up another handful of debris and turned away. And every time she did so, she was more disgusted with herself.

Huffing out a breath, she moved out into the hallway. Hearing footsteps behind her, she whirled around. But it was only Bennett. She nodded distractedly. "I think everyone in town came tonight."

"You know, you never did give me the pleasure of a dance, despite your promise."

"Bennett, you know how busy we've all been tonight. It was worth it, though. We raised enough money to keep the elementary school open another year.'' She went still when he caught her shoulders in his too-smooth hands. ''Bennett, really.''

''Rebecca, you must know how I feel about you.''

''The same way you've felt about every other available female in the county,'' she said pleasantly.

''None of them were like you, though,'' he assured, stepping even closer. ''With your breeding and intelligence—''

''Breeding? I've tried to be nice, Bennett, but I'm simply not interested in you that way.''

''But Rebecca, who else in this little town is in your class? Nothing but ranchers and—''

''People who've given you a livelihood,'' she reminded.

''I suppose you think you're going to score big with the Clays. But you'd do better to set your sights for the old man than Sawyer. Everybody knows that Sawyer doesn't want anything to do with the family holdings. He won't hang around here for long and you'll just be left hanging when he goes.''

It wasn't so different than what she'd thought, herself. But delivered in Bennett Ludlow's snide tone, the statement infuriated her. Not about setting her sights for Squire, which was simply beneath contempt, but about Sawyer's expected actions. ''I'd rather take one minute with Sawyer Clay than a lifetime with the likes of you,'' she said coldly, shoving his hands away. ''I have work to do yet, so get out of my way.''

''Now, listen here, Rebecca. I haven't spent all this time waiting for that ice-princess act of yours to thaw, just to have you fall for Sawyer the minute he comes slouching back into town.''

Disbelief crowded against disgust when he closed his hands around her arms and pressed his lips to hers. She yanked back, stomping her heel into his foot and twisting his wrist in a particularly painful way. "Don't ever touch me again, Bennett, or any other unwilling woman for that matter, or I'll break something the next time."

"If she doesn't it'll be my pleasure to finish the job."

Paling, Bennett backed away from Rebecca, giving Sawyer, who'd soundlessly appeared, a wary glance. He looked like he was ready to say more, but Sawyer lifted an eyebrow, his smile deadly. Bennett huffed and stomped off. Rebecca was so relieved to see the last of him. And so ridiculously touched that Sawyer had wanted to protect her.

Rebecca reached for the trash bag that Bennett had left on the floor, but Sawyer was there first and tossed it into the bin. "Don't say it," she said. "I don't need an I-told-you-so just now."

"Right. How about a final dance, then? They just made the last call."

One minute with Sawyer… "I'd rather go home," she said. "If you don't mind."

If he did, his expression didn't show it. He opened one of the double doors and waited for her to enter first. "I'll get our coats and you can find Ryan."

Ryan was still over the moon, having danced through three consecutive songs with Melanie. Rebecca anticipated an argument, but none came. Probably because she gave him permission to go home with the Fieldings and spend the night there when they invited him.

It took several minutes to say their own goodbyes and work their way to the door; longer actually, than the drive home. Sawyer stopped outside the garage to let her out, and Rebecca hovered on the sidewalk, holding the long folds of her coat around her, but still shivering at the frigid air that swirled around her ankles. The night was impossibly clear and impossibly cold, and she simply didn't want to end it yet.

Sawyer closed the garage door and stopped next to her. "I suppose—"

"Would you like—"

They broke off. Feeling awkward, Rebecca tucked her chin into the turned-up collar of her coat. "Would you like to come in for some coffee?"

"Is that all you're offering?" His teeth flashed in the moonlight and he waved his hand. "Forget I said that," he suggested.

Not likely. So repeating her invitation for coffee was probably foolish, and she did it anyway. After a moment, he nodded, and she silently led the way through the kitchen. She left Sawyer for a moment to hang up their coats, and when she returned, Sawyer was paging through one of the thick photo albums she kept on her bookshelves in the living room.

She swallowed a jab of unease, and was starting a fresh pot of coffee in the kitchen when Sawyer came in. He sat at the table, long legs stretched, his gleaming boots crossed at the ankles. "When you said coffee, you really meant it. Do you always say what you mean?"

Her ears heated. "I try to."

He made a noncommittal sound. He'd propped one elbow on the table beside him, pressing his fingertips against his temple. "Tell me about New York."

"It's a really big city—" She leaned back against the counter at his look. "What do you want to know?"

"How'd you get there from San Diego?"

"What do you know about San Diego?"

"That is where we met, isn't it?"

She hesitated. Then nodded. Wondered how much more he remembered about San Diego, but was afraid of the answer should she ask.

"So how'd you get to New York?" he asked.

"By plane."

"Is this another one of those forbidden areas of yours?"

Yes. But that would only increase his curiosity. "Tom was a partner in a practice there," she said. "I'd known him nearly all my life."

"You wanted to specialize in baby stuff, didn't you?"

She'd once had visions of a neonatal specialty. But life had a way of directing a person on different paths. "I enjoy family practice," she said truthfully. If she stayed in one place long enough, she could end up being one of those country doctors who delivered babies of the babies she'd delivered. She rather liked the sound of that. The continuity of it. Of life renewed, over and over. "In New York I was on staff at one of the county hospitals. It was a good learning experience."

"Too many hours and too little pay," he commented.

She shrugged. "Money is only a means to an end," she said. "It can ease a lot of the world's ills and just as easily it can totally fail to save a person's life."

"Spoken like a woman who has enough green in the bank to be comfortable."

"I still have to earn a living," she countered. "I'm

fortunate that I can earn it doing something that means so much to me.''

"The girl who grew up with the blood of her missionary-doctor parents flowing in her veins," he murmured, rubbing his temple. "Are your parents still out of the country?"

Rebecca swallowed, nervously. "Zaire, these days."

"They must be proud of Ryan."

"Yes. They send us e-mail through the Internet when they can."

"When's the last time you saw them?"

"Before I met you." She realized the coffee was finished and poured two cups.

"They didn't come back when you got married?"

Considering her wedding had been put together in a spare two weeks, they wouldn't have been able to make it, even if they'd planned to. And the last thing she wanted was for Sawyer to start fitting things in a nice, neat, chronological order that would tear her life apart again. "No." She carried her coffee into the living room, stopping by the decorated tree to replace a fallen ornament. He followed.

"What about Tom's parents?"

"They died before I met him."

"So Ryan's never met his grandparents."

Her hand jerked, spilling hot coffee down the front of her dress. She gasped, staring stupidly at herself while the scalding liquid soaked through to her skin, burning fiercely. Sawyer muttered and took her cup, setting it aside and sliding down the long zipper in the back of her dress. It fell forward over her shoulders.

"Pull out your arms," he ordered.

She automatically obeyed, immediately relieved when the dress slipped down her hips and pooled at her feet. And just as immediately mortified. She stepped out of the dress but Sawyer caught her shoulders, bringing her up short when she darted for the hallway.

"Are you hurt?"

She looked down at herself, skin pinkened from the hot coffee. "It's, uh, it's fine."

"I guess I know now what you're wearing under the dress."

She flushed.

"It's a good thing I didn't know earlier," he continued, his voice dropping a notch. "Or I'd really have been in sorry shape."

She wished she'd chosen a different dress. One that required a slip beneath it. At least then she'd be covered in something more substantial than matching bra and panties. She could feel him standing right behind her; could feel that sinfully-soft cashmere against her back.

He ran his warm fingertip over the stretchy lace that held her thigh-high stockings in place and she sucked in a long breath; realized she was just standing there in front of him wearing nothing but lingerie and heels while he explored the little swirls and whorls of that lace edging. Realized, too, that she didn't want him to stop. At that moment, she wanted his touch more than any single thing in the world.

She clamped her fingers over his wrist. Felt his thudding pulse, despite herself. She turned, but he didn't move and now that cashmere was pressed against the black lace covering her breasts.

"If you're gonna ask me to leave, it's only fair to warn you I'm gonna do my level best to persuade you otherwise."

Rebecca didn't doubt that his means of persuasion were considerable. She told herself not to act foolishly.

But inviting him in for coffee had been foolish.

Going to the dance with him had been foolish.

Moving to Wyoming had been the most foolish of all.

"I guess that means I don't have to do my best to persuade you to stay," she said huskily.

His eyes, so darkly blue they were nearly black, devoured her. "Are you sure?"

She managed an uneven smile. "No."

His jaw cocked to one side. He threaded his fingers through her hair and smoothed it away from her face, then cupped her jaw in his palms and lowered his head. "Live dangerously, I always say," he murmured. And kissed her.

Rebecca moaned at the onslaught, fisted her hands in his hair, and kissed him right back. His hands burned over her skin, everywhere; oh, God, everywhere. He knelt at her feet and kissed her stomach, the lace edging of her hose. He wrapped his long fingers around her ankles and lifted, sliding her shoes free. Rose again, shucking his sweater somewhere along the way and her bra, too, she realized foggily. But the sensation of the wall of his chest against her breasts was crystalline clear.

She kissed the hot column of his neck, gasped when he lifted her around the waist and carried her unerringly into her bedroom where an antique lamp cast a dim glow over the ivory eyelet. She didn't even think to protest, and when her feet touched carpet once more, she pressed herself unhesitatingly against him, pulling his head down toward hers with a breathless cry.

When he reached past her and pulled back the

comforter, Rebecca pushed aside a mountain of decorative pillows. When he pressed her back against crisply cool cotton sheets, she pulled him with her. *So long.* The thought cried through her soul and her hands reached for him, unconsciously yearning, when he stood and unfastened his belt.

Rebecca struggled for breath, her gaze greedy on his beautifully male body. His eyes were blue fire when he bent one knee on the mattress and reached for her. Then she was bare, save for the lacy-edged silken hose still covering her from toe to thigh. And his eyes told her he reveled in the sight.

"You're so beautiful." With deliberate movements, he placed his warm palm on her flat belly. "Warm and real." His fingers brushed her breast and her breath stalled, her flesh tightening—tightening with anticipation.

"Sawyer—"

"You've been like a dream in my head," he murmured. "Only you're so much more than that, and I want...you," he finished, his voice deep and rough. "I want you, Rebecca Morehouse."

Rebecca moistened her lips, teetering on a precipice of need and fear. Need won. "I'm right here, Sawyer." She leaned toward him, smoothing her palms over the rigid muscles in his shoulders. Heaven help her, she'd been right there for so very long. "I want you, too."

A muscle ticked in his hard jaw. She brushed her fingertip over it. And still he didn't move. Swallowing, heart thundering, she placed her hand on his, and drew it upward, over the curve of her breast.

His nostrils flared with a hard exhalation, then he settled his long body next to hers, hair-roughened legs tangling with silken-clad ones. She stopped thinking then; how could she think when he touched her so? When his fingertips played her with the skill of a virtuoso?

When he drove her, masterfully, unrelentingly toward one peak, then another, while denying them both the ultimate pleasure of union. Nearly begging for relief, she felt for him, guiding him to her, rejoicing mindlessly at the low groan he gave.

Then he swore harshly and fell back, leaving her blinking with confusion. And realized her phone was ringing.

"I'm beginning to hate that thing," he muttered.

Rebecca scrambled across the tumbled pillows and answered the phone mid-ring. She listened for a moment, pushing her tumbled hair out of her face. "I'll be there as soon as I can." She hung up and turned to look at Sawyer. Her stomach clenched at the sight of him among her eyelet bedding, big and fierce and fully aroused.

"Gotta go out?"

She nodded, already sliding off the bed and rooting through her drawers for warm clothes. She didn't dare look back at him, lest she forget her physician's duty. "You might want to go, too," she said, yanking a thermal undershirt over her head. "That was Jefferson. Emily's water broke. She's in labor."

Chapter Twelve

"She's not supposed to do this until January," Jefferson said. He was looking like a caged lion when Rebecca entered their bedroom, alternating between pacing around the wide bed and sitting beside his wife.

Emily, huffing her way through a contraction, glared at him. "I'll buy a calendar for his first birthday," she said as soon as she could speak again. She hauled in a long breath and blew it out evenly. "I didn't think a few dances would upset the applecart like this."

Rebecca set her bag on the dresser and glanced at Sawyer, who immediately picked up her thought, and herded his brother out of the room. It was a double blessing, Rebecca thought. Jefferson's tension had been palpable, and Sawyer was simply a distraction she couldn't deal with now.

"How far apart are the contractions?" she asked, focusing her thoughts. "Never mind, I can see," she answered for herself just as Emily entered another contraction. Moving quickly, she readied the room as best she could, snapped on sterile gloves, and called Jefferson's name. He must have been waiting with his ear pressed to the door because he was beside his wife in half a second, propping her against his chest. His expression told Rebecca that if he could, he'd have the baby himself just to spare his "Em" the pain.

Ten minutes later, Rebecca helped guide a wonderfully healthy squalling baby boy into the world, and knew that no matter what Jefferson thought, Emily wouldn't give up the experience of bearing the child of the man she loved.

Giving the parents a moment with their newest as soon as she'd examined him, she swiftly cleared away the mess and washed up. She was rolling the kinks out of her neck when she saw Sawyer hovering in the doorway, a sleepy Leandra resting her blond curls on his wide shoulder.

"How's it going?"

She blinked hurriedly and turned back to her tasks. "Fine and dandy," she said over the unexpected lump in her throat. "Leandra, you have a new brother," she said. "Pretty cool, isn't it?"

"Bring her in, Sawyer," Emily said.

Though he turned slightly green at the notion of entering the birthing room, Sawyer did. He set Leandra on the floor, and she scrambled onto her daddy's knee, peering into the baby's face. "He's so small," she breathed.

Rebecca chuckled, taking the newborn for a moment to finish examining him. Busy with the wriggling infant, she didn't immediately notice the start that Sawyer gave. He looked from his brother to his new nephew and back again.

Finished with the baby, she cradled him, her maternal instincts crashing into her professional ones. She brushed her hand gently over the thatch of downy black hair the child possessed; drew the pad of her thumb along the little arm so soft and fresh and perfect; traced the beautiful shape of his head with her gaze. And looked into the face of a baby who would, God willing, grow up to be happy and healthy and treasured in the cradle of his family's love.

She realized that the room was silent and glanced up to see Sawyer, Jefferson and Emily watching her. Finding an easy smile from somewhere, she put it on her face and walked around the side of the bed and put the baby into his father's arms. A muscle worked in Jefferson's jaw for a moment, then he cradled his little son's head in his big palm.

The emotion in Jefferson's ordinarily stern face as he looked at his wife was hard to see, and Rebecca felt silly tears clog her throat. Painfully aware of Sawyer standing so near, she excused herself, quickly gathering up the bundle of disposable cloths she'd already bagged and her other supplies, leaving the bedroom neat and tidier than it'd been when she arrived.

She stowed her things in her Jeep, then went back into the kitchen where she phoned Maggie Clay to let her spread the news to the rest of their family of the early arrival. Then, because Sawyer still hadn't appeared, she found the makings for fresh coffee and started making a pot. If her experience with the Clays proved at all true, she figured they'd start arriving en mass within the hour.

The adrenaline rush fading, Rebecca leaned tiredly

against the counter in the dimly lit kitchen, sipping her own coffee. Ryan's birth swam in her memory. Tom had been there. Had never held it against her that when she'd been in labor with her son, it hadn't been his name she'd cried, though he'd been the one with her, helping her breathe, coaxing and encouraging when, so exhausted with the long labor, she'd felt like dying.

But her son had fought his way into the world and his perfectly formed head had been capped with a wealth of black downy hair and his skin had been—

"Tired?"

She swallowed and brushed her fingers quickly over her cheeks, bracing herself before turning to face Sawyer. "It's been quite a night."

"Yes."

"I called Maggie to spread the word."

"Means they'll be descending soon." He crossed toward her. "It's what they always did. More so now that there're women in the family again." He took the coffee cup from her and set it aside, slid his arms around her shoulders and pulled her against him where her head found its way to his chest. "I remember them, Doc," he said in an even voice that didn't quite hide his absolute relief. "I remember Emily when she was just a squirt of a girl, come to live at the Double-C. I remember tracking down Jefferson four years ago when Squire had his heart attack. I remember my mother." This last came in a voice rough and husky.

On top of a day too full, Sawyer's remembrance was more than she could take. Rebecca twined her arms around his waist and lay against him, tears running silently down her cheek as Sawyer recounted dozens of snippets from his childhood.

Then they heard a door open and suddenly the

kitchen was full of Clays, grown and not-so-grown. Self-conscious at having been found cradled against Sawyer, Rebecca disentangled herself, avoided Sawyer's sharp gaze when he saw the drying tears on her face, and hurried into the hall bathroom where she quickly freshened herself. She checked over Emily and the baby once more, then nodded her agreement when the new mother requested that everyone stop hanging around in the kitchen and family room and come in and see her.

With Jaimie and Maggie there, Rebecca knew that Emily wouldn't be given an opportunity to overtax herself. So she told Emily that she'd come back and check on her in the next day or two if Emily wasn't up to making the trip to Weaver, then headed back down the hall.

She gave the all-clear, and moved out of the way at the mini-stampede toward the master bedroom.

The men, however, didn't stay long, and were already trooping back to their precious coffee in the kitchen by the time Rebecca had buttoned up her coat and found her keys where Sawyer had dropped them on a table when they'd come in.

She hovered in the foyer, listening to the mingling timbre of male voices coming from the kitchen. She easily picked out Sawyer's voice from the others owned by his father and brothers. Heard the bone-deep satisfaction in his tone if not his words that he remembered his family.

Tugging up her coat collar, she quietly walked to the front door and let herself out into the darkness.

He remembered his family.

It was only a matter of time before he remembered all the rest.

* * *

In the kitchen, Sawyer sat around the table and thought about other times when he and his brothers and father had surrounded another table in another kitchen—the big oval table in the kitchen at the big house. They were only one brother short.

"Tristan'll be sorry he missed this," Jefferson said, uncannily echoing Sawyer's own thoughts. Tristan and Emily, who were closer in age than the rest of them, had grown up as best friends, remaining close even after Em had married Jefferson. "He thought he might make it here for Christmas."

"Got a name for the young 'un?"

"I was positive we'd have another girl," Jefferson admitted, his smile crooked. "So we didn't pick out any boy names."

Sawyer absently poured his scalding-hot coffee into a saucer and lifted it to his mouth, letting the conversation flow around him. It was wholly satisfying, he realized, being there. Everyone he cared about, nearly, under one roof. Welcoming another life into the world on a cold winter night.

It hadn't always been that way, he remembered, probing the thought gingerly, like a tongue against a sore tooth. He looked over at his father, who held a sleeping Leandra on his lap as if he'd been doing it all his life. The truth couldn't be more different.

Squire Clay had run cattle, sired sons and buried a wife. He'd been hard and cantankerous and until he'd brought little Emily Nichols into their household to raise, had shown little evidence of softness. He'd raised his sons the same way. And then had found it a betrayal when some of those sons wanted to go their own way.

Sawyer started to tip more steaming coffee into his

saucer, realized that Squire was doing exactly the same thing, and let the saucer sit, empty.

He closed his eyes and remembered the day he'd finally had enough of Squire's autocratic ways.

"You're going to college."

Sawyer's hands curled into tight fists at the flat statement. His old man didn't even look up at him when he said it. Just kept right on methodically hefting sacks of feed out of the pickup bed. "I didn't say I wouldn't go," Sawyer said, feeling his chest tighten until it was hard to get the words out. It was always this way. He thought one thing, and his father commanded another. "I only want to take off a year."

Squire Clay didn't snort with disgust at the idea. He simply reached for another bag of feed and hefted it over his shoulder. "You take off a year, then you can spend it working the ranch," he said flatly.

The ranch. Always the ranch. Sawyer was sick to death of the ranch. It had killed his mother. It obsessed his father. And from the look of things, was coming to obsess his younger brother, Matt, too. Sawyer didn't think any less of his brother for being satisfied with the cows and the dust and the day-in, day-out monotony of it all. Matt liked it. Sawyer didn't. His other brothers were even younger. Yet the five of them, including himself, understood each other.

If they could understand, why couldn't his old man? "It's one damn year," his voice rose embarrassingly and he curled his fists.

"Don't swear at me, boy."

"Don't call me 'boy.'"

Squire heaved the last of the sacks onto the pile and turned to face Sawyer. He thumbed back his dusty hat and stared at him through eyes the pale blue shade of a lake icing over. "You've got five universities knocking on our door, all wanting to get you in their fancy mathematics programs. And you want to take off a year to lollygag around." He lifted his hand before Sawyer could speak. "Explore the world. Call it what you want. It's a pure waste of a man's time."

Sawyer's jaw tightened, and his fists clenched and unclenched. He was nearly eighteen years old—as tall as his father, though the old man outweighed him by a few pounds yet.

"Don't even think it, son," Squire said softly. "Because I'll let you get one good swing and then you're gonna have your butt planted in the dirt."

Sawyer thought it might be worth it. But then, dammit all to hell, his throat tightened and his eyes stung, and he'd be hanged before he'd cry like some baby in front of his hard-as-nails father. It was bad enough that he felt like a fish out of water on the ranch. But he'd had folks from universities all across the country calling on the phone, or driving out to visit him and his father, who "surely must be terribly proud of his son's abilities." What a joke. The old man was proud of one thing only. The Double-C and the ability his sons had— or in Sawyer's case didn't have—to run it.

He didn't want any of it. He didn't want teachers parading him around like some damned freak. He didn't want to spend his days from before sunup to after sundown tending the needs of a bunch of bawling cows. He just wanted…away.

That was all. Away.

Just once he wanted to wake up and smell the ocean. Just once he wanted to look up and see palm trees waving over his head, instead of looking up to see heavy gray clouds overhead, waiting to dump snow on him. He wanted to go to sleep at night not feeling like he was suffocating from expectations and disappointments and a million other things he couldn't even put a name to, but felt pretty sure had to do with being Squire Clay's oldest boy.

He was supposed to be graduating from high school in a matter of weeks. Top of his class. Considering his class consisted of thirty people, that wasn't too damn hard. He was also top of the class for every single student in every single senior class in the whole damn state, and he couldn't figure out why. He didn't work hard at school. It just came easy. So why was everybody making such a bloody fuss over it?

Away. That was what he wanted.

That was what he'd have. No matter what his old man said.

He heard Squire's faint sigh and watched him swing the gate of the truck up into place with a clank and a bang. "Sawyer, if you want to go exploring the world, do it after you get your education under your belt. You're going to college, boy. Count yourself lucky. I never went."

And Sawyer realized at that moment something he'd never thought much about before. His father hadn't gone to college. He'd married Sarah Benedict before either one of them had turned eighteen. Against all odds, he'd built a successful—an unusual thing in itself—cattle ranch from the ground up. He'd weathered the death of his wife and raised their sons by himself. He'd accomplished many things in his life, but college hadn't been one of them. So maybe that was why making sure his firstborn did accomplish it was so important.

"Taking off one year doesn't mean I won't go."
Sawyer's voice was more or less calm. Getting angry
with Squire never did accomplish anything.

"No."

On the other hand, anger wasn't so easily controlled.
Not by a boy who was nearly a man. "It's not like I'm
gonna knock up some girl and get married and end up
punching cows for somebody else for the rest of my
life," he snapped. Then regretted it when his father's
eyes frosted over.

Squire pointed his finger at Sawyer. "If that's some
reference to your mama, you'd best start spitting apologies."

But it was too late now. "Come on, Squire, everybody in town knows I was born a few weeks too early
to be considered a honeymoon baby. You were married
in February. I was born in August. Preemies—isn't that
what they're called—are usually smaller than eleven
pounds—" The words dried up momentarily in his
throat when his father hauled him off his feet, two
white-knuckled hands wrapped in the front of his shirt.
He swallowed a knot of shame and anger and frustration and—dammit—love, for the iron-haired man who
was his dad, but didn't even use the title. "Just 'cause
you never talk about it—or her—doesn't mean other
people don't."

"I loved your mama from the day I met her," Squire
said softly. "And I'll be damned if I'll let anyone, even
her own flesh, speak badly of her."

Squire released Sawyer's shirt so abruptly that he
stumbled backward, nearly falling down and the humiliation of it was more than Sawyer could stand.
"You don't want anyone to speak of her, period," Sawyer said roughly. "She died and you acted like she

never existed—'' considering the bitterness of the words that spewed from him without control or any hint of stopping, he ought to feel some satisfaction at the way the old man flinched at that ''—like you...you blamed her—or something—for having had the gall to die on you.'' Tears burned hotly in his eyes and he hated the weakness, because if there was one thing Squire Clay had instilled in his sons it was to never be weak, and he hated the old man for making him feel as if there were something wrong with him just because he didn't want to devote his life to this godforsaken ranch, and he hated himself for putting that look in his dad's eyes. The look that had been there the day Squire watched his wife being buried—too young, too soon. A look that in the years since had gradually begun to fade. Or maybe it never had faded; it was just that Sawyer had gotten so used to seeing it there.

He gritted his teeth and glared at his father. He'd only wanted to get his father to understand why he wasn't ready to step foot on a university campus come fall—not get into all this...this stuff. He opened his mouth, an apology on his lips, but his father spoke first.

''Get out of my sight.''

The halting apology died unsaid. He turned on his heel and crossed the gravel road to the big house, slamming in through the back-screen door. He went straight inside, up the stairs and yanked down the ladder to the attic. Up there, he blinked at the dust motes and the dim light. He had a backpack somewhere—

His gaze fell on a wooden trunk, years of dust obscuring the details of careful carving. The trunk that, until his mother's death, had resided at the foot of his parents' bed, but which, since her burial, had been banished to the attic. He stared at the trunk, angrily

*swiping at the tears that burned his eyes. The trunk
had an old, dusty padlock that still held it closed—a
padlock that had never been there when she'd been
alive.*

*He reached out, his hand closing over the stock of a
rifle that had been long ago dismantled. He deliberately approached the trunk and the lock that just then
seemed to be symbolic of his whole life—locked up;
locked in.*

*With one mighty crack, he brought the stock down
on the lock and it sprang apart, falling to the floor with
a clatter. Sawyer flipped the latch and yanked up the
lid. The hinges screeched in protest.*

*He tossed the stock aside and crouched down beside
the trunk, wiping his dusty hands on his jeans before
reaching for the neatly folded items inside. A baby
blanket. A dried, crinkly-crisp bouquet of flowers, tied
together with a faded blue ribbon. A shoe box filled
with black-and-white photographs of people he didn't
recognize.*

*A bunch of lacy handkerchiefs with S.B. sewed on
one corner. And a packet of envelopes tied neatly together with a red ribbon that still had a tidy bow in it.
Sawyer sat back, holding the letters in his hand. He
didn't even glance again at the rest of the items as he
slid out the top envelope. He didn't know why he was
suddenly so curious about the contents of a letter his
mother had carefully preserved.*

*A need to connect with the woman who had left be-
hind her family of men so long ago? A need to get back
at his autocratic father, by delving into Sarah's be-
longings that Squire had so deliberately put away but
never completely disposed of?*

Whatever the reason, Sawyer slid the letter out of the

envelope and opened it, catching the small photograph
that fell out with one hand. At first, Sawyer thought the
letter had been written by Squire, because the slashing
letters were similar to his father's style. But as he read,
he realized it was not written by Squire Clay. It was
written by another man.

A man who addressed Sarah Benedict as "My darling Sarah." Who signed the letter with, "Loving you
always, S." Not S for Squire. But S for—he automatically glanced at the photo in his hand. Then looked
more closely. He turned it over, looking at the back,
and felt his whole world shrink down to a pinpoint.

S for Sawyer Templeton.

He turned the photo of the other Sawyer over and
looked at it once more. He could have been looking at
a picture of himself.

He sat there for a long time, looking at the photograph.

Then he replaced everything exactly the way he'd
found it inside the trunk. There was nothing he could
do about the broken lock. But nobody ever came up to
the attic anymore except him.

He found his backpack sitting on top of a box of old
phonograph records. He took it down and shook off the
dust and went back to his bedroom where he threw in
enough clothes to keep him going for a week or so. He
didn't have a lot of cash, but if he could get to Gillette
and the bus depot, he'd make do.

With his backpack hanging from his shoulder, he
took one look around his bedroom. Daniel's checkers
game was sitting on the floor and, muttering an oath
at himself for doing so, he found a sheet of notebook
paper and scrawled a note, leaving it sitting on the
middle of his mattress.

*Then he walked down the stairs and out the front
door, which nobody ever used, and walked until he
reached the state highway. Then he walked some more
and eventually a trucker stopped and he rode the rest
of the—*

"Yo, earth to Sawyer."

He jerked to the present, knocking his hand against
his empty coffee saucer.

The ease he'd felt sitting there with his brothers was
gone, but he didn't so much as betray it with a blink.
And that loss of ease had everything to do with Squire,
who was watching him steadily, as if divining his every
thought.

He set the saucer aside and uncoiled from the chair.
"It's late. Rebecca's probably exhausted."

"She left more'n an hour ago." That came from
Matthew, who was sprawled in the chair to Sawyer's
right.

After everything, she'd left without a word. He
couldn't believe how hard that hit him. Without waiting
a beat, Jefferson handed Sawyer a set of keys. "Take
Em's pickup," he said.

Sawyer palmed the keys, nodded to the others and
strode toward the door. He stopped short, though, long
enough to turn around and bid goodbye to his sisters-
in-law. "You did good, Em." He kissed the top of her
head when he went back to the master bedroom to find
the women and their daughters cooing over the newest
family member.

Despite the fact that she'd brought a baby into the
world within the past few hours—beside the fact that
she was obviously exhausted, her chocolate-brown eyes
were radiant. She smiled serenely and caught his hand.

"Now that you've come back to us, I hope you decide to stick around a while."

He shrugged, noncommittally. There were several things to resolve before he decided what he was going to do. He peered into the sleeping baby's face. "For such a tiny guy, you sure do cause a huge fuss," he murmured.

Emily raised a mock fist. "I'll give you tiny—"

He lifted his hands apologetically and escaped the feminine laughter that rained over his head. What did he know about babies?

He knew the navy. He knew the SEALs, was still heavily involved with the black ops team which he'd led and bled for. He knew his particular branch of intel, the men and women under his command, the increasing frustration he'd been dealing with over a bureaucracy more interested in being politically correct than just doing what was right. But babies?

What he knew about babies would fill a thimble, he thought as he drove Emily's fire-engine-red pickup back into Weaver. What he knew about Rebecca Morehouse, apparently filled even less.

How could she just leave like that? Without a word of goodbye. Without a thought.

By the time he'd made it back to town, his temper—rather than cooling during the drive—had simmered until it bubbled in his veins thick and hot. He parked on the snowy concrete slab next to her garage and without thought went right through her unlocked kitchen door, back to her bedroom, where she was a still form in the bed that *they'd* torn to pieces less than six hours ago.

He flipped on the overhead light, crossing to the bed and planting his hands on either side of her when she rolled over, gasping and blinking at the sudden light. "How could you walk away like that?"

Her face, bare of cosmetics, was unutterably vulnerable and his extreme grip of anger eased.

Her lashes shielded her golden brown eyes from the unrelenting light. And from him. "I thought you'd want to stay there," she said at last. "You remembered—"

He pushed away from the bed with a derisive sound. "Rebecca, if I came even close to believing that—" He broke off, scrubbing his hands over his face, then shoving his hands into his pockets to keep from reaching out for her again. Where was his control? He was supposed to be a man of control. Isn't that what his men called him? "Concrete Clay"—unyielding, unswerving, unrelenting in his pursuit of justice in a world too filled with injustice.

He'd spent years cultivating that control, starting with the moment he'd hitched a ride out of Wyoming to make his own life, his own future, ironically becoming the type of man Squire had raised him to be. He'd had less than a handful of occasions when he'd lost his control.

An innocent medical student named Becky Lee, whom he'd known better than to get involved with, considering the dangerous life he'd chosen, had been one.

Testifying in the court-martial of a man he'd served with, trusted once, and finally had to take down, another.

And now, back with sweet Becky Lee, all grown-up, with a very definite mind of her own, he didn't seem able to find his control on so many levels, it scared the Beelzebub out of him.

He'd done a lot in his life; had fought fights that didn't usually end with a pretty bow wrapped around them. He'd snooped and spied and delved and probed into people's lives, their business activities, their personal relationships. On occasion, he'd even taken lives—with deliberate, deadly accuracy.

But Rebecca Morehouse saved them.

"This is one of those times I'm sure God is up there having a grand old laugh," he muttered.

She pushed herself up on her pillows, holding the comforter to her neck like a shield. He noticed that her hand was shaking when she pushed her lustrous hair out of her eyes. "Sawyer, what are you doing here?"

"I want to finish what we started."

Her slender, elegant throat worked as she swallowed. "Not tonight dear, I've got a headache." Expressed in her husky, not-quite-steady voice, the joke fell flat.

"I'm not talking about making love with you." His lips twisted, his eyes running over her. "Though, God knows, I intend to do that, too."

Rosy color flooded her creamy cheeks and he became distracted for a moment by the way she pressed her soft lips together, as if she was holding back words—or remembering the sensation of a kiss. "I might have something to say about that."

"Yes, you will," he agreed. "Something along the lines, perhaps, of 'I don't care what you do, Sawyer, I only care about now. About us.'"

He watched the blood drain from her face, and had to force himself to continue. Because if he didn't, if they didn't move beyond what he'd done in the past, then any hope of a future with her was already dead. And a future with her was exactly what he wanted. Somehow. Some way.

He'd known it the moment he'd watched her holding Jefferson's newborn son—not holding the baby as the physician who'd just delivered him into the world, but as a woman; a mother.

But before a future, they had to deal with the past. So he pushed out the words even as the memories coalesced. "That's what you said, and I knew you were too young to really know what you were talking about. But I wanted you more than any single thing I'd ever wanted in my life. So I overlooked the fact that I was ten years older than you. And I overlooked the fact that there was no room back then for a future together. And I overlooked the fact that you were a total innocent when it came to men. I took that innocence. I took you. For those—what, four months?—you were mine, and I was yours."

"You were the navy's," she corrected flatly. "I was...'shore leave.' Don't pretend it was more than that for you."

"I went back to look for you."

Her eyes widened for a moment, then her lips twisted. "So the sex was good."

"Dammit, Rebecca, don't do that. Don't reduce what we shared to something—hell, to something *base*. It wasn't like that."

Rebecca couldn't believe what she was hearing. "It wasn't?" She certainly hadn't thought so. But he'd cleared her up on that point. "Obviously you don't remember quite as much as you think you do."

"I remember that you split San Diego during the time I was in Malaysia. You disappeared. You left school. Why did you do that, Rebecca? Is that when you took up with Tom? He was that visiting lecturer who had the hots for you, wasn't he? He was probably old enough to be your father.''

She wouldn't cry. She would *not*. There'd been a time ten years ago when she hadn't been able to get through a day without resorting to tears. But that time was over and gone. And right now she was unutterably weary from the events of the day. ''I owe you no explanations,'' she said evenly. ''You walked away from me, Captain. You made it clear.'' Oh, God, he'd made it painfully clear. ''So please don't try to romanticize it now, so long after the fact. We had a...*good time*.'' Her voice cracked. ''And that's all we had.''

''Dammit, Bec—''

''No.'' She couldn't handle this. She threw back the comforter and slid from the bed, yanking the hem of her flannel nightshirt down around her thighs as she hurriedly crossed to her dresser and her grandmother's antique jewelry box sitting on top. She opened it and pushed her fingertips past her wide silver wedding band and a swirl of pearls, then pulled out a microcassette.

Her breathing was harsh as she turned and slammed it against his chest. ''A good time,'' she repeated. ''You said—God, it wasn't even twenty-four hours ago—that you said you wouldn't hurt me again. Well, you won't hurt me again because I won't let you,'' she vowed. ''But do me the c-courtesy of calling it what it was.'' She turned away, angrily brushing at the tears that were burning down her cheeks. ''A...good... time.''

Sawyer's hand closed over the tiny audiocassette. ''I couldn't offer you a future, Bec. I warned you going in of that. I'm not blaming you. I was older. Had more experience ten years ago than you do, even now. You were the eternal optimist and I knew it. I should have known you'd believe you could change that—change me. Who I was. What I did.''

Her jaw ached. She wanted to hit him upside the head and the violence of the urge shocked her. "Your back must ache constantly under the weight of that ego you cart around."

An indefinable shadow haunted his dark blue gaze. "Rebecca, I'll admit that the memories are still a little patchy. But I do remember the calls you made to me."

"The calls you couldn't be bothered to answer."

"If you weren't trying to hold on to what we had, then why did you keep trying to reach me, even though I was half a world away from San Diego? If you didn't believe that what we'd had could continue, why did you keep leaving messages with my C.O.? With every person who could conceivably reach me? You managed to find out where I was based, and that was classified information. That took twenty-three calls, Doc. Twenty-three."

The hot words on her lips nearly escaped in her shock that he'd known, and remembered, such a detail. But how could she tell him why she'd kept calling? Why she'd swallowed her humiliation over and over again to get in touch with him?

"You're mistaken," she lied right through her teeth, and felt her face heat because of it. "Confusing me with one of your other...shore-leave girls."

An expression remarkably close to pain darkened his carved features. Over the past ten years, she'd done a fair job of convincing herself that Capt. Sawyer Clay didn't feel emotional pain. She knew she'd been somewhat mistaken, because he *had* been suffering through his amnesia. But had he been feeling pain, true pain, because of her?

Not likely.

Not possible.

Not in a million years.

She stood in the doorway of her bedroom, leaning her back against the doorjamb, making it obvious that she was waiting for him to leave. "You said it yourself. I was young." She forced a shrug she was eons from feeling. "Fortunately, time is taking care of that."

She knew he was angry. Knew it in the stillness of his shoulders. In the set of his jaw. And the way his voice, when he spoke, was soft. Evenly paced. "Make no mistake, Doc, whether you're twenty-three or eighty-three, I'm gonna want you. And you're lying to yourself if you think I'm gonna believe you don't feel the same way about me."

His words pierced her like well-aimed arrows. And still she didn't move from her position at the doorway. But holding his gaze took more strength than she possessed and she dropped her own to the muscle ticking in his tight jaw.

He exhaled a short, harsh breath. Stepped through the doorway, and stopped right next to her. "I never would've taken you for a liar, Rebecca. I guess it's just one more thing I've been wrong about in my life."

He moved past her, down the hall. Her knees weakened and she leaned her shoulders back against the wall. After a moment, she heard the kitchen door open and close. Then all was silent again.

Her knees gave, and she slid down the wall to sit on the floor. She would have cried, if she'd had any tears left.

But the pain went too deep for tears.

And as far as Rebecca could see, there was no end to it in sight.

Chapter Thirteen

Filled with too much energy, too much frustration, Sawyer paced the square confines of his motel room. His head felt as if it was in a vise. His chest ached. His eyes were dry from lack of sleep.

He'd been in worse shape and in considerably worse, deadlier, situations.

Only none of them had ever hurt him down in his soul. He flipped the microcassette Rebecca had shoved at him between his fingers. He was kidding himself if he thought she'd ever forgive him for the past.

Why should she? In her place, he doubted he'd feel any differently than she. He'd met her, bedded her and left her. Oh, yeah, he'd taken a few months while he was about it. Four months that had never really left him, except in the aftermath of his recent accident.

He set the cassette on the table situated beneath the window. It was light outside. Another day.

He wished he knew what the hell to do with it.

He pulled aside the drape, looking toward the other end of the building. Toward the entrance of Rebecca's office.

All was still. Quiet.

It was Sunday morning in Weaver. Not exactly one of the world's hot spots. The interesting thing was, just then, he figured that was okay. That a quiet, still, snowy morning in Weaver was not an altogether bad place to be.

God, he was talking himself in circles, he thought with disgust, and turned away from the window. He stripped and took a shower, dressed in the last clean outfit he possessed and drove in Emily's truck out to the big house.

Surprisingly enough, everything was silent there, too. Of course, everybody had been over at Jefferson's for a good portion of the wee hours. And it was too early yet for them to drive into town if they planned to go to church.

Moving quietly, he grabbed a quart of milk from the fridge and carried it with him down the hall beyond the stairs to Matthew's office. He passed by Squire's open bedroom door, automatically noting that it was unoccupied. But he hadn't driven all the way out there to talk to his father.

He sat down in the chair behind Matt's wide, somewhat-messy desk, and flipped on the computer. This is what he'd come for. Answers. Of the type he could deal with.

There were things in his memory that still evaded him. He'd be damned if he'd keep waiting for them to reappear in their own sweet time. He'd be damned if he'd ask again for answers his family wouldn't provide. Or couldn't.

It took a few minutes for the computer to boot, then another few to log on to the Internet. He thumbed open the milk carton and absently drank, while he logged his security code and accessed the files he'd been working before the accident.

The information he found there was pretty much what he expected. He'd been integral to the court-martial of Admiral Jonathan Ingstrom. It was Sawyer's investigation—more than two years of grinding hard work—that had finally put the nails in the coffin of Ingstrom's career. The reason Sawyer had scheduled a meeting with his old contact, Coleman Black, was to thank him for his discreet assistance in gaining a key piece of evidence. Considering he and Cole rarely met publicly, it was no wonder that his some-time associate had been suspicious when he'd missed the meeting.

Then, Sawyer came across the obituary notice of Ingstrom's wife, and he felt a familiar stab of remorse. He couldn't regret taking Ingstrom down. The man had been dirty to the core, and Sawyer hated that *his* navy had turned a blind eye to Ingstrom's activities. But he did wish there'd been some way to spare Mitzi the trauma she'd endured over her husband's public humiliation. The night after her husband had been stripped of his commission she'd swallowed too many of her prescription tranquillizers and hadn't awakened in the morning.

Sawyer sighed and entered another file. His own. And there it was. Photos of the wreckage that had once been a car. His head pulsed painfully, and Sawyer still couldn't recall the accident, even though he was looking at graphic evidence of it. Black ice. A blown tire.

A tree and an embankment. Nobody else had been hurt. Nobody had been at fault.

Just an accident. That changed his life when it could easily have taken it.

"I thought I heard someone back here."

He dragged his attention from the computer screen. Realized that more than two hours had passed. "Matt."

His brother glanced at the computer screen when he rounded the desk and did a double take. "Is that…?"

Sawyer closed the file. "I could answer," he said blandly. "But then I'd have to kill you."

Matthew snorted. He continued reaching past Sawyer for the stack of breeding records that he'd come in for. "You need to muck out some stalls. Get rid of that load of bull you carry around with you at the same time."

He ignored that. Arms propped on the desk, he watched his brother for a moment. "You ever think about Mom?" he asked abruptly.

If Matthew was surprised, his expression didn't show it. "What about her?"

"Think she was happy with Squire?"

That did surprise Matt. "Yeah. I do." His eyes sharpened. "I thought you said you'd remembered."

"I did."

"Then you oughta know better'n me what she was like around Squire. He loved her. He buried most of his heart with her. Why?"

Sawyer shrugged dismissively. "No reason."

"You haven't made inconsequential comments in decades." Matthew watched him for a moment. "Talking to the old man isn't as impossible as it once was, you know. He's mellowed since his heart attack. Even he and Jefferson have made some peace between them.''

"Thanks to Emily."

"Mostly. But not entirely. He wants us all home, on the Double-C. Including you.''

Sawyer knew that. But the fact was, he wasn't like his brothers. But for reasons they knew nothing about. For reasons he'd discovered when he'd been an angry teenager, determined to find his own way in the world, whether it followed the path Squire set out or not. He logged off the computer system and stood, walking past his brother down the hallway. "I couldn't do what you do, Matt. Or Daniel or Jefferson, for that matter.''

"And I couldn't do what you've done. Never wanted to. But who cares? We're all still bound to this place, 'cause it's our roots, no matter how far we walk. How far we drift.'' Matthew tapped the stack of records against his leg. "I just drifted differently than some of you." He looked up suddenly, uncannily sensing Jaimie standing above him on the landing before she even called down to him.

Sawyer continued on alone into the kitchen, decided he didn't want to sit at the big oval table that seemed to hold such a wealth of memories that just a few days ago he'd been aching to have, and shrugged on his coat, heading outside instead.

His breath clouded around his head as he walked along the snowplowed road that separated the big house from the corrals and barns. But no matter how far he walked, how badly he wanted to outrun the memories that he'd been so desperate to regain, they stayed with him.

His mother's death on Christmas Eve so many years

ago. The contents of that old trunk in the attic. Walking away from Becky Lee.

There was no more road. He stopped walking and stared out at the snowy fields—and at the mountains in the distance. He'd been away from the Double-C for more years than he'd lived there—visiting only sporadically as his schedule had allowed. His real life had been elsewhere.

He blew out a long breath, wincing at the pull in his ribs, the biting-cold burn in his lungs when he inhaled the frigid morning air. He slowly turned, squinting against the morning glare, as he looked back. At the big house—stone and wood and built to withstand generations. Barns and corrals and stables.

Matthew was right. It didn't matter how far he went. Or for how long. His roots were tamped deep, immovably, in this snow-covered land. He'd be hanged, though, if he knew when that had become a satisfying thing. Something to find comforting. When had it become something he'd needed to accept, and not something he'd needed to escape? Did it have to do with Rebecca? With his increasing cynicism over his naval career? Did it have to do with the sheriff's frequent suggestions that the town could use a man like Sawyer?

"You're getting old, man," he muttered to himself, striding back the way he'd come. When he entered the kitchen this time, the rest of the household had risen. He stood in the doorway, taking in at a glance the homey scene. Matthew, with Sarah on one knee while he forked country-fried potatoes in his mouth and paged through the paper. Jaimie at the sink, humming some song in a slightly off-key tone.

She turned to the side, setting a plate in the drainer, and the sunlight shining through the window over the sink cradled her pregnant body in a golden glow. She'd married his brother four years ago come April.

He remembered the wedding perfectly.

Sarah asked something, Matthew answered and Jaimie turned back to the table, sliding her hand over her husband's shoulder in a curiously intimate movement. Then Sawyer realized Matthew's hand had slipped around his wife's narrow back and rested on the swollen bulge of their child.

His vision pinpointed, focused on Matt's hand and that pregnant swell.

Awareness blasted through him. Holy hell.

Jaimie laughed over something and the moment passed, though it remained frozen in Sawyer's mind. She noticed him standing in the doorway and waved him in for some breakfast. But he shook his head and told them he was heading back into Weaver.

He was nearly to the borrowed truck when Matthew caught up with him. "What's wrong?"

"Nothing."

"I suppose you're getting ready to blow town. Now that you've got your memory back, you can get your medical release and get back to work."

Oddly enough, Sawyer hadn't been thinking about that. Which, in itself, was totally out of character. He climbed behind the wheel, starting the engine with a controlled touch. "I've got things to clear up first," was all he said. "See you later."

Matthew hesitated, as if he wanted to say more. But he didn't. Just backed up from the truck and watched while Sawyer wheeled around and headed back toward town.

The closer he got, the tighter Sawyer's nerves coiled.

He'd been so stupid. Wrapped up in his own feelings, his own memories.

He pulled into Rebecca's parking lot and sat watching the entry of her office. Even though cold air seeped into the cab, he felt himself sweating. Felt the hair on his neck prickle. And knew he was finally on the right track. He knew why Rebecca had looked as if she'd seen a ghost when he'd walked into her office last week. Why she'd looked as if she'd wanted to pass out when he'd told her he'd remembered everything after Emily's baby was born.

He knew the truth now, with every atom of his being. With every black fiber of his soul.

He got out of the truck and walked around the building.

Rebecca opened the kitchen door before he reached it. She didn't look surprised to see him. She looked tired and worn and so beautiful it made him hurt deep down inside where he didn't like to look.

The breeze blew. He watched her shake her head slightly, clearing the gleaming strands of brown silk from her eyes. Eyes that held the truth of what he'd finally figured out.

She leaned against the open doorway. Her arms, covered in butter-colored cashmere, were crossed, giving the appearance of casual interest. But he knew better. He knew that if she weren't leaning against the immovable support of that doorjamb, she'd collapse.

"He's my son," he said.

Her lashes lowered for a moment. But only for a moment. Then her gaze, golden brown and glazed with pain—pain he'd caused—met his. "Yes."

The affirmation, even though expected, was a small pebble—dropped in the center of his soul. Rippling out, wider and wider, deeper and stronger, and shaking the foundation of his being. He gripped hard for his voice. "Where is he?"

"He doesn't know."

Sawyer remained standing where he was. Because if he went one step closer, he was going to throttle her. Or take her. Either one was unacceptable. "Where is he? Still at his friend's? The Fieldings'?"

Her steady gaze wavered.

He spun on his heel. He heard her boots on the walk as she hurried after him. Braced himself for her to reach out and stop him, but she didn't. She jogged in front of him and stood in his path. "Don't do this, Sawyer. He's just a boy."

"My boy."

She caught his sleeve. "He'll be hurt if you just blurt it out because you're angry with me."

"I won't lie to my son," he gritted.

"Let me talk to him first."

"You've had nine years to talk to him. He has a father, and a right to know it."

She winced as if he'd physically struck her. "He had Tom," she said unsteadily, pulling back her hands. "And he still grieves for him."

"I think you're the one doing most of the grieving." Sawyer shoved his hands into his coat pockets. His jaw ached. "Did Tom know, or was my son another lie of yours—one you passed on to him because you didn't have the guts to tell me the truth?"

She paled. Drew herself up. "Tom gave us his name. His love. And you can blame me for not telling you the truth when I learned I was pregnant, but you know good and well that you have your own share of responsibility in that. Twenty-three calls, Captain. Do you think I tracked you around the world with phone calls just because I liked humiliating myself? I knew I came a poor second to your career. I knew that somewhere around the tenth futile call. And I still kept trying to reach you. To tell you about the baby. Then you finally left that message on my answering machine, and I knew there was no point.''

"No point? You carried my son, and there was *no point?*"

"You didn't want a family. A wife. You told me so yourself the very first time we went out. Remember that night, Sawyer? Do you remember that secluded little place on the beach? You built a fire in the fire pit, and we ate cold lobster with our fingers and shared a bottle of wine? And you stared at the ocean and told me she was your first love. You wanted me to understand that your work was dangerous, and you wanted me in your bed. Do you remember?''

He did. And each memory cut like a knife.

"So you passed my son off as another man's.''

Her throat worked. "Bastard.''

She'd never know the truth in her harsh branding. He didn't know who he was angrier with—himself or her. Or the absent Tom who'd been a father to his son when Sawyer had not. Who was remembered as a father by his son. "You should have told me.''

"When?''

"How should I know?'' He turned away from her, realized he was heading toward her kitchen door, and turned again. "When I came back here. When we made love last night.''

"We didn't—''

He silenced her with a look. "Cut the technicalities, Doc. We made love last night just as much as we made love that night on the beach with the surf pounding at our feet and the stars shining over our heads.''

She shivered and he cursed himself, anew. She didn't even have on a coat. Just that soft yellow sweater that draped her full breasts and black jeans that emphasized the lean length of her endless legs, but neither of which offered much protection against the cold morning. "Go inside," he said wearily. "Before you catch pneumonia and I've got that on my conscience, too.''

Stubborn woman. She didn't move. Just hugged her arms tighter around herself. "Don't tell Ryan, Sawyer. Not like this. Please.''

"Go inside, Rebecca.''

"You'll break his heart when you leave.''

"I won't leave.''

Her expression tightened. "That's exactly what you *will* do, Captain. You don't want small-town life. You chafe against the ranching heritage of your family. You want the world at your fingertips. Your team and your intelligence networks are your family. I understand that. But my son won't.''

He hated the chunks of truth in her words. But they were old truths. Based on old facts. Things were different now. "He has a right to know. You can't hide this, Rebecca. How could you move here, to Weaver, and think you *could* totally escape me? Ryan will learn the truth—whether from me or someone else—and he will never forgive you for keeping it from him.''

"You know nothing about it," she snapped through chattering teeth. "You only know what you want. What you think. But this is about Ry—''

"I know everything about it," he clipped harshly.

"A boy needs to know his father. His *real* father. Good, bad, or indifferent. He needs to know—"

"That he's loved," she cried. "That he comes first. The only thing that comes first with you is your precious career. Sawyer, why can't you just let this be? You know the truth. Isn't that enough for you?"

"Until my son knows the truth, it'll never be enough." He realized he was rubbing the pain in his chest, and deliberately pushed his hand instead into his pocket.

"You're being unreasonable," she accused. "And totally selfish—"

"Me! You've had him for nine years. Pretended he was another man's for a good portion of that."

"I pretended nothing." Her nose was blue with cold. "Tom knew everything. He loved us anyway."

"Hell, he was just a real saint, wasn't he? Just a real upstanding guy."

"Say what you want, Sawyer. It won't change the facts. Tom and Ryan and I *were* a family, no matter what you want to believe. Ryan will always remember Tom as his father."

"And if Tom hadn't died?"

She looked away.

"You'd have just kept on living a lie," he guessed roughly. "And one day the truth, somehow, someway, would have come out. And Ryan's whole existence would be ripped from beneath him. That's being *real* unselfish, Rebecca. Not only has he lost *Tom,* he'd think I'd never wanted him."

"Ryan would know that Tom loved him. That's what matters. That's what he would remember. What he'd know. Tom wanted him. Tom loved him."

"And you never gave me a chance to love him! The

truth matters too. Make no mistake, it matters a helluva lot more than you're willing to admit.''

"You don't know—"

"I know." Pushed beyond endurance, he caught her arms and pulled her up to his nose. "I know because it is exactly what happened to me."

Her lovely eyes blinked in confusion. "What?"

His gaze lowered to her lips. He swallowed and let her loose, turning away. Rubbed the sharp ache in his chest again. "I was seventeen when I learned that Squire Clay isn't my real father."

Rebecca stared at Sawyer's back, unable to contain a gasp of shock. "But of course you're Squire's son," she said after a moment. "You're so much like him it's uncanny."

He grunted. "Yeah, well, I guess it goes to prove that environment has a lot to do with some traits."

Some note in his voice stayed afloat in the wave of panic and pain and...and yearning that she'd been drowning in since she'd opened her kitchen door to find him standing outside. She'd sensed he was there before she'd even opened the door. Had known, too, before she'd seen his expression that he'd realized the truth about Ryan.

That note in his voice, though—resignation colored with fruitless wishes and unanswered prayers—broke over her when nothing else possibly could. She walked around him, unreasonably saddened to see the lines etched in his stark face. The hand that he probably didn't even know he was rubbing over his heart.

And despite everything—the past, the present, the future—she wanted to soothe him. No, not just wanted. *Needed.* "Tell me."

She expected him to refuse. Expected him to brush

it all off and return to the most basic of his demands. To see her son and claim him as his own.

But he didn't. And Rebecca had to admit that she didn't know Sawyer as well as she'd been telling herself all these years. Because he did tell. And her heart broke all over again.

Only this time it wasn't because of him.

It was *for* him.

Chapter Fourteen

In the end, they came to an agreement of sorts. He wouldn't tell Ryan the truth right now. And she'd allow Sawyer to spend as much time as he wanted with her son. Their son.

Now that he'd told her his own history, she understood his unrelenting inflexibility a little better. But she knew that sooner or later Sawyer would insist on Ryan knowing. No matter how much she wanted to deny it, she knew that he wasn't being unfair.

She didn't understand, though, why Sawyer hadn't discussed his long-ago discovery about Squire. Ever. She'd asked, but his answer had contained only the holdover logic of an angry, hurt seventeen-year-old boy. And as the years had passed, he'd become less and less interested in delving into the issue. If it hadn't been for his accident and the resulting injuries that had brought him back to Wyoming, back into Rebecca's life—which he'd promptly turned topsy-turvy—he still wouldn't have given it half a thought.

She wasn't sure she believed him on that score. But she knew she had no leg for argument, considering that her move to Wyoming had occurred only after Tom's death.

Dropping her head back against the chair, she sighed and closed the photo album she'd been paging through. Baby pictures of Ryan. The album containing the informal snapshots from her wedding day sat on the floor beside the chair.

Let go of the past. Accept the past.

Both things had been recommended by people who loved her. Tom. Delaney. She'd even told herself the same things at one time or another. So why couldn't she do either one?

Because she didn't want to let go.

Rebecca slowly leaned over and picked up the photo album with the wedding snapshots. Her heart ached a little that she had to look at the photos to truly remind herself what Tom had looked like. The tall, nearly gangly, man he'd been, with a shock of auburn hair and gentle brown eyes. He'd been good and kind and sweet and supportive. Incredibly gifted in his field. She'd come to love him and missed him still.

But then, he'd never taken her from the heights of heaven to the depths of hell, either.

Rebecca carefully adjusted a photo that was a little bit crooked. She hadn't wanted the heights and depths. She'd wanted stability. Security. A man who was there, when he said he'd be there. A man who put her and her son first; even before his precious career.

But did he really put you first? The question that

Delaney had pointedly asked the last time they'd spoken popped impertinently into Rebecca's mind.

How many times had Tom had to adjust their evening plans because his surgical skills were needed in some emergency?

Rebecca drew in a shaky breath. Tom had saved lives.

Sawyer had done the same. They'd just had different means of doing so.

Tom had been as committed to his career as Sawyer. Except that Tom had embraced the future. He'd *wanted* a wife. A son. More children if they'd only been lucky enough to conceive one together.

Whereas Sawyer had most definitely *not* wanted those things.

What was it with a world that was so topsy-turvy? A man who wanted the future, only to be ripped painfully from their lives. And a man who didn't want the future, to be dumped so thoroughly into their existence.

She was no closer to finding an answer to that than she'd ever been. Also no closer to knowing anymore why she'd ever moved to Weaver in the first place.

Surely she hadn't moved to Weaver to resolve the past. Or had she?

Life is too short.

The words whispered through her mind. She'd said them to Squire Clay at the dance. He'd told her to remember them.

They'd been the last words Tom had spoken to her before he died. She could pretend that he'd been speaking personally. But doing so would dishonor his memory in ways he didn't deserve.

He'd been telling her to do what was right. To let Ryan know that he still had a father, despite Tom's fate. To *live,* because life, in the end, was simply too short to waste.

The buzz of the telephone jerked her out of her solemn thoughts. She closed the pages of the wedding-album and went over to answer it.

Ryan wanted to spend the rest of the day with the Fieldings, who were driving into Gillette to finish their last-minute Christmas shopping.

Knowing she was the biggest coward on the planet, Rebecca agreed.

When she'd hung up, she turned away from the phone. Her attention snagged by the gaily decorated Christmas tree in the corner—the dozens of ornaments that Ryan had made in school projects over the years, and the few bulbs that she and Tom had collected during their marriage.

Both mingled together on a tree selected by another male—the one man who had been the instigating reason for either one of the other two being in her life at all.

Life was too short.

Rebecca slowly gathered up the photo albums that chronicled Ryan's infanthood through his recent school activities. She pulled her coat on over her shoulders and with her arms filled with the leather-bound albums, walked down to the end unit. After their confrontation, she'd been aware of the sheriff's car coming by. A few hours later, when she'd been hovering in her office, making a mishmash of a supply order, she'd seen Bobby Ray drop off Sawyer in front of his room. So she knew he was back.

When Sawyer answered her knock, she held the albums out for him. "If there are any photos you want to keep," she said through a throat raw with emotion, "add them to that bottom album there. You can keep it."

He took the books, his hands brushing against hers, making her chest ache even more. "What if I decide I want them all?"

She swallowed. "Then I guess you can have them all," she whispered.

His blue gaze darkened. "Why?"

She swallowed again. Still the lump in her throat wouldn't budge. Tucking her hands in the pockets of her coat, she controlled the urge to look away from his intent gaze. "I'm trying to do what's right," she said finally.

"And giving me carte blanche with your photo albums is what's right?"

It sounded almost silly, put that way. "I can't give you those years," she said. "But I can give you a piece of them with those photos."

"And does that clear your conscience?"

Rebecca winced. "It's not like that." He turned inside for a moment, setting the albums on the round table underneath the window. She realized her chance for escape was gone when he turned to her in half a second and pulled her inside the comfortably warm room.

"Then tell me what it is like," he suggested in a low voice. "Tell me how you expect me to respond, here. Is this an olive branch you're extending? A sign of the truce we've more or less reached? A tidbit to placate me? Keep me happy enough that I'll hold off just a little longer on forcing the issue with Ryan?"

Rebecca looked away, not answering. She had no words. The albums sat on the table, covering part of the microcassette she'd given him. The cassette had been split in two, little curls of narrow brown audiotape swirling over the table.

"I listened to it," he said, obviously following her gaze. "I borrowed a player from Bobby Ray."

"Sawyer, don't."

" 'Becky Lee, you've gotta stop calling,' " he quoted his ten-year-old message back to her. "We had a good time, but now it's over. Time to move on. My team needs me and...well, Bec, you just gotta stop calling."

She felt ill. Physically ill, because she realized at that moment that saying the words now hurt him as much as they'd ever hurt her.

She wanted to turn and run. She wanted to put her arms around him and hold him. Kiss away the lines of strain around his dark blue eyes and let his touch make her forget the past that would forever stand between them. Make her forget that there was still no future for them.

All she did, though, was sink weakly down to the nearest surface. The foot of his neatly made bed. "It was a long time ago."

"Not so long that you don't still hate me for it."

Staring at her fingers twisting together on her lap, Rebecca shook her head slightly. "I already told you that I don't hate you, Sawyer. I just—just don't want Ryan hurt."

"This isn't all about Ryan, Doc. You know it as well as I do. If it was, you wouldn't be sitting there looking like your insides are knotting, and I wouldn't be standing here needing to bury myself in you like I need blood in my veins."

Her gaze flew from her hands to his face.

"You just can't come into a man's room and sit on his bed without inspiring thoughts, Doc."

She bounced up from the foot of the bed as if she'd developed springs in her rear. "I didn't come here for this."

"What did you come for?"

"To give you the albums. To try to solve—"

"We can't solve the past, Bec. It's done. Right or wrong. Ryan is our son and you kept that truth from me, right or wrong, because of things I'd said. Things I'd done. We can't solve that. Can't settle it. It just is. Just like it just *is* that I can't be in a room without wanting you, and that—sweetness—doesn't have a damned thing to do with the past. It…just…is."

It always would be.

The words weren't spoken, but she shivered as if they had been.

"Where is Ryan?"

She touched a trembling hand to her throat. "I gave him permission to go to Gillette with the Fieldings."

"Trying to keep him away from me?"

Annoyance trickled through her. "I said I wouldn't keep you from seeing him whenever you wanted."

"Just not today."

"I'm not ready to tackle this with Ryan yet. Are you?" She spread her hands. "For heaven's sake, Sawyer, you and I cannot even get through a conversation with each other. So, yes, when I was presented with a reprieve for today, I took the easy way out. Shoot me. In the meantime, I know he's having a ball with the Fieldings."

"There's only a few days until Christmas."

"I'm aware of that."

"You and Ryan will come with me to the big house tomorrow evening. They're planning a big old meal and stuff for Christmas Eve."

Panic spiraled through her. "But you said you wouldn't blurt the news right away."

"It's Christmas," he said inflexibly. "We'll be there. Like a family, whether we admit it aloud or not."

"I see the captain is alive and well."

"What's that supposed to mean?"

"Just that you're awfully full of orders, here. What if Ryan and I already have plans for tomorrow?"

"Do you?"

"That's not the point." Frustration made her voice rise and she pressed her lips together, grappling for composure. "I'm not going to just barge in on a family celebration," she explained more calmly.

"Ryan *is* family. You'd make life a lot easier for us all if you'd start accepting that."

"I accepted that ten years ago when I had a positive pregnancy test and you were halfway around the world, refusing to accept my call." Rebecca rose, tugging the lapels of her coat together. "And I've spent every day since trying to provide a stable life for Ryan, because I didn't want him to ever know that his natural father didn't want him."

"I didn't know about him," Sawyer said tightly. "I'm sorry. I was the selfish, self-absorbed bastard you remember. If I *had* known, things would have been different."

"How?" Rebecca poked her finger into his unyielding chest. "How? Would you have requested assignments that kept you in this country? In this hemisphere? Would you have been around to go to my childbirth classes? To be there in the delivery room when Ryan was born? Or when he was three and already learning to read, confounding his preschool teachers with his mind, his precocity? Or when he was only six and smaller than most of his classmates, determined to prove that he could keep up with them and broke his collarbone playing sports with boys twice his size?"

Sawyer was so still, his words so soft. "I suppose Tom was there for all that. You sure didn't waste any time finding a substitute father for my son, did you?"

"Yes, Tom was there. He never let us down. He loved Ryan."

"And you."

She lifted her chin, instinctively backing away from the waves of tension radiating from his still body. "And me."

"Did he love you well, Rebecca? Move you? Make you tremble? Make you—" his head tilted, his eyes blue flame "—burn? Make a baby with you?"

She bumped the edge of the bed, wobbled, but held her ground. "I'm not going to discuss this with you."

"I haven't been a saint," he murmured. "Ten years is a long time. There have been women."

"I'm sure there were."

Sawyer nearly smiled at her tart retort. Only he couldn't find one humorous thing about this situation. "None of them were you," he admitted, as he watched the pupils of her eyes dilate, then disappear beneath the protective layer of lowered lids and long, soft lashes. "None of them made me think about changing my existence…my life."

"Oh, please—"

"Don't interrupt me, Doc," he warned. "Or you'll suffer the consequences."

Her lashes flew up, her expression torn between wariness and challenge. "I'll remind you, again, that I'm not under your command, Captain."

His senses heightened even more. He deliberately touched her jaw with his thumb; brushed across her lower lip, making her shift uneasily. "You were the one in my dreams. Sweet Becky Lee." He watched her suck in her lower lip for the barest second. "The only one who made me feel things I was afraid to feel. Want things I'd spent a lifetime convincing myself I didn't want."

"Sell it to the next girl. I'm not buying."

"Do you remember Rabbit?"

"What?"

"Rabbit Gonzales. My swim buddy."

"I— Yes, I remember him."

"He was married. Two kids."

"What does he have to do with—"

"He died on that one op I had about a month before I went to Malaysia. Remember when I was gone for that week?"

Rebecca nodded.

"He left his pretty wife a widow—his little kids without their daddy. Because he was a SEAL. Because he tried mixing two lives that didn't mix. And I didn't want to do that to you."

Her throat worked. Her coat rustled when she sank down again on the foot of the bed. She knew the relationship between swim buddies was a near-sacred thing. "I'm sorry about your friend. I didn't know. I know you were...changed after that week away. But you didn't tell me why."

"I didn't tell you because I knew you would think that we could be different. That was you. Optimistic, thinking you could change the world for the better."

"So, instead, you waited until you were on the other

side of the globe before you dumped me.'' Her lips twisted. "Gosh. Thanks."

He'd consumed more liquor before he'd made that phone call than he'd ever consumed in his life. He'd gone so far as to write down exactly the words he needed to say, because he'd known that the moment he heard her voice, he'd likely lose it, and he couldn't afford that. Instead, he'd gotten her answering machine, and the words he'd rehearsed—careful explanations, inarguable realities—had dried up. He'd stumbled over the words that would end things.

He'd never realized how harsh, how cold and unfeeling, he'd ended up sounding. "I looked for you when I returned to California."

Her hands spread, palms up in her lap, but she didn't look at him. "So you said."

"Despite what I'd said on that message, what I believed, I couldn't stay away." There was no point in protecting either one of them, anymore, from the deeds of the past—not when there was a nine-year-old boy who bound them so intimately together.

He realized a tear had fallen to her soft, vulnerably exposed palm. And damned if he didn't feel his own eyes burning in their sockets. Concrete Clay. What a joke.

He crouched down at her level. Folding her slender hands in his. "You had withdrawn from school," he continued. "Quit that part-time waitressing job you had. Moved from your apartment with no forwarding." His jaw clenched and he consciously relaxed. "I realized that I'd succeeded."

"You could have found me," she said, almost soundlessly.

He couldn't deny that. His resources were considerable, and he'd been tempted—God, so tempted—to track her down. "And only hurt you more if I did. That's what I believed, Rebecca. If I'd known about the baby—"

"I'd have known that you were with me only because you felt responsible for Ryan." She carefully slid her hands from his. "I couldn't compete against your career then anymore than I can now."

"Forget my career, would you? I've already—"

"You put your career between us before, Sawyer," she interrupted, her eyes glistening. "Maybe, like you say, you thought you were protecting me. I don't know anymore. All I know is that there was always a third party in our...our relationship, and she came before the rest of us. Even you, it seems. So, no. I can't forget your career. It's as much a part of you as being a physician is part of me."

"You don't know how wrong you are." She was slipping away from him. He felt it. And it hurt even more than it had hurt when he couldn't remember his own face. "I've always loved you, Becky Lee. I'm not leaving Weaver."

She closed her eyes for a long moment. When she opened them again, he knew he'd lost. "My name is Rebecca," she whispered. She rose and he let her. She walked to the door, pausing after she opened it to an afternoon that had grown gray with snow-laden clouds. "You will leave, Sawyer. I'm going to sign your medical release and fax it to your C.O. Your memory is fully returned and your other injuries are nearly healed. There's no reason you cannot return to active duty."

Sawyer stared at the closed door for a long while

after she'd walked out. He'd come to Wyoming to find his way back to his life.

Except that he'd just seen the one woman who gave meaning to his existence walk out of it.

Chapter Fifteen

"*I've always loved you, Becky Lee.*"

Sawyer's words kept playing in her mind. Making her heart ache. Making her stomach churn. There'd been a time in her life when she'd have given everything in her soul to hear those words from Sawyer.

But that time was long passed.

Wasn't it?

Now, sitting in her living room, listening to the wind howl outside, Rebecca felt more alone than she'd ever felt. And Suzanne Fielding had just called from Gillette to say they'd decided to wait out the storm. Ryan would be gone until tomorrow. Christmas Eve.

She'd faxed that medical release just as she'd told Sawyer she would. There was nothing to keep him in Weaver. Only his newfound knowledge of Ryan.

When the phone rang beside her elbow, she automatically answered it. "Dr. Morehouse."

"Merry Christmas, Rebecca!" Delaney Vega's lilting voice greeted her. "You're sounding a little like the Grinch, I think. Those wild, wild west holidays stressing you too much?"

It was so good to hear Delaney's voice. So good that Rebecca realized she was crying before she could stop it. She wiped her cheeks, picturing her friend sitting in her ultrachic glass-and-chrome high-rise apartment, a glass of white wine at her fingertips and bunny-rabbit slippers on her feet. "I was supposed to call you back," she remembered.

"Yes, but I'll just hope that you were busy with the Christmas dance and maybe a romantic man who was keeping you too occupied to phone."

Rebecca sighed miserably. "You have no idea."

"Oh, dear. I'm not liking the sound of this. Just tell me my favorite honorary nephew is all right."

"Ryan's fine." Rebecca realized she was sitting there in the dark. But getting up to turn on a lamp seemed too much work. "It's his, uh, his father." And the whole story came tumbling out.

Silence hummed on the line for a moment after she'd finished. "I see."

Rebecca sat forward in the recliner, reaching for the throw pillow that ordinarily sat in it. Sawyer always tossed the pillow on the floor when he sat in the chair. Fresh pain accosted her and she shoved the pillow behind her back. "That's your professional 'I see,' Delaney."

"I'm not sure you want to hear what the friend in me would say."

"You think I should just welcome him into our lives with open arms, with no regard for his coming-and-going ways."

"Rebecca, if you really didn't want something like this to eventually occur, you would never have moved to Weaver. You wanted to get Ryan away from the city, from your apartment filled with memories of Tom and away from the group of friends he'd fallen in with, I understand that. But Weaver? Couldn't you have found another small town that needed a physician?"

"But Weaver—"

"Was the one place in this world where you could put your life on hold after Tom died," Delaney finished gently. "A place where you could justify remaining emotionally uninvolved with the people there—specifically the Clays. A place where you could be on the fringe of people who would care if you'd only let Tom go."

"I let Tom go," Rebecca defended. "I don't even wear my wedding ring anymore."

"Sweetie, you never did wear your wedding ring. Well, hardly ever. You kept it in your grandmother's antique jewelry case with your other irreplaceable treasures because you said it was too difficult to wear on your finger when you were constantly using sterile gloves."

"It's got that diamond. It always tore the gloves," Rebecca muttered.

Delaney laughed softly. "Rebecca, as a therapist, I'd spend hours getting you to explore the real reasons you didn't wear that ring, but I'm not your therapist. I'm your friend. So here's my Christmas present to you, friend. Let Tom go. He died, but you didn't. You moved to Weaver because it was, ironically enough, a safe place for you to go. A—a waiting zone, if you will. Because this man you've never shaken from your heart had a life pretty much separate from the town and his family who live nearby. But you also moved there, because deep down inside you, you knew that this day would one day come. And you could close a wound that's been open for ten long years. Well, sweetie, that day has come.''

It was so true, Rebecca realized with dismay. So ridiculously, pathetically true. ''I don't know what to do about it,'' she admitted.

''Ah, now that's one I can't help you with. Even though I am the most brilliant friend you've got.''

''It hurts,'' Rebecca said after a moment.

''Which tells you that you're alive and well,'' Delaney said gently. ''Do you love him?''

No matter how close she and Delaney were, no matter how many times, good and bad, they'd shared, she couldn't answer that one. ''He's calmer now,'' she said. ''Not as…driven. But that's probably just an effect of his accident.''

''Or the passage of ten years. I'm sure you're not the same now as you were ten years ago, either, Rebecca. Good grief, ten years ago you probably had visions of joining your parents overseas and curing the world of all its ills!''

''There was nothing wrong with that.''

''Not a thing,'' Delaney agreed swiftly. ''Except that it was your parents' call. Not yours. I think your calling in life is making house calls on kids with the mumps and delivering babies and helping the aged live and die with dignity. I think your calling is getting involved in people's lives. Their whole lives, Rebecca. You're a family doctor. A good one among an unfortunately dying breed. Now get your own family in order. Heal thyself, friend.''

If only it were so easy. Rebecca felt a wry smile

curve her lips. "One of these days, I'm gonna turn the tables on you, Delaney, and make you look hard at the things you're avoiding in your own life."

Delaney laughed. "Oh, sweetie, there's not enough hours in the day for that. Do me a favor, will you?"

"Depends on what it is." She reached out and turned on the lamp beside the chair.

"Take a hard look at Sawyer *now*. At the way you feel *now*. Don't view the situation through glasses clouded by the past."

"I don't wear glasses."

"Ha-ha. Oh, look. It's past midnight here. Christmas Eve has arrived. Please tell me that you're having Christmas dinner somewhere, so that I don't have to worry about you and Ryan dying of ptomaine."

"Actually, we have been invited somewhere," Rebecca admitted. "I'm not sure he still wants to take us, though. And I'm not sure I *want* to go."

"Because you're afraid you won't enjoy yourself?"

Rebecca shook her head. "Because I'm afraid that I will."

They talked for a few minutes more before hanging up. Rebecca pushed out of the chair, feeling older than she should. She took a long, hot shower, and afterward pulled on warm leggings and a soft flannel shirt. She wrapped the last few Christmas gifts for Ryan that she'd kept hidden in her closet. She washed the few dishes in the kitchen, then mopped the floor.

But, for once, she didn't kid herself. What she was doing was putting off what she knew she should do. That she couldn't leave things with Sawyer the way she had.

She didn't believe there was a future for them. She couldn't go that far. But she could, at least, come to some resolution over Ryan. And she couldn't do it with her on this end of the building, and Sawyer on the other.

Taking a quick breath, Rebecca pulled on boots and a coat and let herself out the front office door, which was considerably closer to Sawyer's room. Snow tickled her nose as she quickly crossed the parking lot, to knock on his door. Only he didn't answer. Not when she knocked. Or pounded. Or called his name.

Finally, the cold made her return to her office where she strongly considered using her master key. But her pride wouldn't let her. So she locked her office and went through to her private quarters. She tucked the presents she'd wrapped under the tree and pretended that she didn't mind Sawyer ignoring her.

The phone rang just as she'd finally admitted that she might as well turn in. She picked it up, half expecting to hear Delaney on the other end. But it wasn't Delaney. It was Judy Blankenship. Roy had gone after Dylan. And this time he had a gun.

Rebecca ordered Judy to stay right where she was. She grabbed her medical bag and her master key and ran down to Sawyer's room, unlocking it without a second thought.

Only he wasn't there. The room was totally cleaned out. No black leather duffel bag. No used towels. No sign that Sawyer had ever even been there except the ruined microcassette that sat in the middle of the small round table.

She sucked in a pained breath, swearing at herself. She'd known. Dammit, she'd *known*. So why be shocked now?

Why feel as if her life had just been wrenched in two?

She'd faxed his medical release, and he'd wasted not one minute—not even enough time to say goodbye.

She yanked the door closed and ran around to her garage, stopping cold when she heard the sharp, unmistakable echo of a gunshot rip the still night. *Oh, my God.*

The tires of her Jeep spun and skidded as she wheeled out onto Main, gunning for the sheriff's office. There was a crowd of people around the brick building. Judy ran toward her as soon as Rebecca threw the truck into Park and started toward the crowd. "They're all inside with the sheriff," she said, panic-stricken. "Roy was just out of his mind. I couldn't calm him down. Phyllis came over and said there was no way on earth she was letting her boy get tricked into marrying our Taylor and—"

Rebecca listened, pushing her way through the people. If the parents would just let Taylor and Dylan be, she herself believed that the kids would find their own way just fine. She made it to the door of the sheriff's office and knocked on it loudly. "Taylor, it's Rebecca Morehouse. Is everyone okay in there?"

"They won't answer or let you in," Newt Rasmusson observed. "We've already been trying." He looked like a circus clown in his striped thermals and heavy wool coat. "Phyllis said she'd shoot anyone who tried to break in. Already shot off a round. Don't know what they did to Bobby Ray. He hauled 'em all in when he found Roy traipsing around like a maniac."

Rebecca ignored him, pounding on the door again. If Sheriff Hayes had lost control of the situation, it could only be because something terrible had happened to him. Adrenaline pumped through her and she turned, spying Bennett. "Who all is in there?"

Even Bennett appeared shaken by the night's events. "Bobby Ray, Roy, Phyllis. Dylan and Taylor. Sawyer."

Rebecca gasped, her stomach clenching. She pressed a shaking hand to her mouth and turned once more toward the building. Sawyer would know what to do. *Had someone been shot?* If there was a way to diffuse this nightmare, Sawyer would use it.

She closed her eyes, wishing the sound of that shot would stop repeating over and over in her head. She looked up at Bennett. "Is there another way inside?"

Bennett rubbed his gloved hands together, stomped his feet. "There's a window around back," he said. "Leads into the breakroom. But it's small and always locked, and you're crazy if you think any of us are going to let you try to go in there."

The crowd was growing. Ruby and Hope Leoni were there. The minister from the church, Jolie Taggart and her husband, Drew. Feeling utterly helpless, Rebecca rested her palm flat against the locked door. "Please be all right," she whispered. "Don't leave me again."

Taylor was crying softly, and Dylan was a tensed coil of young testosterone ready to explode. Roy Blankenship and Phyllis Reese were squared off on opposite sides of a desk, both of them holding shotguns, and Bobby Ray was lying on the floor beside Sawyer, his face contorted in a spasm of pain.

Sawyer wasn't all that sure he didn't feel some sympathy for Roy wanting to protect his teenage daughter, especially against Phyllis's nasty accusations that Taylor was trying to trap her son with this pregnancy business. But he sure in hell didn't like sitting smack dab between two shotguns aimed over his head.

He also didn't like knowing that Rebecca was standing on the other side of the heavy door. Until he got the weapons away from these two fools, *everyone* standing inside or outside the office was in danger. He'd tried reasoning with both parents, to no avail. Now, Sawyer only hoped to God that Bobby Ray wasn't having a heart attack.

He moved off the chair, crouching beside the older man. "How you doing, Bobby Ray," he asked quietly.

The sheriff moaned, unable to answer, and Sawyer quietly swore. "Dylan," he spoke to the boy who was nearly a man, and was aware that everyone jumped. "Come over here and help me with the sheriff."

"Don't you move, Dylan," Phyllis screeched.

"Oh, Ma!" Dylan yelled. "You want to shoot me like you tried to shoot Mr. Blankenship?" His deep voice broke and he sidled around the rear of his out-of-control mother.

"You keep your mouth shut, Dylan," she hissed. "None of this would be happening if that tramp hadn't taken advantage of you."

"Phyllis, I swear if you call my girl a tramp one more time, I'm gonna shoot you just for the pleasure of shutting that vicious mouth you've burdened this town with for the last two decades."

Dylan crouched down beside Sawyer just as Bobby Ray cried out, clutching his chest. Then he fell back, deathly still.

Sawyer swore, not quite so silently this time and felt for a pulse. He yanked open the sheriff's puffy down vest and started CPR, making sure Dylan was watching his actions. "You people are fighting over who is trapping whom when you're all gonna benefit when that little baby is born," he said tersely. "Can't you think beyond your own noses to your grandchild? To your son and your daughter who you claim to love?'' Sawyer would give everything he possessed to regain the years he'd lost with Rebecca and Ryan.

"That boy is going to do right by my little girl,'' Roy said tightly.

Taylor cried. "Daddy, I don't want to get married. Why can't you listen to me?''

Beside him, Sawyer felt Dylan wince. He grabbed the boy's big hands and planted them over Bobby Ray's chest. "Don't stop,'' he murmured firmly. Dylan's eyes were scared but his gaze didn't waver. And he didn't stop the CPR. The kid had more guts just then than Sawyer had when he'd been the same age— running away from the life that hadn't been exactly the way he'd figured it ought to be.

Phyllis and Roy were screeching like two idiots at each other, and Sawyer knew that the sheriff needed Rebecca. Immediately.

Sawyer needed her, too.

He just needed to get them all out of this insane situation so that he could tell her so.

When the thumping on the outside door began again, startling Phyllis and Roy, Sawyer moved swiftly. He could hear Rebecca calling his name through the heavy wood even as he deftly disarmed Phyllis. She clawed at his shoulder and he pushed her down into a chair with a firm hand. He didn't take his eyes from Roy as Taylor darted around to her dad and yanked at him. Sawyer cursed even as he dove for the floor, taking Phyllis with him just as Roy's shotgun discharged when Taylor jostled him.

Phyllis lay sobbing weakly against the tile floor, but she was unharmed. Everyone was unharmed except for the wall clock that had been shattered with the shot. Everyone except the sheriff, who was still on the floor.

Moving fast, Sawyer took the shotgun from Roy, who was staring at the clock as if he couldn't imagine how it had gotten shot to pieces. Sawyer unlocked the door and scooped Rebecca against him for a hard kiss before he turned her to see the distressed sheriff.

She rushed over to Dylan and took over. She was in control of the emergency so capably that Sawyer felt a lump in his throat. He was so damned proud of her.

He had to get it through to her that he was in this for the long haul. But getting through to her was going to have to wait for a while.

At least until they took care of Bobby Ray. Sawyer cradled the two shotguns under his arm and wearily locked both Phyllis and Roy into cells at opposite ends of the hallway. Taylor and Dylan were holding each other as if they would never let go. He hoped they didn't.

Leaving Newt to disperse the crowd who'd gathered, Sawyer locked up the guns and went to Rebecca's side. "What can I do?"

She gestured and moved to Bobby Ray's head and lowered her mouth over the sheriff's. Sawyer knitted his hands together and held them over the sheriff's chest, pressing rhythmically when Rebecca told him to.

By the time the emergency helicopter arrived, which Rebecca had had the foresight to summon, Bobby Ray was stabilized, and Sawyer was exhausted. But Rebecca kept right on going, issuing instructions as she ran alongside the stretcher and the EMTs who carried Bobby Ray toward the chopper that had landed in the nearby park. Leaning against the cold brick building, Sawyer watched Rebecca hug Bobby Ray's tearful wife and help her into the helicopter that would take them to the hospital in Gillette.

And then it was all over.

The helicopter took off. The townsfolk went back home. They went to their beds, to their phones to continue gossiping, to their chores. It was nearly dawn.

Rebecca started walking down the middle of the street toward Sawyer. Her heart was beating unevenly and her breath was choppy. She wanted to run into his arms and kiss his unharmed face. She wanted to yell her head off at him for scaring her half to death.

He walked toward her and she knew that her life was never again going to be simply content. Her feet dragged to a halt when she was within arm's reach of him.

"I loved Tom," she said baldly. "I was...content. And he was happy." Her eyes burned. "But he was never you. And he never...moved me the way you did." She held her blowing hair out of her eyes. "I don't know where you and I go from here, Sawyer."

He closed the distance between them and his hand, big and warm and gentle, cupped her cheek. "As long as you admit we're going somewhere," he said huskily, "we'll figure it out."

Rebecca leaned her cheek into his hand. Then she was in his arms and it was the only place she wanted to be. "Take me home, Sawyer."

"I'm going to stay there with you if I do, Bec."

She pressed her lips to his hard jaw that was cold from the night air. "Yes. I know."

A sigh shuddered through his broad frame and he turned her toward her Jeep, driving them home in silence. When they arrived, Sawyer stopped in the middle of her living room where the lights of the Christmas tree glittered colorfully. "And I used to think nothing exciting ever happened in Weaver."

Rebecca pressed her cheek to his chest and felt a weary tear slide down her cheek. "Nothing much did, Captain, until you came back to town."

He kissed her with such gentleness that another tear followed the first. Forgetting about the bedroom just a few yards away, she unfastened the buttons of Sawyer's denim shirt. She pushed it from his shoulders, forgetting years of anatomy, and remembering only the incredible pleasure of being a woman. And of touching this one man. The shoulders with such muscle. The corded neck. The supple skin that covered his narrow waist.

A shiver danced across her shoulders and she frowned slightly, wondering when he'd removed her shirt. "Nice moves, Captain," she murmured, reaching for the button fly of his jeans, moving her fingers with indecent haste as her weariness was replaced with breathless need.

"Great hands, Doctor."

Then there was nothing between them but the glistening red, blue and green light cast by the Christmas tree. Drowning in pleasure from the strong sweep of his palms down her back, over her body, she shuddered and murmured approvingly when he tossed the pillows from the sectional couch onto the floor and drew her down with him, over him.

Needing him more than she needed anything, she guided him—sobbing softly as his flesh found its home inside her—stretching, pulsing, living.

Now that he was part of her, she caught her breath, her furious hurry stilling. She bit her lip, looking down into his face. So male. So strong. His blue eyes burned into her and she breathed his name. "I love you," she whispered, the relief of it making her weak. "I love you."

His jaw worked. He touched her cheek. Her lips. Curled his hand behind her neck and drew her down to him, making them both groan with pleasure at the movement. "There's no more darkness inside me, Bec. Not anymore."

He caught her lips with his. His hands slid to her hips because they had to move. Had to. And there was no more need for words.

Because their hearts, thundering against each other, said it all.

Chapter Sixteen

They managed to make it to the bedroom eventually. Even managed to get a few hours of sleep when they finally collapsed. Because even though the spirit was willing to make love endlessly, the turmoil of the past days had finally caught up with the flesh.

It was nearly noon when Ryan came bounding in the kitchen doorway, his arms full of shopping bags, and a new ball cap perched on his head. He didn't seem to see anything unusual in finding Sawyer, freshly showered and wearing nothing but his jeans, sitting at the table, paging through the day-old newspaper—just chattered a mile a minute about the "cool" basement that Mrs. Fielding's brother had.

Rebecca, however, was a mother above all. She caught her son in her arms and kissed his cheek, hugging him to her. Thanking God and every other kind spirit for what she had.

Ryan disentangled himself after only a moment, though. "Jeez, Mom," he complained good-naturedly. "Give it a rest, would ya?"

Rebecca caught Sawyer watching her over Ryan's head. She pushed her fingers into the pockets of her slacks and couldn't help but smile when her son turned to Sawyer, anxious to show off the purchases he'd made in Gillette.

Rebecca went back to the peanut-butter sandwich she'd been fixing. Ryan pulled open the refrigerator and made an impatient noise. "Mom, I told you that you had to thaw the turkey in the refrigerator. And it takes like two days. It's still in the freezer. What're we gonna eat?"

"We're gonna eat at the big house later today," Sawyer said easily.

Ryan's eyes lit up. "Really? Cool." He sidled over to Sawyer. "Who's cooking?"

"My brothers' wives," Sawyer said. He tapped Ryan's cap. "They're good cooks," he promised.

"Cool," Ryan repeated. Then he frowned, looking up at Rebecca. "No offense, Mom."

Rebecca couldn't help laughing. "Delaney was relieved at the idea, too." She waved at the clutter he'd brought in with him. "There's wrapping paper, tape and ribbon on the dresser in my bedroom. Why don't you get these things taken care of?"

He nodded, gathering up everything and carrying it with him down the hall.

Sawyer tugged her over to his lap. "Who is Delaney?"

"Delaney Vega. She's got a psychiatric practice in New York. We've been friends for years."

"Oh, female. So I don't have to be jealous."

She snorted softly, sighing faintly when he kissed the curve of her shoulder. "As if you're the jealous type."

"You wouldn't want to test that out," he said softly, nudging aside the collar of her shirt so he could taste her skin. "It would be upsetting for us both."

She shivered with delight. "Ryan could come back in here any—ah—minute."

"He can get used to his parents kissing each other," Sawyer murmured. He turned her until she faced him and did just that.

Rebecca opened her mouth to his. Loving the taste of coffee, the rough glide of his tongue, the mobile press of his lips. She loved him. But she still needed air, and she broke the kiss, dropping her forehead to his shoulder. "Thank God you were there last night with the sheriff. He's going to survive because you kept him alive. I was so frightened when I heard the shots."

"Me, too."

He kissed her mouth closed. "Only a fool doesn't feel afraid when there are loaded weapons being waved around by people on the edge."

He cradled her face in his hands, looking her straight in the eye. His eyes were so blue, so intense. "You are an incredible doctor, Rebecca. I was in awe of you."

Rebecca's eyes flooded.

Sawyer made a rough sound and shook his head, kissing her thoroughly.

"You cleared out of the motel room," she said, a few minutes later.

His fingertips massaged the arch of her spine. "Made it halfway to Jefferson's place before I turned around and came back. Was at Ruby's nursing a gallon of coffee thinking of plans to get you back when I heard the ruckus at Bobby Ray's.''

"I hate to think what might have happened if you hadn't been there.''

"I'm gonna be there a lot more often,'' he said.

She frowned, lifting her head to look at him. Whiskers blurred the sharp angle of his jaw, tempting her lips. "Where?''

"The sheriff's office.''

"I don't understand.''

He shrugged—then set her off his lap and stood, crossing his arms across his bare, golden chest. Rebecca took the chair he'd just vacated and watched him; realizing, with a start, that he was nervous.

"I'll be working there,'' he said, giving her a crooked grin. "You can start calling me Deputy instead of Captain.''

She blinked. "Excuse me?''

"At least until they arrange a special election. Then, mebbe, it'll be Sheriff. Bobby Ray's been working on me for the last week. He wants to retire. Seeing what's happened, I'm certain he'll do it now, rather than later.''

"When did he appoint you deputy?''

"Yesterday.''

"Before I'd signed your medical release.''

Sawyer tugged on his ear, not entirely sure he liked the glint in her golden eyes. "Yeah. I started to tell—''

"Before I'd admitted that I loved you. Before...everything.''

"I told you I wasn't gonna leave again, Bec. I don't know. The accident—I cursed it, because of the amnesia. Still can't remember how it all even happened. But it brought me back here. To you.'' He rolled his shoulders and told her about the court-martial case. About his weariness of it all. "I've got twenty-five years in the service, Bec. I did the best I could do while I was there." He shook his head. "But it's time I did my best at something that matters more. Becoming the sheriff means I won't have to hang around you all day long driving you up a tree. I would have found something else, if not that—because I wasn't going to leave you again, no matter how much you expected me to. I want you to be my wife." He watched tears collect in her eyes. "Hell, sweetness. Don't do that. I should've told you yesterday, but every time I opened my mouth, nothing came out the way I wanted—"

He caught her when she sprang out of the chair and into his arms.

"I *want* to be your wife. Captain, Deputy, Sheriff— whatever you are. I love you."

Relief made him weak. Holding her, though, made him strong. Stronger than he'd ever been without her. "I love you, too, Rebecca."

"So does this mean that you guys are gonna date now or something?"

They both whirled to see Ryan watching them, his young face wreathed in smiles.

"Or something," Sawyer said, tucking Rebecca's silken head against his chest. "That okay with you?"

Ryan made a production of considering that. "Yeah. It's cool."

Rebecca sniffled against Sawyer and pushed out of his arms, linking her hand with his. "There's something else that I hope you'll think is cool," she said.

Sawyer went still. And listened as Rebecca calmly told Ryan that Sawyer was his biological father. That she'd loved Sawyer years ago, but circumstances hadn't let them be together.

Ryan tilted back his ball cap and looked up at Sawyer when she was finished. And Sawyer thought he'd never prayed more in his life that he measured up.

"I got your blue eyes," his son said after a moment. Sawyer nodded. He realized he was crushing Rebecca's hand in his and consciously loosened his grip.

"I miss my dad," Ryan said. "My—ah—other dad."

"I know you do, Ryan."

Ryan nodded. "He told me when I was little that I was lucky 'cause I had two fathers when some kids only had one. I guess he meant you, huh."

Rebecca pressed her hand to her mouth.

And Sawyer found himself thanking a man he'd never known—a man who'd been a better man than he—for loving this boy. For being there for them both. "I guess he did," he agreed rawly. "And you're smarter than I am because you've realized something that I, in my whole life, didn't." He held out his hand to his son, whom he knew had a good dose of man in him despite his youth. "Is it okay if I marry your mom, then?"

Ryan's jaw cocked to the side in a manner so similar that Sawyer couldn't believe he'd missed it before. Then his son tugged on the bill of his ball cap, put his hand in Sawyer's and shook it solemnly. "It's okay with me," he said slowly. "But you guys gonna kiss and have babies and junk like that?"

Sawyer's eyes met Rebecca's. "It's a distinct possibility," he admitted.

Ryan thought about that for a moment, then squinted up at Sawyer. "What do I call you?"

"Whatever you want."

"Like Captain? Or Sawyer?"

He nodded and found himself wondering if Squire had ever yearned this badly for a young boy to call him dad.

Ryan tugged again on his cap. "Well, can I ask one more question?"

"Sure."

"Can you cook? 'Cause I think Mom has got, like, a mental block when it comes to reading a recipe."

Rebecca made a face. "Oh, thanks."

Sawyer laughed. And when his son's eyes met his, he figured that his family was going to come along just fine, regardless of what Ryan called him. "I do a mean lobster," he said.

Rebecca giggled and wrapped her arms around her two men. "Lobster and peanut butter sandwiches. Who could ask for anything more?"

They could hear a dozen voices and Christmas music and laughter before they even walked in the kitchen door of the big house later that evening.

Rebecca brushed nervous hands down the front of her black velvet dress when Sawyer helped her off with her long coat in the mudroom. Ryan was still outside by the truck, petting Matthew's golden retriever. "You sure this looks all right? I'm not overdressed, am I? You think they'll like us?"

He grinned wickedly, knowing exactly what she wore beneath the formfitting dress. "You look great. You've known these people for two years, Bec. Why are you so worried?"

"Because I've never been anything but the town doctor to them before," she said under her breath.

He tilted her head up. Her hair was slightly mussed from the breeze outside and she'd chewed off her lipstick before they'd made it halfway to the Double-C. "You're beautiful, and they'll love you as much as I do." He narrowed his eyes. "I hear Tristan's voice," he said. "He's still unattached. He can love you *almost* as much as I do."

Her cheeks colored. So he kissed her for good measure. The squeak of the inner door told him somebody was standing there watching, but he didn't care. He was going to marry this woman at the earliest possible opportunity.

"Let the doc breathe, son," Squire said blandly. "Don't want to suffocate her now that we've got her here."

Rebecca gasped and jumped away from him, touching her hair, her lips, the picture of self-consciousness. Sawyer tucked her fluttering hand in his and glanced out the back door. "Come on in, Ryan," he called.

Ryan trotted inside and stood next to Sawyer, shrugging out of his coat, which he dumped on the pile of coats already sitting on the washing machine. "Cap, Ryan," Rebecca prompted.

The boy rolled his eyes and doffed his cap, tossing it on top of the coats. "Merry Christmas, Mr. Clay." He stuck out his hand at Squire. "I'm real glad we're here."

Squire's head tilted slightly. Then he grinned, shaking Ryan's hand in return. "I'm real glad you're here, too," he said. Then looked at Sawyer. "All of you."

He backed into the kitchen, throwing his arm wide. "Follow the noise," he suggested. "Tristan arrived just a little while ago. The girls are upstairs ogling the new baby. Boys are in the basement shooting pool. Ryan, you play much pool?''

Ryan's eyes widened. "You got a pool table here? That is totally cool."

Sawyer watched his father close his big hand over his son's shoulder and guide him toward the stairs that would take them down to the rec room. He didn't even realize what he was seeing at first as he followed Rebecca into the kitchen. "Did Ryan get a haircut?"

Rebecca nodded, busy setting the tray of peanut-butter-and-chocolate-chip cookies Ryan had made that afternoon on the table. "Finally. He and Eric got them when they were in Gillette. They went to a 'stylist.' Apparently that's more acceptable than the barber in Weaver."

"He's got a white streak on his nape."

She turned to him, smoothing the hem of her dress down her thighs. "Yeah. I wouldn't mention it much to him, though. He's rather sensitive about it. That's why he likes to leave his hair long and constantly wears a cap. Hides the streak." She turned her head toward the sound of female laughter. "I want to see the baby," she admitted. "Do you mind?" Her eyes shone like amber.

"Go ahead," he said. "Hold him and think about the notion of having another one of your own."

Her lips parted. "Oh?"

"I'm not getting any younger." He couldn't resist kissing the surprise on her lips. "Only this time let's get the marriage license taken care of first." Thoroughly satisfied with the glazed look in her eyes, he grinned and left her standing there in the middle of the kitchen to follow his son downstairs.

Squire was leaning against the wet bar, watching

Tristan help Ryan select a pool cue from the rack of them on the wall. Sawyer stopped next to him, leaning over to grab a frosty long-neck from the collection of them in the stainless-steel ice-filled sink. He thumbed off the cap and tossed it onto the counter. "Who is Sawyer Templeton?"

Squire's eyebrows rose. "Your mother's half brother," he answered. "Why?"

Sawyer just shook his head, smiling faintly as he lifted the bottle to his lips. It didn't matter anymore. It had ceased to matter when Ryan had spoken so simply about the luck of having two fathers. Perhaps one day he'd ask for the whole story of how he came to be named after an uncle he'd never known existed—perhaps.

Ryan was staring up at Tristan with fierce attention as Tristan pointed to the balls with his cue.

"That's how I went gray," Squire murmured after a moment.

"I remember," Sawyer replied.

"Started at my nape and spread up. Boy'll be totally gray by the time he's thirty, just like I was. Like my grandfather before me. Looks like the trait has continued to skip a generation."

"I expect you're right, Dad."

Squire smiled. "You'll be a good sheriff, son."

"News travels fast."

"Always did." Squire reached into his pocket and pulled out a narrow gold band with a trio of small diamonds. "It's not fancy, son. But it was your mama's. She'd want you to have it."

"The wedding ring you gave her."

Squire nodded. "Thought it might come in useful for you," he said. "I got it out after I saw you and the doc dancing the other night. Be happy, son. Cherish every day.''

Sawyer picked up the ring. "I plan to," he said huskily. Then turned when he heard footsteps on the stairs. He realized, too, that every male in the room looked up as the women descended.

Emily came first, holding her son who *still* didn't have a name, along with Leandra who importantly carried the requisite diaper bag. They went over to Jefferson and caused a smile to light his stern features.

Maggie, who was trying to tie the matching ribbons on the backs of her daughters' dresses—J.D. and Angeline. One was fair and one dark. But all three of them swooped on Daniel, who hitched both girls up in his arms even as he kissed his new wife.

Jaimie, with Sarah clattering beside her, was laughing gaily as she reached the bottom step. She shot a knowing look toward Sawyer and Squire, looped a slender arm around Matthew's neck and kissed him boldly right in front of everyone.

"Makes a man feel good deep down, to see his sons happy," Squire said. "Well, almost all of them," he added, glancing at Tristan, who turned away.

Sawyer nodded, his attention focused on the shapely legs, clad in off-black silken hose, descending the steps. Saw Rebecca's eyes skim over the heads before landing on him. Realized that her expression lit in the same way the faces of his brothers' wives did when they looked at their husbands.

Gloria Day and her twin daughters, Nikki and Belle, were the last to descend. Gloria smiled at Sawyer, cast a challenging look at Squire, and accepted a glass of wine that Tristan was busily pouring now that Ryan was clearly in command of the pool table. The Day twins immediately headed toward Tristan as well, but his little brother didn't seem unduly disturbed by the attentions of the college students.

Rebecca slipped her arm behind Sawyer's back, and he reminded himself that standing there in the middle of his considerable family was not an appropriate place to want to make love to her.

But he couldn't help it. He kissed her ear, murmuring his thoughts. She colored and shifted, standing in front of him. But the look she gave him from beneath her lashes was purely female. Purely satisfied.

Squire cleared his throat and just that easily, silence fell over the room. They could hear the faint strains of "O Holy Night" from the sound system upstairs.

Sawyer wrapped his arm around Rebecca's shoulders, holding her back against him, closing his eyes for a moment as he inhaled the fragrance of her hair.

When he opened his eyes, though, it was to find Squire looking at him. "We haven't really celebrated Christmas in this house for a long time," Squire said. His gaze moved from Sawyer, touching on the rest of his sons in turn. "Because it was a time of loss for us, though your mama would never have approved of my feeling that way. But that's the past. And I hope the future sees a lot more of these celebrations. All the women in this room have had a part in that," he went on, his gaze turning finally to Gloria, who was watching him steadily. "And so it seems appropriate that during this season that Sarah always considered blessed, I move into the future, too, to count the blessings of my life with the woman who has brought Christmas back into my life. The woman I've finally asked to be my wife."

"Hallelujah!" Daniel said fervently.

Rebecca turned in Sawyer's arms and kissed his jaw. "What a Christmas," she whispered. "But I like your idea of having our own newborn next year."

"I'll do my best to oblige," Sawyer murmured. "I want to see you get big and round with our child. Next year we'll have another child for Christmas. It'll be our new family tradition."

"What're you two whispering about over there?" Squire demanded.

Sawyer smiled widely for his family. But his intent blue gaze was for Rebecca, alone. For the med student who'd loved him even though he'd warned her not to. For the young mother who'd raised his son finely and decently. For the woman who filled all his dark areas with light. Who challenged him and loved him and accepted nothing less in return. "Nothing," he said, sliding the delicate ring on Rebecca's finger. "Except you're gonna have to work fast if you want to beat us to the altar. Life's too short to waste. Isn't that right, Dr. Morehouse?"

She looked up from the ring that fit perfectly. Her lips were smiling when he covered them with his own. "That's right, Deputy Clay," she said against his kiss. "That's exactly right."

* * * * *

Don't miss the heartwarming conclusion to this family saga when Tristan comes home for Squire's wedding and finds himself walking down the aisle as well, coming only to Silhouette Special Edition in Summer 2000.

PAMELA TOTH
DIANA WHITNEY
ALLISON LEIGH
LAURIE PAIGE

bring you four heartwarming stories
in the brand-new series

So Many Babies

At the Buttonwood Baby Clinic,
babies and romance abound!

On sale January 2000: **THE BABY LEGACY**
by Pamela Toth

On sale February 2000: **WHO'S THAT BABY?**
by Diana Whitney

On sale March 2000: **MILLIONAIRE'S INSTANT BABY**
by Allison Leigh

On sale April 2000: **MAKE WAY FOR BABIES!**
by Laurie Paige

Only from Silhouette **SPECIAL EDITION**
Available at your favorite retail outlet.

Silhouette®
Where love comes alive™

Visit us at www.romance.net   SSESMB

If you enjoyed what you just read,
then we've got an offer you can't resist!

Take 2 bestselling love stories FREE!
Plus get a FREE surprise gift!

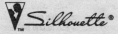

**Start celebrating Silhouette's 20th anniversary
with these 4 special titles by
New York Times bestselling authors**

Fire and Rain
by Elizabeth Lowell

King of the Castle
by Heather Graham Pozzessere

State Secrets
by Linda Lael Miller

Paint Me Rainbows
by Fern Michaels

On sale in December 1999

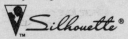

Celebrate Silhouette's 20th Anniversary

With beloved authors, exciting new miniseries and special keepsake collections, **plus** the chance to enter our 20th anniversary contest, in which one lucky reader wins the trip of a lifetime!

Take a look at who's celebrating with us:

DIANA PALMER

April 2000: SOLDIERS OF FORTUNE
May 2000 in Silhouette Romance: *Mercenary's Woman*

NORA ROBERTS

May 2000: IRISH HEARTS, the 2-in-1 keepsake collection
June 2000 in Special Edition: *Irish Rebel*

LINDA HOWARD

July 2000: MacKENZIE'S MISSION
August 2000 in Intimate Moments: *A Game of Chance*

ANNETTE BROADRICK

October 2000: a special keepsake collection, plus a brand-new title in
November 2000 in Desire

Available at your favorite retail outlet.

Where love comes alive™

EXTRA! EXTRA!

**The book all your favorite authors
are raving about is finally here!**

**The 1999 Harlequin and Silhouette
coupon book.**

Each page is alive with savings that can't be beat!

**Getting this incredible coupon book is
as easy as 1, 2, 3.**

1. During the months of November and December 1999 buy
any 2 Harlequin or Silhouette books.

2. Send us your name, address and 2 proofs of purchase (cash
receipt) to the address below.

3. Harlequin will send you a coupon book worth $10.00 off
future purchases of Harlequin or Silhouette books in 2000.

Send us 3 cash register receipts as proofs of purchase and
we will send you 2 coupon books worth a total saving of
$20.00 (limit of 2 coupon books per customer).

Saving money has never been this easy.

Please allow 4-6 weeks for delivery. Offer expires December 31, 1999.

I accept your offer! Please send me (a) coupon booklet(s):

Name: _____

Address: _____ City: _____

State/Prov.: _____ Zip/Postal Code: _____

Send your name and address, along with your cash register receipts as
proofs of purchase, to:
In the U.S.: Harlequin Books, P.O. Box 9057, Buffalo, N.Y. 14269
In Canada: Harlequin Books, P.O. Box 622, Fort Erie, Ontario L2A 5X3

Order your books and accept this coupon offer through our web site
http://www.romance.net
Valid in U.S. and Canada only.   PHQ4994R